Yet some part of Samantha seemed willing to ignore the fact that he was everything she'd sworn to avoid in men. He could be smooth, too smooth, and he was entirely too handsome. The possibility that any man could be so successful and so adored by women without letting it go to his head was ridiculous.

So why did she feel as if some invisible cord were pulling her toward him? As if there was an electric tingle in the air whenever he was near? Why did her mind want to keep drifting to last night and the way she had felt when he held her and touched her?

Sam tried to tell herself that she'd been single too long, that she was having some kind of old-maid reaction. But it was so easy to imagine Derek turning to her, reaching for her, drawing her closer, covering her with his body . . .

Oh, jeez, she had it bad!

Other Avon Contemporary Romances by
Sue Civil-Brown

CARRIED AWAY
LETTING LOOSE
CHASING RAINBOW
CATCHING KELLY
TEMPTING MR. WRIGHT

ATTENTION: ORGANIZATIONS AND CORPORATIONS
Most Avon Books paperbacks are available at special quantity discounts for bulk purchases for sales promotions, premiums, or fund-raising. For information, please call or write:

Special Markets Department, HarperCollins Publishers, Inc., 10 East 53rd Street, New York, N.Y. 10022–5299.
Telephone: (212) 207–7528. Fax: (212) 207–7222.

SUE CIVIL-BROWN

NEXT STOP, PARADISE

AVON BOOKS
An Imprint of HarperCollinsPublishers

This is a work of fiction. Names, characters, places, and incidents are products of the author's imagination or are used fictitiously and are not to be construed as real. Any resemblance to actual events, locales, organizations, or persons, living or dead, is entirely coincidental.

AVON BOOKS
An Imprint of HarperCollins*Publishers*
10 East 53rd Street
New York, New York 10022-5299

Copyright © 2001 by Sue Civil-Brown
ISBN: 0-380-81180-4
www.avonromance.com

All rights reserved. No part of this book may be used or reproduced in any manner whatsoever without written permission, except in the case of brief quotations embodied in critical articles and reviews. For information address Avon Books, an Imprint of HarperCollins Publishers.

First Avon Books paperback printing: September 2001

Avon Trademark Reg. U.S. Pat. Off. and in Other Countries, Marca Registrada, Hecho en U.S.A.
HarperCollins ® is a trademark of HarperCollins Publishers Inc.

Printed in the U.S.A.

10 9 8 7 6 5 4 3 2 1

> If you purchased this book without a cover, you should be aware that this book is stolen property. It was reported as "unsold and destroyed" to the publisher, and neither the author nor the publisher has received any payment for this "stripped book."

Prologue

At five-thirty in the morning, Colonel Wellington James Albemarle, formerly of the Welsh Fusiliers, led his ragtag band down the beach for their morning march. Known as the DustBuster Brigade ever since a small supernatural problem at the Paradise Towers condominiums, the six stalwarts, all in their seventies, had become a common sight on the early morning beach—for those awake enough to see them.

They marched along the sand, the dark waters of the Gulf of Mexico to their right and the hotels, condos, and small beach houses to their left. The first lightening of the midsummer sky etched the darkened buildings in a misty sort of gray. The white sand beach stretched ahead of them, looking like a wide, glowing ribbon.

Albemarle, as usual, hummed "Men of Harlech" as they marched. Well, he didn't exactly hum it; he rather blew it out of the side of his mouth, between his lips, so that it sounded more like a kazoo.

He wore his usual tropical uniform: a khaki shirt, neatly pressed and tucked in, complete with military creases, and knee-length khaki shorts above knee-high green socks and chukka boots. On his head, he wore a pith helmet, a little worn about the edges. And under his arm he carried his swagger stick.

The five other men of the DustBuster Brigade were not quite so natty, in their odd assortment of baggy shorts and tropical print shirts, but they stepped smartly enough, considering arthritic knees and ankles and the fact that they marched on sand. Of course, Lester Mankin was out of step as usual, but none of them troubled to point that out. And Albemarle, leading the group, never looked back long enough to notice.

Along the way they broke formation from time to time to clean up trash left behind by careless tourists. At midsummer the trash level was low. In January they were kept quite busy by the larger crowds.

Not that there were no tourists in the summer; it was merely ebb tide in their flow, and by the time the brigade had reached the south end of the barrier island, near the private condos where beach access was limited, they had collected five huge bags of loose trash. In January they might have found twice or three times that much.

Behind them stretched the pristine beach, clean now of all detritus except what the sea washed up. A good morning's work.

That's when Colonel Albemarle saw the footprints.

They so stunned him that he stopped dead, and his band nearly ran into him, bunching up and precariously balancing so they wouldn't fall.

Then they all saw them.

"Blimey," said Colonel Albemarle, who didn't usually resort to such vulgarity.

"Holy shit," said another of the men, only to receive a withering glare from the colonel, who believed that gentlemen didn't swear.

They stood there staring in disbelief at the largest, strangest set of footprints any of them had ever seen.

Finally, Lester Mankin, who elbowed his way to the front of the group, gave a low whistle and spoke for them all.

"It's a sea monster!"

There was trouble in Paradise Beach.

1

Police Officer Samantha Bartlett was bored. Paradise Beach wasn't that big, and she'd spent most of her shift cruising up and down the boulevard looking for drunk drivers, which seemed to be ninety percent of the trouble on the island. This night she'd picked up her last one at around two A.M. In the four hours since, she'd had nothing to do except commune with the night air and trade an occasional comment with the dispatcher, Harv Neilson.

But that's why she had chosen to join the Paradise Beach Police Department, rather than some larger organization. Six years after graduating from college with a degree in psychology, she'd realized her corporate job was unfulfilling. An urge to do something more important had begun to plague her, and community policing had struck her as the perfect way to meld her education and her desires.

She'd chosen this place because here she wouldn't have to face an unending stream of drug dealers, murderers, thieves, but would be dealing for the most part with good people. She would get to know those she was sworn to serve and protect.

And she had. Unfortunately, that meant a lot of boring shifts. A wild Saturday night usually meant picking up a half dozen DUIs, ejecting a few obstreperous patrons from bars, and settling a handful of fights. Thievery usually amounted to shoplifting.

Most nights, she wondered why they even needed a police force here.

On the other hand, she got a lot more respect wearing a 9mm Glock on her hip than she'd ever gotten in the corporate world. Without the gun and the thick gun belt that concealed her waist with all its pouches and accoutrements, she was a slender woman, a little over five eight, who boasted curves in all the right places. Those curves and her auburn hair with its shiny red highlights had, she was convinced, caused her to be taken less seriously in the business world. Even now, people sometimes wanted to dismiss her, but all she had to do was settle her hand on her belt, reminding them she was a cop. Boredom had its perks.

She was yawning hugely, her gray eyes watering, when the call came from the dispatcher. The early birds were just beginning to pull out of their parking spaces beneath their raised condo buildings, heading for their jobs across the Intracoastal Waterway in St. Petersburg or Clearwater or Tampa. Traffic was on the rise, little by little, and there'd probably be a fender bender before her shift ended.

She half-heard what the dispatcher said. Her yawn checked in midstream and she blinked, sure she must have misheard.

"Say again, Harv?"

His sigh was audible. "I'm just telling you what I've been told. Down by Seaview the DustBuster Brigade found some footprints on the beach. Strange, very large footprints. According to Lester Mankin, they must belong to a T. rex."

"Good grief."

"Yeah," Harv said, reading her tone correctly. "Somebody's been tippling again. Anyway, you gotta check it out."

"Sure. I'm on my way." T. rex footprints on Paradise Beach. She turned her patrol car around in a hotel parking lot and headed south and half-wished they *would* be dinosaur footprints. At least it wouldn't be boring.

Derek Peter Todd, known as Derek Diche to his millions of television-viewing fans, was also bored to tears. Which was why he was listening to the police scanner at six in the morning, local time. Although for Derek it was eleven A.M., biologically speaking, since his home was in England.

After years of traipsing around the world, first as a news correspondent and now as the host of his own mystery-debunking TV show, he'd learned one thing: to leave his biological clock alone. If he stayed in a locale long enough, as he had sometimes as a correspondent, his inner clock gradually came into alignment with local conditions. If he was just there for a brief period ... well, it was better to eat his breakfast in the evening in Nepal, and film in the middle of his biological night because the sun happened to be up, than it was to do it the other way around.

So, when he was on short jaunts like this, he obeyed his inner imperatives. Which had his aunt, Mary Todd, remarking that he was an odd guest indeed. Not to mention a little troublesome.

But Mary said it as if she rather approved, so he didn't let her complaint bother him. Besides, as he'd learned in only two days, his aunt owned the patent on "odd."

Which was how he came to be listening to her police scanner—a rather odd thing for a woman in her eighties to own, he thought—and heard about the T. rex footprints.

Right up his alley. Just the kind of thing he was forever on the lookout for. A ray of interest in the boringness of a quiet sun-filled beach community. Not that Derek was an adrenaline addict or anything; he just loathed boredom.

Ignoring his stomach's demand for a midday repast—he'd breakfasted at one in the morning—he picked up his microcassette recorder and digital camera and headed out to his rented Range Rover. The Seaview Condominiums were down south, he seemed to recall, not far from here.

He paused just long enough to pull a fake mustache and some adhesive out of the glove box and paste the strip of fur to his upper lip. His strongly etched features, his handsome face, were entirely too well known on this side of the pond, where his program captured a significant share of the ratings when it aired six times each year.

He didn't want to be identified. At least not until he decided whether it was worth getting his crew down here.

The eastern sky grew rosy as Samantha passed by the Seaview building, where the mayor lived, and parked at the back of the private lot. She could see the figures of the DustBuster Brigade spread out from the high tide mark all the way to the water's edge, as if they were guarding a corridor.

The scent of the salt water and rotting seaweed filled her nose on humid morning air as she crossed the boardwalk and walked across the sand. She didn't really expect to find the elderly gentlemen drunk. They were all solid citizens, if a bit eccentric, and while they might have a drink in the evening, she seriously doubted any of them would tipple at this hour of the morning.

What she expected to find was a hoax. The kids had been out of school for a month now, ample time to scheme up a good prank.

Colonel Albemarle greeted her by coming to attention. "Good morning, Officer Bartlett."

"Good morning, Colonel. What's this about a sea monster?"

The colonel frowned at Lester Mankin. "That's *one* person's opinion. However, we did find evidence that someone—"

"Or some*thing*," interrupted Lester unrepentantly.

Albemarle glared at him. "Some*one*," he repeated heavily, "seems to be trying to disrupt the peaceful atmosphere of our fine little town."

Lester rolled his eyes. "That's not what you thought when you first saw it," he insisted. "None of us did. They're too deep."

"Let me see," Samantha said, bypassing the colonel and approaching the guarded area.

What she saw *did* give her a moment's pause. Well, all right, several moments' pause.

A set of reptilian footprints started about halfway up to the high tide mark, made their way just above the washed-up line of seaweed and detritus, where they circled widely in dry sand and returned to the water. Between the four-toed footprints, which seemed to have claws on the front of each toe, there was a deep groove, as if a tail had dragged.

"Hmmm," she said.

"Hmmm," echoed the others.

"It looks almost like a gator," she remarked.

"Too big," said Lester. He stepped up beside one of the prints, which dwarfed his foot, and stepped heavily on one foot. Then he stepped back. "See? I weigh two-thirty. Whatever made that print made it a lot deeper. It had to have been much heavier."

The colonel harrumphed, but didn't sound quite convincing.

Sam scratched her head. "Well ... the sand's not as wet right now. That would make a difference."

"That much?" Lester asked.

"I don't know." Although the truth of the matter was, wet sand didn't compress as easily as dry. Therefore, whatever had made those deep prints must have been extremely heavy. But she didn't want to say that out loud. The chief would have her hide if she started a panic. "It has to be a prank. Remember that thing that happened in St. Pete forty years ago? Monster footprints on the beach?" Sam knew about it only because the local paper had printed a story about it last year, revealing at long last the identity of the hoaxster.

A few of them nodded.

"It turned out to be a prank."

Movement in the corner of her eye caught her attention, and Sam turned to see another man approach. She didn't recognize him, so he must be a tourist. Although, as he drew closer, she began to think there was something familiar about him.

He had his hands shoved into the pockets of his khaki chinos, and his air said he was just out for an early stroll, but for some reason Sam didn't believe that. Of course, she reminded herself, he was probably just curious about the odd group out here and what they were doing.

She couldn't blame him for that.

"Hi," he said as he reached them. Then he gave a long, low whistle as he saw the footprints. "Good heavens, what did that?" He had a British accent.

"A prankster," Sam said firmly.

"Did you catch him?"

"Not yet." The sense of familiarity was growing, and she wondered where she'd seen him before.

He wasn't a very tall man, maybe a little under six feet, but his physique suggested someone who exercised religiously. Broad shoulders, narrow hips—she liked narrow hips on a man—and an easy stride that suggested he was comfortable in his body.

As he came closer, she saw that he had blue eyes—a startling contrast to his dark hair—and a face constructed of clean-cut lines. He was probably photogenic as hell, she thought irrelevantly.

"This is really cool," he said, sounding entirely too disingenuous. He just, drat him, happened to have a camera dangling from his neck and started to snap pictures.

Sam wanted to tell him to stop, because some instinct told her this wouldn't be good for the beach community if it got widely bruited about, but she couldn't think of a legal reason to stop him. It was a public beach, after all.

And he was careful to take pictures of Albemarle and the DustBuster Brigade, who puffed up quite nicely for him, standing straighter than most of them had probably stood in ten or twenty years.

This was getting out of hand, and she had a feeling the chief wasn't going to be too happy with her. But what could she do to stop him?

Then, in an instant, she recognized him. "Diche," she said, pronouncing his name to rhyme with "tick."

He stopped snapping pictures and looked at her. "I beg your pardon?"

Yup, that carefully cultivated British accent was as familiar as his face was beginning to be. "Derek Diche," she said, voicing his name with scorn.

"That's *deesh*," he corrected her. "It's French."

"About as French as you are. What are you doing here?"

"Vacationing." He smiled, and his mustache was suddenly lopsided. "Taking some scenery photos. A pleasure to meet you, Officer. And since this is a hoax, you certainly won't mind if I just snap a few more?"

As if she could prevent him. Because now he had become a member of the press, far worse than any mere tourist.

"What are you going to do with them?" she demanded, wishing she could keep her voice more level. But he'd always infuriated her, which was the prime reason she watched his program. So she could sit and kibbitz and mutter and criticize him and his methods. He didn't know the first thing about *real* investigation.

"Nothing, probably," he said amiably enough. "As you say, it's probably a hoax, and unless you can find the pranksters, there really isn't much of a story, is there?"

He could make a story out of anything, she thought darkly. As long as he could find a way to make money out of it.

But she still had no legitimate reason to stop him. How very annoying.

Sighing, she let him snap away, reminding herself that the next high tide would wash the whole mystery away. And if Diche were ill-advised enough to make a mountain out of this molehill, all he'd get for his trouble was a few high school students snickering at him.

And Paradise Beach would go back to its peaceful state of ordinary craziness.

He finished his photos and turned to give her that wide, warm smile he was so famous for. Her body turned traitor, leaping in response to it despite the objections of her brain. Electric tingles danced along her nerve endings in the most annoying way, and goose bumps rose on her arms. It was an allergic reaction, she told herself sternly.

"Hey," he said. "Can I buy you a coffee?"

"No." The refusal came out sharply, mainly because she was suddenly feeling desperate. She caught herself, realizing that she had been unforgivably rude, even to Derek Diche. "I'm on duty," she elaborated.

"Not forever, surely. When do you get off?"

She knew his type, she thought. The type who were attracted to women wearing uniforms and gun belts. A type that seriously turned her off.

"No, thank you," she said firmly, offering no further explanation. Then she looked at the prints again and hoped this would be the last she'd ever see of them.

"It's only a cup of coffee," he cajoled. "Hardly an assignation."

Her head snapped around and she glared at him, sorting through the catalogue of her mind for something withering to say. "You know," she said in a deceptively sweet voice, "you're smaller in real life. Shorter."

Damn him, his smile never wavered. "I know," he said agreeably. "They insist on using camera angles to make me look taller. Something about creating an air of authority." He spread his arms. "The real me. Five-foot-ten."

Samantha, who was five-foot-eight, didn't find him intimidating at all. Well, except for some very fine musculature. "Your mustache is falling off."

That got his attention. He clapped his hand to his upper lip, looked a bit sheepish, and tugged the strip away. "Sometimes I don't want to be recognized."

"A strange thing, for a man who spends his life making a public spectacle of himself. I'm going to get my camera."

It was at least an official, police-type of thing to do, although she figured they weren't going to make any great effort to find the pranksters. Nobody had done anything illegal, after all. But taking photos would be another way to make Diche look foolish.

When she returned from her squad car, she was carrying not only her 35mm camera and flash, but a ruler and tape measure. Unlike Derek Diche, Samantha Bartlett knew something about proper investigation.

With the help of two of the brigade members, she stretched the tape beside some of the footprints so their measurement would be in the photos. Then she took the ruler and stuck it into the sand to indicate the depth. She photographed a number of the prints individually, then stepped back to take pictures of the entire trail from several angles. And finally, she collected several small vials of sand and labeled them with time, date, and distance below the high tide line.

Of course, no one was ever going to use all this stuff, but she felt she was giving Diche a little comeuppance, showing him how a proper investigation was run.

Diche watched the entire operation with a smile. "You're very good," he told Samantha.

"It's my job."

"Would you like to come to work for me?"

"Are you always this annoying?"

"I doubt it. Most people seem to like me well enough."

Most people, thought Samantha as she packed up her gear, were probably sadly lacking in intelligence. "Well, that's it," she said, and thanked Colonel Albemarle and his crew for their help. "Back to work."

Without once glancing at Diche, she marched across the beach back to her car.

When she was out of earshot, Derek turned to Colonel Albemarle. "Is she always this prickly?"

"Officer Bartlett? I should say not, old chap. One of the pleasantest people you could ever hope to meet."

"Hmmm," said Derek.

"Hmmm," agreed Albemarle.

2

Derek stayed a few minutes longer on the beach, chatting with Colonel Albemarle and his crew. He took down names and phone numbers in case he should need them later, although he was pretty sure at this point that he was looking at a hoax.

He was far more interested in Officer Bartlett, and that worried him. In the four years since his wife's death, he'd steadfastly avoided dating, despite the increasing opportunity to do so. No feminine wile, no scanty dress or magnificent bustline had managed to break through his defenses, and he preferred it that way. One heartbreak was enough for a lifetime.

It seriously annoyed him that the first woman to get under his skin in all these years had managed to do so in a matter of minutes, and by the simple expedient of being... prickly.

Of course, he told himself as he trudged back up the beach to his car, no one liked to be taken in instant dislike by a total stranger.

But, as he had to remind himself time and again these days, he wasn't a total stranger to many people on the globe anymore, which put him at a decided disadvantage. Everywhere he went, people knew him, or thought they did, from his program.

While he was usually greeted with backslapping or delighted smiles, his recognizability was a twin-edged sword. Someone like Officer Bartlett could take him in dislike from his show before she had exchanged a single word with him.

Which was an unusual reaction, but within the realm of possibility, nonetheless.

He wondered what her first name was.

And he wanted to kick himself for wondering.

His stomach growled insistently, so he decided to go back to his aunt's house. The likelihood that any restaurant in Paradise Beach would be serving something that passed for lunch at this hour was slim indeed. He had, however, stocked Aunt Mary's larder with provisions to make sandwiches at such moments, and a roast beef with lettuce and tomato sounded very good.

Mary Todd was up and about when he returned, sitting at the breakfast table in the bow window that offered a view of the boulevard and the dunes and water beyond. Mary, he thought, had been quite intelligent. She owned most of the barrier island, and had been careful about which patches she leased for development or sold. Which created a rather interesting hole in Paradise Beach, a hole that preserved Mary's view of the beach and Gulf across the boulevard.

She had permitted a parking area to be built across the boulevard for public beach access, and by afternoon it would be full or nearly so. But the cars didn't disrupt the view much, and the public restrooms had been put off to the side, out of her way. The view had even been enhanced by the planting of a few palm trees.

From the breakfast nook, it almost seemed as if she were alone on the beach.

As he entered the side door from the driveway, Mary was indulging in crullers and coffee.

"I don't suppose you'll join me," she said without preamble.

"Actually, I think I shall. But I'd rather make a sandwich."

She waved a queenly hand, as if giving him permission. "You were out early."

"I was listening to your police scanner."

Her sharp, dark eyes took on a sparkle. "Heavens, don't tell me something actually happened last night. What was it? A juicy murder? A major robbery?"

He had the distinct impression that a headline-making crime, the gorier the better, would amuse her. "Uh, no," he answered as he gathered his sandwich-making supplies: deli roast beef, thinly sliced Irish Swiss cheese, cherry peppers, tomatoes, and lettuce. His mouth was already watering.

"No?" She sounded disappointed. "I suppose there was another fender bender on the boulevard, then."

"Oh, much more exciting than that. Sea monster footprints."

"Sea monster footprints?" She arched her thin white brows. "Who was drunk this time?"

Derek began to understand why his elderly aunt had a police scanner. How else would she keep up with the dirt on everyone in town?

"No one," he said. "Colonel Albemarle found them. Quite impressive, I must say. But, of course, it's a hoax."

"Of course." But her black eyes started sparkling again. "Pass me the cordless phone, will you?"

He wiped his hand on a paper towel and obliged her. Then he listened with amazement as Mary dialed a number and said, "There are sea monster footprints on the beach, Carl. What are you and the city council going to do about it? It's your job to protect the safety of the residents, you know. I don't care to see Paradise Beach looking like Tokyo after a visit from Godzilla."

Derek nearly choked. Forgetting his sandwich, he leaned back against the counter and folded his arms. When she hung up, he asked, "Why did you do that, Aunt Mary?"

She gave a dry little laugh. "It's unhealthy to grow too complacent, boy. Besides, this is an election year. These dratted politicos need something to argue about besides drunk driving laws. Now take me out to see the monster prints."

He almost laughed. Instead, he forced himself to sigh as if he disapproved. "*After* I have my lunch."

"Good heavens," she muttered. "What is the world coming to when a healthy boy can't wait a half-hour for lunch to please his elderly aunt?"

He made the sandwich anyway. Now that his aunt was up to something, it might well be his last meal.

Police Chief Blaise Corrigan was shaving before his bathroom mirror when the phone rang. His bride, Jillie, was curled up around his pillow, still deeply asleep. She didn't need to open her bookstore until ten, and now that she was pregnant with their first child, he hoped she would cut back her hours even more.

Hurrying so that the ringing wouldn't wake her, he wasn't exactly thrilled to hear the mayor's voice on the other end of the line. "What are you going to do about the monster footprints, Blaise?"

For an instant, Blaise wondered if he might still be in bed dreaming. He pinched himself and winced. No, unfortunately he was wide awake.

"What footprints?" he asked.

"I can't believe you don't know about it. You and your department are charged with the responsibility of protecting this town, Corrigan."

Things were always about to get bad when the mayor started calling him Corrigan. "Has anyone other than you called the department?"

"I'm sure they have. I've already had three calls this morning about it. The good people of Paradise Beach are frightened, and well they should be. It's not every day a tyrannosaurus walks on our beach."

Blaise wondered if the mayor had at long last slipped over the edge into madness. "Um . . . the tyrannosaurus is extinct."

"You think so? Haven't you seen *Jurassic Park*? God knows what those damn gene scientists are up to. Get your butt out here and look at the beach behind my condominium. Then tell me what the hell you and your department are going to do about it!"

Sam was just finishing up her reports on the night's activities, ready to head home to bed, when the day dispatcher called her over. Harv, lucky devil, had already gone home, and Wilma Johnson had taken over at the console.

"Hellzapoppin'," Wilma said succinctly.

"What? I'm off duty."

"Not yet, you aren't. Chief says to get down to the beach behind Seaview on the double."

Sam sagged. "Not the footprints."

"Reckon so. He needs some crowd control. And an explanation."

"Great." Diche had to be behind this. He was stirring up trouble to make a mountain out of a molehill for his program. If she ever saw him again, she was going to . . . going to . . . well, shooting him seemed a little extreme.

Rubbing the scratchiness out of her eyes, she smothered a yawn and went back out to climb in her patrol car. This wasn't fair. She'd put in her shift. Unfortunately, the Paradise Beach Police Department wasn't exactly huge and they all had to pull overtime occasionally. This was apparently one of those occasions.

Crowd control. Criminey. What in the world had Diche done?

By the time she was tromping across the sand again from the parking lot behind the Seaview, there were four other cops there in addition to the chief, who was looking pained and listening to a wildly gesticulating mayor. The mayor, short, plump, and balding, was still wearing brown silk pajamas with garish yellow stripes. Twenty or so of the town's other residents were also out there, gawping at the footprints. Colonel Albemarle and his brigade had long since disappeared.

"It's a hoax," she heard Corrigan say to the mayor as she approached.

"Are you an expert?" the mayor demanded. "Get me an expert who'll tell me that."

"Look, there really are no tyrannosauruses left."

"Maybe not. Maybe it's something else. Whatever it is, it's huge and it was up here last night while I was sleeping, and I don't like it."

Corrigan sighed. "Maybe we should call out the marines."

"Hell, no," the mayor said. "Didn't you see what the military did to New York in the latest *Godzilla*? If you think I want those helicopters blowing holes in my condo, you have another think coming."

Sam exchanged looks of sympathy with Corrigan, and thanked heaven she was only a patrol cop.

"Then," said the chief, "just exactly what do you want me to do? I can't exactly shoot something I don't see."

"Of course not," grumbled the mayor. "But I want some experts out here to check these footprints. Investigate, man. You should investigate!"

"I already am," Sam hastened to say, wanting to help her boss. "I took photos and measurements and samples of the sand."

The mayor glared at her. "And then what?"

Sam was stumped. The *and then what* had been a plan to ignore the whole thing as an obvious hoax.

"We're going to send everything to a specialist at the university," Corrigan said.

"That's not enough," the mayor insisted. "I want an expert out here before high tide washes away the evidence."

Corrigan folded his arms. "I'll see what I can do."

"That's not good enough. We need protection."

"Fine. I'll ask the sheriff to lend us the SWAT team."

"What? And make me look like a fool?"

Corrigan smiled. "You don't need me to do that for you."

"Damn straight." The mayor paused a moment, realizing what Corrigan had walked him into. His cheeks reddened. "I want these prints protected. I want experts out here. And I want everyone to keep quiet about it. Just imagine what news of this would do to the tourist trade!"

"I take it you've never watched *Jaws*," Corrigan remarked. He turned and looked at the footprints again. "They're small, you know."

"Small? You call these small?"

The chief's voice grew dry. "Well, they're not as big as the footprint in *Godzilla*."

The mayor glared. "So? It's a baby. Did you

see what those babies did to Madison Square Garden? Oh, my God, they're born pregnant!"

This new disaster seemed to overwhelm the mayor and he fell mercifully silent. A moment later he turned and started to walk away. Over his shoulder he called, "I want a full report of your plans on my desk by noon."

"What are you going to do?" Sam asked the chief, keeping her voice low so the sound of the surf and crying gulls would prevent others from hearing.

"Pray for high tide," he said. "And hope that we don't have a volcano under the boulevard by tonight."

Driving a lavender golf cart wasn't exactly Derek's idea of traveling in high style, but Aunt Mary insisted on it. As it turned out, it was a good idea because he was able to drive right over the dunes and down to the footprints, saving his elderly aunt the trouble of walking in the sand. Of course, he thought wryly, he could have just let her travel on her broomstick. He was growing increasingly certain that she must have one stashed somewhere.

They arrived just as the mayor was storming off the beach. He was quite plainly upset, but he paused long enough to say to Mary, "Thank you for telling me about this, Miss Todd. It's obvious the police were planning a cover-up."

"Well, of course I told you," said Mary, her dark eyes shining with delight. "We wouldn't want to let an opportunity like this slip by, would we?"

"Opportunity?" the mayor said, looking confused.

But Mary didn't answer. Rapping her nephew's arm lightly with the head of her ebony cane, she said imperiously, "Drive on, boy. I want to see them."

Leaving the mayor in their dust—er, sand—Derek obligingly headed for the footprints. Who'd have thought he'd spend his vacation Driving Miss Todd?

The thought made him chuckle. The entire scene made him chuckle. Six cops, including the elusive Officer Bartlett, and about twenty local denizens were milling around the footprints. This promised to be rich.

As they approached, he saw Officer Bartlett, her auburn hair looking fiery in the early sunlight, say something to the officer beside her. The man turned to look at him, and it would have taken a lesser intelligence than Derek's to realize that Officer Bartlett's comment had been unflattering.

He wondered why she disliked him so. And why he even cared.

"That's the police chief, Blaise Corrigan," Mary said to her nephew. "A fine, upstanding man. Pity I have to make his life difficult sometimes."

"Who's that beside him?" He felt, rather than saw, his aunt's speculative look.

"Samantha Bartlett. Nice young lady."

Samantha. Now he had a name to put to his nemesis. A name he rather liked. Curvy, willowy, altogether an enticing nemesis. *Down, boy,* he told himself sternly. The command didn't work.

The morning sun was already hot, promising an even hotter afternoon, but the ceaseless breeze made it bearable. Samantha Bartlett looked cool, however. Wary, but cool.

"Good morning, Miss Todd," the chief said. "Mr. Diche."

At least he pronounced the name correctly. He did, however, have the same wariness about his face that Samantha did. Not good. Derek preferred to maintain pleasant relations with local authorities. It made life so much easier.

"I came to see the footprints," Mary said bluntly. "They seem to have the mayor all in a bother."

Blaise gave a small shrug. "You wouldn't know anything about that, would you?"

Hah, thought Derek. Someone else who knew his aunt well.

"*Moi?*" Mary asked innocently.

"Someday," said Blaise, "I'm going to understand why the Fates have afflicted me with you."

Mary cackled her brittle laugh. "You know why, boy. When life gets too easy, the soul gets sluggish. The arteries harden. I'm protecting your health."

"Funny," said Blaise, "I'd have said exactly the opposite."

Mary ignored him. "So these are the footprints, eh?" She climbed out of her golf cart and, attempting to use her cane for balance, walked closer to look at them. "It's a hoax, of course."

"Of course," said Blaise.

"Definitely," said Samantha.

"Pity," said Derek. Everyone looked at him. "One likes a real mystery every now and then."

"The only mystery," Samantha said, "is which of our high school miscreants had this brainstorm."

"Well, I am purely disappointed," said Mary, who clearly was not. "These are puny."

"Puny?" Samantha looked at the tracks. "Your idea of puny and mine must be different."

Mary waved her cane. "Well, look at them. They're certainly not big enough to drive a truck into. Nor even a tricycle, come to that. When I heard about monster footprints, I imagined something more impressive."

"They're still large," said Derek. "Very large. And look at the distance between them."

Mary arched her brows at him. "Are you saying these are real?"

"Of course not. But I do find it very interesting that the hoaxers left behind these prints and didn't leave any of their own among them."

All of them looked down at the tracks.

"Hmmm," said Mary.

"Hmmm," agreed everyone else.

Blaise raised his eyes to the heavens and sighed. "I guess I need to call that expert."

The Sunshine Skyway Bridge was, as Derek's aunt had suggested, a marvel of modern engineering. Worth the forty minutes of slogging through traffic on Gulf Boulevard, which seemed like an endless passage of strip malls, condominiums, hotels, and hardly even a glimpse of the Gulf for which it was named.

But the bridge itself. Wow. He'd grown accustomed to amazing sights in his travels, but this was right up there with anything he'd ever seen. Towering three hundred feet over the mouth of Tampa Bay, suspended from its center by cables that stretched out like an inverted fan, it seemed somehow too fragile to stand—yet he felt no qualms in crossing it as an oil tanker plied its way north, far beneath him.

Still, his thoughts were only partly on the bridge. The footprints *were* a hoax. They had to be. Everything in his training and experience virtually screamed it. And yet some inner voice kept whispering . . . *What if it's real?*

His professional reputation to the contrary, in his innermost thoughts, he was driven by that very question. *What if it's real?* And as such, he'd been doomed to a life of dissatisfaction. It was never real. Reality remained a drab and predictable progression of physical laws, both revealed and bound by the disciplined collection of hard evidence. It was mathematical, not magical. His quest for magic had lain forever beyond his reach.

Oh, some things defied prediction or explanation. Samantha Bartlett's reaction to him, for example. He'd barely said hello and she'd turned into a porcupine, rewarding any approach with a stinging quill that said, *Go away!*

So why didn't he? Now, there was a mystery. What drew him to her like a moth to a flame? Even now, when he'd intended to get away for an hour or two to ponder whether the footprints might justify a program, his thoughts found their way back to the cool, prickly deputy and her warm, entrancing eyes. Eyes he could lose himself in. Eyes that held magic in their gaze.

It had been a long time since he'd looked at a woman this way. And, by some perverse law of the universe, she was unreachable. Downright hostile. Maybe that was the ultimate magic of the universe. Whatever his quest, it was always out of reach.

Samantha let out an oath as the soap slipped from her fingers and landed squarely on her little toe. Finally, a shower. The day, tagged at the end of a night shift, had been endless. Chief Corrigan, seeing the exhaustion in her eyes, had posted another deputy to watch the footprints for the afternoon. But she'd be back on footprint watch in six hours. Time enough for a quick sandwich and what would seem like an even quicker night's sleep.

Time enough to dream. Dream of . . . what? Derek Diche was a two-bit TV hustler who made his living peddling factoids to the gullible. He sold pseudoscience with a smile. But what a smile. Yes, he was shorter in person than he appeared on the screen. But when his eyes found her and that face opened up . . . What did the pundits call that attraction? Q-Factor? Whatever it was, he had it.

Too much of it.

Was she taking extra time washing herself? No. Absolutely not. It'd been a long, hot, exhausting day. Her fingers were not taking extra care to find relaxing touches that eased away the tension that had knotted her muscles. And she was most definitely not trying to make herself . . . presentable. No. She would crawl into her bed alone, and there was no need to be presentable for anyone. Most assuredly not Derek Diche. Although, despite her best efforts, she found herself wondering how his touches would feel.

Her fingers disagreed. Finally she willed them to move on to scrubbing and rinsing.

The sandwich could wait. She needed to sleep it off, disappear into a place that wasn't tainted by whatever evil spell that . . . man . . . could cast with merely a smile. She tucked her hands beneath her pillow, keeping them out of trouble.

But when the alarm buzzed, and her mind reluctantly surrendered a dream she could only barely remember, she realized Derek had followed her into sleep.

That was enough. She would make it her personal mission to bury Derek Diche.

3

Derek had an incredible intelligence network, which was why he showed up at the Paradise Beach police station just one minute before the expert arrived from the university. Samantha was there, and didn't look exactly thrilled to see him.

"What are you doing here?" she asked without preamble.

"I understand a professor is arriving to look into the tracks." He smiled his winningest smile. "You wouldn't want to keep the media in the dark, would you?"

It was quite apparent she would, but she refrained from saying so. He imagined her teeth would get sore from biting back the words.

"There's nothing to see," she pointed out.

"Nothing that would interest TV. The prints were washed out by high tide this morning."

"I know. But I'd like to hear what the expert has to say."

She scowled and pointed him to a plastic chair just inside the door. "Wait there."

Then she marched down a hallway and disappeared.

Sam knocked on Blaise Corrigan's door and entered before he even asked her to. "Guess who's here," she said to the chief.

"The expert?"

"Worse. Derek Diche. He somehow discovered the expert was coming."

Blaise leaned back in his chair and folded his hands over his flat stomach. "What is it you want me to do, Sam? Throw him out? He *is* a member of the media."

"Media. That's a joke. He's an entertainer. A one-man, three-ring circus."

"That may be. But it also remains that he's a debunker, and I could use a good debunker right now."

"The mayor?"

"And the whole city commission, and half the business owners." He sighed. "Keep Diche happy, Sam. I don't care what it takes."

"Me?" She was horrified.

"You. You're the most diplomatic officer I've got."

Her, diplomatic? "Not around Diche, I'm not."

"Work at it. Make him happy. See that he gets what he wants. It'll be the fastest way to settle this whole mess down."

Sam had her doubts about that. "He'll just stir things up, Chief. Everybody in town will get camera happy."

"Fine. Let them talk to the cameras." He sighed again and leaned forward. "Trust me, Sam. They're not going to want to look like hysterics on national TV."

She hoped he was right. "Can't you ask somebody else? Anybody else?"

"Who?"

It galled Sam to admit it, but she couldn't think of anyone. Anybody except her would succumb to Diche's world-famous charm, not to mention his perceived importance as a television personality. "You owe me," she told Blaise.

"You owe *me*," he retorted. "This is a cream-puff assignment."

If only she would be that lucky, thought Sam as she headed back to the reception area. Somehow she didn't think that dealing with that man was ever going to be easy.

She found Diche involved in conversation with Ben Franklin. Well, it wasn't really Ben Franklin, just a rather stocky, overly muscled guy with a severe case of male pattern baldness and a severe overgrowth of the hair he had left circling his skull. Exactly like Benjamin Franklin's portrait.

"Samantha," said Diche, who was suddenly making free of her name without invitation, "this is Professor Harold Plum, the marine biologist we asked for."

Three things struck Sam, leaving her momentarily speechless. Professor *Plum*? Not really! And why was Diche introducing her to *her* expert? And why was he saying *we*? The police department had asked for an expert. Diche had nothing to do with it. Obviously he was the worst kind of encroacher. *Cream-puff, my foot!*

Then she realized that Professor Plum was looking at her rather oddly, his hand extended for the requisite shake. Gathering her remaining wits, Sam stuck out her own hand and shook his. "Professor. Thanks for coming. I'm Officer Samantha Bartlett."

"Samantha," said Derek, as if she were a precocious child of whom he was proud, "is the investigating officer."

She resisted an urge to send him a withering glare.

"Well, I must say I'm curious now," the professor said, rubbing his hands. "To find Derek Diche involved . . ." He nodded as if he approved. "You do a splendid job of setting the record straight on so-called mysteries. There's far too much superstition and misapprehension running amok in the world today."

"Why, thank you," Derek said modestly. "I owe it all to scientists like yourself, of course."

Oh, man, thought Samantha, *a mutual admiration society.* If she let this go on, the saccharine would nauseate her. "Let's go to my desk," she said firmly. "We think it's a hoax, of course, but it would help us a lot if we have an expert to agree with that opinion."

"Well, of course," said Plum, who seemed predisposed to find exactly that. "If the tracks are as large as you said on the phone, it can't be anything else."

They reached her desk and Sam pulled up a couple of chairs.

"I thought," said Derek as he sat, "that there were still a great many mysteries in the ocean." Sam wondered what kind of craziness he was leading up to.

"Oh, certainly," said Plum. "The sea floor is awfully deep and there are many places we haven't fully explored yet. Surprises still await us. But whatever you're talking about here would have to be an amphibian, which means it would have to be a surface dweller. No surprises left there."

"Why would it be an amphibian?" Derek asked.

"Nothing else would have crawled up on the shore and returned to the sea."

"Duh," said Samantha under her breath. Only Derek heard her, and he favored her with an amused look. She wondered if anything in the world got under his skin.

Bringing out the eight-by-ten glossy prints she had made from the film she had shot yesterday, Sam handed them to Plum. He took them, moving through them slowly, saying, "Mm-hm," from time to time.

"I also took sand samples," she said, passing him the specimen bottles. "Some from inside the tracks, some from beside them. We discovered the prints about three hours after high tide."

He nodded and continued to scan the photographs. "Obviously," he said presently, "this is a hoax."

"It is?" Sam was already looking forward to her freedom.

"Most certainly. These tracks don't resemble any known amphibian's or marine mammal's. However . . ."

He trailed off and studied the prints more closely. Samantha found she was almost holding her breath. That "however" had her on tenterhooks. Derek, too, apparently, since he never took his eyes off Plum.

"Well," said Plum finally, "I don't know. May I take these back with me? I'd like to have some of my colleagues review these photos."

"Those are your copies."

"Good. It's really odd. . . ."

"Odd?" prompted Derek.

"Odd," Professor Plum said. "Extremely."

Sam looked at Derek, and found her frustration echoed in his gaze. "Professor . . . what's extremely odd?"

"Well, the depressions. They're very clear. Almost crisp."

"Meaning?" It was like pulling teeth from a reluctant rhinoceros, she thought.

"Well . . ." He hesitated. "Clearly the sand was wet. Dry sand wouldn't make a clear impression, as you know. Nor would very wet sand. So these prints were made when the sand was just damp enough. . . ." He handed a photo to Sam. "See how they look more blurry nearer the water and above the high tide mark? And the same thing coming back. You can see exactly what I mean about the varying dryness of the sand."

"Yes. Of course." Curbing her reluctance, she passed the photo to Derek. "It's what you would expect."

"Precisely." Plum nodded approval.

"So . . . why is this bothering you?"

"Well. . . ." Again the hesitation. "I really need to talk to some of my colleagues about this, but . . . well, I'm not an expert on this, you know."

"We understand," Sam said, resisting an urge to demand the information he was so reluctant to share.

"It seems to me . . . I may be wrong, but . . . well, it would require something *very* heavy to make prints of this depth and clarity. Damp sand is so hard to compact. Which is of course why I always jog just above the waterline when I'm on the beach."

Sam nodded. Derek nodded, too. Then Sam asked, feeling a most unpleasant sensation in the pit of her stomach, "How heavy?"

He shrugged. Then shrugged again. "I don't know. A ton?"

"A ton!" Derek repeated the estimate five minutes later, after Professor Plum had departed with the samples and photos. "A ton! Can I buy you some coffee?"

"You don't give up easily, do you?" Sam asked. But her mind was hardly on his invitation.

"Actually, no. It's the main reason for my success. I'm relentless. So . . . coffee? And food. It's suppertime in England."

"I need to talk to the chief."

"Then I'll buy you lunch, dinner, dunch, whatever you want to call it. Say yes, Samantha. We need to talk."

And she was assigned to him. Drat him. And drat Corrigan, too. "Sure," she said, pretending utter indifference. "I'll be right back."

Talking sounded innocent enough, she thought, as she headed for the chief's office. It also occurred to her that there were probably a billion women who'd give a great deal to be invited to eat with Derek Diche. Well, she wasn't one of them.

"A *ton*?" Corrigan repeated.

"That's what he said, Chief."

"Oh, my God."

"Yeah."

He rubbed his face as if wanting to wipe something away. "Well, that puts paid to the idea of teenage miscreants."

"He could be wrong."

Corrigan looked at her from beneath lowered brows. "You haven't been in Paradise Beach for long, Sam. Trust me, the impossible happens here. I suppose I'm going to have to tell the mayor about this." He looked like a man contemplating his own execution.

"I don't know," said Sam. "You could always wait. Plum was just guessing and wanted to talk to some of his colleagues."

"That's a good excuse. I may use it. What about Diche? Tell me he isn't getting a film crew down here."

"Not yet. He's taking me to lunch."

Corrigan nodded. "Good. Keep the genie in the bottle, Sam. I'm counting on you."

But as she left his office, she found herself wondering just what genie she was about to let out.

God's air-conditioning, the ceaseless breeze, was keeping Paradise Beach at a comfortable eighty-eight degrees. Well, comfortable except for the humidity. This close to the water, very little was ever really dry, and two weeks ago, when her air-conditioning unit died and the repairman hadn't been able to fix it for five days, she'd been sprouting mildew inside the shoes in her closet.

The humidity was the main reason she didn't suggest the beach bar. Five days without a.c. had made her dedicated to the concept of mechanically iced air.

She chose the restaurant at the island's biggest hotel, figuring that there, at least, they wouldn't run into beach residents who might ask questions.

Big mistake. They had barely been seated at a table with a beach view when she realized that Derek Diche was an eminently recognizable man. Too recognizable. Worse, his sitting with a local cop was apparently occasioning a lot of whispering. Before she had the chance to do more than read half the menu, five people had approached to ask for his autograph, each of them using the opportunity to tell him which of his shows they liked best, and to air a complaint about one of the others.

Sam looked at him when they were again alone. "How do you stand it?"

He shrugged. "It keeps me in touch."

"You mean you like the ego strokes."

"Well, that, too." He smiled almost boyishly. "It's sort of my own rating system."

Sam blew a disgusted breath.

He pretended to be wounded. "Really," he said, "it's all just part of the game."

"Right." She resumed her study of the menu and reminded herself to watch it. Blaise didn't want her to alienate Derek. All she had to do was keep her teeth together and smile for the next thirty minutes or so. Easy enough.

But almost as soon as she made the resolution to be on her best behavior, Mort Horn showed up. Mort was the owner, publisher, editor, and sole employee at the Paradise Beach *Weekly Gabber*. Sam usually liked him well enough, but this afternoon she was most definitely *not* happy to see him.

"Hi, Sam," he said cheerily enough. He was a fiftyish, graying, bowling ball of a man who was more of a gossip columnist than a reporter. "Mr. Diche, it's a pleasure. I'm Mort Horn, editor of the local paper."

A grandiose description for a collection of ads, a police blotter report, and a regular tongue-in-cheek listing of the latest foibles foisted on the community by the city commission. Also known as the city council. Paradise Beach was a bit schizophrenic about that. Sam sometimes wondered if the mayor's cronies had an official designation.

"Pull up a chair," Derek said with a big smile. "Sam and I were just about to order lunch."

Oh, great. Corrigan was going to *love* this.

Mort pulled up a chair, sitting at the end of the table and pulling out his notebook. "I've been hearing all about the sea monster footprints on the beach," he said. "I take it you're here because they might be real?"

"I hate to disappoint you," Derek said smoothly. "I'm here on vacation."

"Ahh." Mort made a note of that, as if the president had just issued a foreign policy statement. "What's your opinion of them?"

Sam couldn't keep silent. She and Derek spoke at the same instant.

"They're a hoax," Sam said, even as Derek pontificated, "I don't know."

Mort's head swiveled between them. "Which is it?"

"A hoax," Sam said firmly. "A practical joke. No known amphibian or sea mammal could have made the tracks."

Mort barely gave her comment a squiggle on his pad. Instead he looked at Diche. "You disagree?"

"I wouldn't say that. All I said is that I have an open mind, unlike some folks."

It was that tag that got to Samantha. She wondered how he'd look with his tongue wrapped around his head. "You heard what the expert said."

"Yes, I did. I also know he said something would have had to weigh a ton to make those tracks."

Oh, God. Mort was scribbling that down. This town was going to get as hysterical as the mayor. How could she salvage the situation, now that Diche had let the cat out of the bag?

Mort looked at Diche, asking, "Are you going to investigate?"

And Derek looked at Sam, smiling broadly. "I may just do that."

Maybe she should staple his mouth shut. Mort got up, thanked them both, and walked away. Considering how few questions he had asked, Sam had a pretty good idea of what kind of story he was going to tell.

"Well, that's great," Sam said, snapping her menu closed. "You can hold yourself responsible for this."

"Responsible for what?"

"By the time Mort gets done, we're going to have had a flying saucer invasion from Mars. The aliens will be ten feet tall, weigh a ton, and dine on helpless little puppy dogs and old ladies."

A laugh burst out of Derek. "No!"

"Yes. And you're going to be responsible for the subsequent hysteria."

Derek shook his head. "Not I. I'm a debunker, remember. I don't believe in little green men. Or big green men, come to that. I can't help what others do, but I'm serious about this stuff."

"Right. You expect me to believe that, when you've faked snowstorms on the side of Everest while looking for the ever-elusive Yeti."

"Hey," he said, holding up a hand, "that was a clearly marked dramatization of the weather up there."

"Yeah. I saw it. You managed to come off looking like Superman surviving Kryptonite."

He shrugged. "That wasn't the point of the demonstration."

"No? Then how about that time you wrestled that poor anaconda?"

"I wasn't wrestling him; he was sleepy. But how better can you give people an idea of what we're talking about when we talk about a giant anaconda?"

"How about a little computer magic?"

He shook his head. "It's not the same."

"In your mind, maybe."

His smile had vanished, and he was looking at her with those incredibly blue eyes. Blue eyes that were giving her the uncomfortable feeling that he was hurt. Derek Diche? Hurt by *her*? Not in this lifetime. Nevertheless, she squirmed in her chair.

"You just met me, Sam," he said levelly. "You don't know me."

"I know your show."

"My show and I are not the same thing."

All of a sudden she felt as if she'd stepped off a cliff and couldn't do anything to prevent her fall. "Maybe not," she said finally. Maybe she was going overboard.

"I don't think you're reacting to *me*," he said after a moment. "Maybe you're reacting to someone else in your life."

"Oh, spare me the penny psychoanalysis. I just don't like your show. Maybe I'm wrong to think the show represents you personally, or maybe I'm not. Time will tell, won't it?"

"I suppose it will." He sighed. "Make your selection, Sam. I suddenly have an urge to get on with my life."

Now she was wounded. Which was ridiculous, wasn't it? Because she'd been wanting to shed him since the moment she met him. But somehow that remark had cut her to her quick.

Worse, she felt maybe she deserved it. After all, Regis didn't sit around in real life asking, "Is that your final answer?" Why should she think Derek was as one-dimensional, egotistical, and self-important as he seemed to her on a scripted program?

She forced herself to meet his gaze. "Truce?"

He hesitated. "Is that possible?"

"I think so."

"Fair enough. Truce. What are you having?"

Keeping in mind the fact that her bathroom scale had crept up two pounds, she ordered a chef salad with dressing on the side. Derek wasn't kidding about suppertime. He ordered a steak, baked potato, and steamed broccoli. When the waiter departed, they were left with nothing to do except look at one another or look out the window at the Gulf beach. Sam chose the window.

"It's pretty," he remarked.

She glanced at him and found he was looking at her. She felt her cheeks heat, just a little, and hoped he couldn't see it.

"What made you decide to become a cop?" he asked.

"I wonder how many men get asked that question."

"I have no idea. I didn't mean to offend your feminist sensibilities."

"You didn't." But he had, and that wasn't his problem, it was hers. Sighing, she leaned back in her seat. She wasn't ordinarily this hypersensitive; something about Derek seemed to bring out the worst in her. "I'm sorry. I seem to be irritable."

"That's quite all right. We all have irritable days."

"I became a cop because I was bored with feeling like a useless cog in a huge corporation."

He nodded. "The cog feeling is something I'm familiar with. Unfortunately, most of us are precisely that."

"But you're a wheel."

He smiled wryly. "I'm only as good as my most recent ratings. I'm as disposable as a paper napkin."

"I hadn't thought of it that way."

"Most people don't. They see fame, fortune, a name that pops up on a thirty-second commercial fifteen or twenty times over a week, and they get envious. It never occurs to them that they might never hear my name again."

"But it occurs to you?"

"Quite often. It keeps me humble."

Sam wasn't inclined to think he had a humble bone in his body, but anything was possible. "So why did you get into this business?"

"Because," he said slowly, "I'd had more than enough of being a war correspondent."

Sam sat up a little straighter. "You were? Really?"

"For thirteen years, from Afghanistan to Beirut to Kosovo. I started in print, then moved to IBN and the telly. It was a lot easier to be inconspicuous as a print journalist, let me tell you. Running around with a cameraman and a satellite truck gives you a high profile."

She thought she heard a touch of sorrow in what he said, maybe even a touch of bitterness. "Do you miss it?"

"Absolutely not. The things that human beings do to each other are . . . well, more unbelievable than the monster footprints, if you want the truth."

"I know." Even quiet little Paradise Beach had given her some experience of that.

"Anyway, what I'm doing now is fun." He smiled, as if to dismiss the demons she suspected might be lurking beneath the surface.

She had some food for thought when she and Derek parted ways after lunch. Unfortunately, her newfound rapport with him didn't survive the next morning.

4

The jangle of the telephone awoke Samantha from a sound sleep. The room was still dark, although she could see the gray light of predawn lining the blinds over her window. "Bartlett," she said sleepily into the phone.

"Get down to the beach now, Sam," Chief Corrigan said to her. "The DustBuster Brigade has found an egg."

"An egg?"

"Just get down there."

She struggled out from beneath a tangle of sheets and blankets that seemed to explain why she'd been having a crazy dream in which she wrestled with a huge anaconda while Derek stood on the sidelines shouting directions. Didn't it figure? Did he come to her rescue? No. He just stood there and told her how to do it.

Men.

Then the possible Freudian interpretation of the dream struck her, and her cheeks flamed, waking her fully in a rush.

No! Not possible. It didn't matter how gorgeous Derek was. It didn't matter how much a part of her longed to get wrapped up in his... anaconda. Which thought promptly made her mad at herself. *Sheesh!* She was losing it.

She crawled into the fresh uniform that she'd laid out last night and tried not to feel too icky from all her exertions in her sleep.

Minutes later she was cruising down the boulevard in her patrol car, wondering what unpleasant surprises the sea had cast up this time.

An egg. How many people got haled out of bed at dawn because someone had found an egg on the beach? Nobody but her, she was willing to bet. And she'd get down there and discover it was nothing but a clutch of sea turtle eggs that some hyperactive imagination had turned into something alien.

Well, maybe not, she amended as she drew near the condominiums. One of the DustBuster Brigade was waiting at the edge of the street, signaling her wildly. Hmm.

Once again she pulled into the parking lot and drove to the rear of it. Howie Crenshaw, who'd waved to her from the sidewalk, came trotting up, huffing and puffing in his attempt to catch up with her.

"Watch it, Mr. Crenshaw," she said. "You'll give yourself a heart attack."

"If I didn't have one from that egg, I'll never have one." He spread his arms expressively. "It's huge!"

She was sure he was exaggerating, but she nevertheless revised her estimate upward from a typical sea turtle egg. Maybe a few more inches in diameter?

"Come on," Howie said impatiently as she locked her car. "The guys are waiting. What if it hatches before you get there with your gun?"

Visions of shooting an egg filled her head, along with images of egg yolk splattering the faces of the Brigade. No, she didn't think so. One person in town with egg on his face would be enough. And she knew exactly who she wanted that person to be: Mr. Anaconda.

But she quickly revised her opinion as she took two steps on the sand, then saw the egg.

The pale, gleaming orb sat near the high tide mark, half as tall as a tall man. Her mind immediately balked. That couldn't possibly be real.

She must have spoken aloud, because Howie Crenshaw answered her. "That's what we said, too. Wait until you touch it."

Touch it? Her skin began to crawl. Surely that wasn't a part of her job, touching some weird egg tossed up by the sea. But even as she quailed inwardly, she realized she was the cop and was supposed to control the situation. She cleared her throat cautiously. "Uh... were there any footprints this morning?"

"Nope," Crenshaw told her. "Nary a one. The thing could have been tossed up by the tide. Or left there at high tide."

Samantha walked warily toward it. Not as big as the eggs in *Godzilla*, thank goodness. Nor as ovoid. This was rounder, more like a fish egg.

It had to be some kind of ball or balloon, she told herself. Well, not a balloon. Too heavy.

The rest of Albemarle's brigade watched her approach. She noted that they stood a safe distance away from the egg. Typical: Six stalwarts who marched on the beach every day to the tune of "Men of Harlech" were going to let the female cop approach the thing.

But... did she really have to *touch* the thing? She could just imagine her call to Blaise if she didn't, though. She had to be able to tell him something besides that there was a big white glob on the beach.

Remembering suddenly that Crenshaw had already mentioned touching it, she felt her backbone stiffen. She wasn't more cowardly than these guys, and anyway, they'd apparently survived touching it.

She stepped up to the four-foot-high egg and laid her hand on it.

Yechh! It was cold. Slimy. She wanted to wipe her hand on her pants.

"Caviar," she said. It was all she could think of.

"Caviar?" repeated Albemarle.

"Sure." She sniffed her hand. "It even smells like it."

"Great," said Lester Mankin. "Maybe one of the hotels could use it for a banquet."

Sam and all the rest of the men merely looked at him. Sam keyed her radio. "Get me the chief."

Corrigan was patched through to her. "Well?" he said.

"It's caviar," she said. "One giant—and I do mean *giant*—egg."

"How giant is giant?"

"Four feet or so in diameter."

"Damn." He was silent, and for a few moments static was all she heard. "So you can't haul it away?"

"I don't think so. I'm not sure we should, anyway."

"Why not?"

"Well . . . it might be of scientific interest."

"Hmmm."

"Hmmm."

"What happened to the cop who was so sure this was a hoax?"

"I'm still sure the tracks were, Chief. But this . . ." She shook her head and stepped back a little from the egg. Had it moved? She wasn't sure. "Umm . . . it stinks. And . . . uh . . . I think it might be moving?"

Blaise groaned. "Why couldn't this have happened to St. Pete Beach?"

"Beats me."

"Okay. Cover it. Put a tarp over it. Something. Just get it out of sight before the mayor sees it."

"Uh . . ." Sam eyed the egg again. "What good is that going to do? He's going to demand to know what's under it."

"So let him demand. Put up tape around it, keep everybody away, and guard it until I can get some scientists out here, okay?"

Sam stifled a sigh. Guard the egg. It wasn't exactly what she had in mind when she'd decided to become a cop.

"And don't let Diche see it," Corrigan said. "That's all I need."

Just then Sam heard a sound from behind her. Turning, she groaned. "Too late, Chief. It's too late."

"Hmmm," Derek said.

"Hmmm," the lady cop answered.

"Hmmm."

"We've done that part," Sam said.

"Yeah. Ummmm. Wow."

It was, he knew, a totally unscientific reaction. But then again, nothing he'd ever seen had prepared him for this. A professional debunker with nothing more to say than "Hmmm" would not do.

"Who found it?" he asked, searching for a safe footing within his mind from which to proceed.

"What are you doing here?" she demanded.

He was getting rather tired of this woman, possibly the only person in the entire English-speaking world who didn't like his show, treating him like some lowlife who ought to be in a cell. "Taking my morning constitutional."

"Really? With a minicam?"

"You never know." He shrugged, not bothering to tell her that he'd come down looking for more footprints. What she didn't know wouldn't make her angry, and she was already looking like a hornet that had been swatted by a stupid picnicker. "Besides, it works better than dumbbells. Heavier."

She lifted both brows dubiously. "If you're a gentleman," she said, "you'll give me the videotape."

"Why?"

"Because I don't want this town to be made to look foolish on national television."

"Nobody's done anything foolish."

But he'd spoken too quickly, because the mayor, clad in blue silk pajamas, was hotfooting it across the sand toward them. Derek almost felt sorry for Sam, but that didn't keep him from lifting the camera to his shoulder and filming the mayor's barefoot prance across the sand as he tried to avoid stepping on seaweed and shells.

"What the hell is this?" the mayor thundered as he reached them.

"Caviar," Sam said with a shrug.

"Caviar! Who do you think you're kidding? I eat caviar all the time. This is bigger."

"No duh," Derek heard Sam say under her breath.

"It's some kind of fish egg," Sam continued aloud as if it were a matter of supreme unimportance. "That's *all* it is. Now, if you'll excuse me, I need to cover it and cordon it off."

The mayor rounded on her. "Where were you when this thing was left here? Some police force. I'm sleeping soundly in my bed, and wake up to discover that you've allowed a catastrophe to occur right outside my window."

"It's hardly a catastrophe. Sir. It's just an egg."

"Just an egg?" The mayor's hands flew up. "*Just an egg?*" Heedless of Derek's camera, he went into a full-scale rant. "If you think that's 'just an egg,' you need your eyes examined! 'Just an egg' is tiny. No bigger than a hen's egg."

Colonel Albemarle cleared his throat. "The ostrich egg—"

"I don't want to hear about ostrich eggs," the mayor roared. "Eggs are small. Caviar is smaller still. My God, can you imagine the size a hen would have to be to lay this egg?"

Derek had to admit the idea kind of boggled the brain. The hen that laid this egg would probably be peeking into the mayor's third-floor window while she laid it. "Thirty feet?" he suggested.

"At least," said the mayor, stomping his bare foot on the sand, then letting out a howl as a broken seashell bruised his arch. He grabbed his foot and began to hop in circles—all the while being watched by the unblinking eye of Derek's camera.

"Maybe it's not an egg at all," suggested Lester.

Everyone looked at him, even the mayor, who stopped hopping but still held his foot, looking rather like an overweight blue flamingo.

"Maybe," said Lester, "it's an alien spaceship."

The mayor groaned and let go of his foot. "Shut up right now, Lester. We don't need any more panic."

Derek, peering through the viewfinder, said, "I wasn't aware anyone was panicking except you, Mr. Mayor."

The mayor glared at the camera. "Put that damn fool thing away." Then he rounded on Samantha. "I want the marines out here. Today!"

Sam watched him limp up the beach. Derek lowered his camera and looked at her. "Rough morning, Sam. Can I buy you breakfast?"

She turned slowly and looked at him. "Sorry. I've been assigned to guard an egg."

Then he really *did* feel sorry for her. But not so sorry he didn't feel the twinges of excitement that were beginning to light up his life again.

A real mystery. A real, honest-to-God mystery, and it was unfolding right before his eyes. What more could a man ask for?

Sam was able to cordon off the egg without any problem. She had all the necessary supplies in her trunk, supplies she hadn't needed once in her entire time with the police. The DustBuster Brigade, under Colonel Albemarle's bluff direction, helped her, while Derek filmed their every move.

"You know," Sam finally said to him, "you're wasting videotape. This footage couldn't be good for anything but a sitcom."

"You never know," he replied, his stock answer. The problem was, he usually *did* know, which was why he'd become so famous as a debunker. If you looked hard enough, from a skeptical, scientific perspective, you could always find a rational explanation for even the craziest thing. But that "always" bothered him. Part of him was perpetually looking for some mystery, some wonder or magic, that wouldn't yield to the scientific mind or the Amazing Randi.

So far, no luck.

And wasn't Sam cute? She stationed herself on a dune, once she had the egg surrounded by the cordon of yellow police tape. She sat on the sand, forearms resting on her knees, and looked as if she would rather be almost anyplace else in the world. The DustBuster Brigade evidently agreed, wandering away as the morning began to take full hold and a heavy line of clouds to the west suggested that Sam's post might become extremely uncomfortable before too long.

She looked dejected, and he felt another pang of sympathy for her. Apparently she couldn't see how marvelous this event might turn out to be.

Switching off his camera, he lugged it up the dune and sat beside her, the camera on his lap so sand wouldn't get into it.

"It's exciting," he remarked.

"For *you*, maybe."

"No, really," he persisted, looking at her. "Think about the possibilities."

"Let's see. First there's the possibility that you'll make Paradise Beach the laughingstock of the English-speaking world by proving it's just an extremely large ping-pong ball."

"I don't think so." He was a bit taken aback by her indictment. "I don't do that. Haven't you seen the program? I simply investigate startling mysteries or events and find logical causes for them. I don't make fun of the people who misinterpret what they've seen or experienced. And I certainly don't invent ridiculous explanations. Besides, it doesn't feel like a ping-pong ball."

"What are you going to do? Wrestle with the egg?"

"Afraid not. That would only make *me* look ridiculous." Her mouth was maddening, he realized, his thoughts caroming off in entirely the *wrong* direction. Every time she made that little moue of disgust at him, all he could think about was kissing her. Quickly dragging his gaze from those lush, unpainted lips, he looked at the egg.

After a moment, he shifted uncomfortably, moved the minicam to a more strategically concealing location, and said, "All right, that was the first terrible thing that could happen. What's the second?"

"That egg could hatch before my very eyes?"

He found, much to his amazement, that he shared a bit of the same trepidation. One didn't know, after all, exactly what the contents of that egg were. He cleared his throat. "That would be exciting," he said stoutly. "Thrilling. The introduction of a hitherto unknown species."

"Right. And with my luck it would stand ten feet tall, have a voracious appetite, and huge teeth and jaws. And it would climb right into the mayor's bed with him in the middle of the night. While I'm watching it."

"That *would* be bad," he agreed, eyeing the egg in a new light. "Unless, of course, it *eats* the mayor. Does he always run around in his pajamas?"

"That seems to be a recent development."

He thought he heard a tremor of amusement in her voice, so he stole a look at her, and discovered that her eyes were actually sparkling, and a small grin curved that delicious mouth. Worse yet—he sighed and shifted the minicam . . . again—trust the old zoom lens to act up at entirely the wrong time.

"So," she said after a moment of rather pregnant silence, "why of all places on earth did you decide to vacation here?"

She didn't have to sound as if a plague of locusts had just visited itself on the helpless town, he thought, a little disgruntled . . . mainly because he didn't like the way his body was developing a mind of its own—and at such an awkward time. "My great-aunt lives here," he said between his teeth.

"Your great aunt? Who's that?"

"Mary Todd."

"Ah," she said. "That explains a great deal."

He felt a flicker of real irritation. "What's that supposed to mean?"

"Well, you know your aunt."

"Actually, I don't. My father went to England half a lifetime ago. He settled there, and this is the first time I've met Aunt Mary."

"You poor dear. Well, that exonerates you."

"Exonerates me from what?" He frowned at her, feeling the family escutcheon was being sullied.

She shrugged. "I just mean that you're not closely related to her other nephew."

"The other nephew? I presume you mean the one who lives hereabouts? I haven't met him, I'm afraid. And I don't believe my father kept in touch with him." That embarrassed him a little, his out-of-touch, far-flung family. It didn't somehow seem . . . familial.

"Just as well. He keeps trying to have Mary committed so he can get his hands on her property."

"Does he, now?" The idea appalled him, even though he was quite sure Mary knew how to handle this other nephew. "How very tacky."

"Tacky?" she repeated. "Tacky is what *you* do. What *he* does is criminal."

The camera was no longer a strategic necessity. Nor, he decided, was his sympathy. "I'm out of here," he said. "Enjoy your guard duty."

Feeling rather miffed, he walked away. So he was *tacky*, was he? The woman was going to drive him mad.

Sam sat on her dune, feeling the rising sun bite into her exposed forearms and face. She was going to look like a lobster before noon, and she didn't have any sunscreen with her. Of course not. That was just one more screwup in a screwed-up day.

Finally she radioed the chief. "I'm burning up," she said without preamble. "I need some relief or some sunscreen. Whichever."

"I'm sorry, Sam," he said, not sounding contrite at all. "I don't have anyone to spare right now. A group of French tourists is having a knock-down, drag-out fight with a Spanish-speaking family."

"Why?"

"Who knows? You wouldn't happen to speak French or Spanish, would you?"

"Sorry. I studied German."

"Then I need you right where you are. I'll see if I can get some sunscreen over to you."

"That might be a good idea, if you don't want me in the hospital for the next week." Although, now that she thought about it, being treated for sunburn would get her off this boring, ridiculous duty.

"Did you cover the egg?"

"With what?" she asked Corrigan. "I don't have a tarp. Besides, how do we know that covering it won't damage it somehow?"

"Good point. Which would be the worse headline? *Beach community kills helpless egg*, or *Beach community invaded by monster egg*?"

"There's no contest there. The tree huggers are militant." Given that she was a tree hugger herself, she was sure of it. "On the other hand, there's the mayor."

Corrigan's voice turned glum. "I know. He wants the marines."

"At this point, so do I. I'm burning up."

"Rescue is on the way."

She signed off and scanned the beach. It was a beautiful morning, and she really should try to enjoy it.

But that grew more unlikely as she realized that people were beginning to approach the egg. They were still a distance away, moving rather hesitantly, but headed directly toward her. Great. Just her and a crowd of frightened beach residents. This could get hairy.

She reminded herself of the Texas Ranger motto, *One riot, one Ranger*, and told herself to stiffen her spine. *She* had the gun, after all.

A crowd began to gather in ones and twos. Word was getting out. At first they were silent, except for murmurs among themselves, and they hung a safe distance back. Sam began to relax. They were just curious, and she couldn't blame them. This may not have been what Corrigan wanted, but unless he ordered her to close the beach—and she was sure the mayor would flay him alive if he did that—there was nothing she could do about it.

"Hey, Sam," yelled a resident she recognized but couldn't put a name to, "what's the department going to do to protect us? Aren't you going to shoot it?"

And then it began. The tree huggers versus the self-anointed militia, one side screaming to protect this priceless egg, the other side demanding an air strike.

An air strike? Lord. Sam stood up, put her hand on the butt of her gun, and approached the feuding crowd.

"Cut it out!" She bellowed the words in the deepest voice she could manage, and was relieved to watch the crowd fall silent.

"Now, look, folks," she said in a more reasonable tone of voice, "we've got experts on the way to determine what this thing is and what we should do about it. In the meantime, I'm sitting here with a gun. If Godzilla shows up, I'll shoot him. Her. Whatever. Okay?"

"With that little peashooter?" one man asked, scoffing.

"Now, just take it easy," she said in what she hoped was a tone of clear authority. "It's an egg. Maybe. It certainly isn't harming anyone or anything right now. So relax until you've got a reason to stop relaxing."

The crowd subsided with mutters—among them, "If it hatches it might be too late"—but Sam chose to ignore them. Her orders were clear: Protect the egg until someone with greater expertise decided what to do about it, or until it posed a threat. And right now, huge and repulsive though it was, it was still just sitting there minding its own business.

"Cool," said a too-familiar voice behind her. She spun around and saw Derek standing there, filming the entire scene. He lowered his camera and grinned at her. "When do you start swaggering like John Wayne?"

"Oh, cut it out," she snapped.

"Okay." Bending over, he picked up a white Styrofoam container and offered it to her. "I brought you breakfast. I know, don't bother saying it. You loathe me and everything I stand for. I must be crazy. But..." He shrugged. "You haven't had breakfast."

Sam looked down at the container in her hand and felt the most unwelcome tightening of her throat. She'd been abominable to this guy from the instant she set eyes on him, but he'd brought her breakfast. She didn't know what to say.

"It's okay, you don't have to thank me." Then he lifted his camera and started filming the crowd again.

"Uh, Derek?" Sam said. "That camera might incite more trouble."

He lowered it and looked at her. "You're right. I'll stop."

She had to give him credit for that. She retreated to her sand dune and opened the breakfast he'd brought her. Scrambled eggs, bacon, sausage, toast. Maybe he wasn't the scum of the earth after all. Or... maybe he was just trying to buy her goodwill. It wouldn't be the first time some jerk had pulled that.

But she was still hungry, and decided to take advantage of the unexpected manna anyway. "Thank you," she said to Derek, when he sat beside her.

"Quite all right."

She ate with one eye on the crowd, which, it suddenly struck her, were beginning to look like a group of zombies from *Night of the Living Dead*, or some other such movie. They milled stiffly, not even speaking to one another any longer, looking suspicious or frightened according to individual temperament. It wasn't the way they were eyeing the egg that worried her, it was the way they were eyeing each other.

"Cracks in the social structure?" Derek mused, apparently noticing the same thing she was.

Sam immediately felt defensive of her fellow Paradise Beachians. "They just don't know what to make of it."

"Who does? But it's interesting how many of us revert to our most primitive state when we're frightened."

"You have experience of that, I suppose." She'd meant the remark to be teasing, but a shadow crossed his face, surprising her, and she felt she had trod on a sensitive place.

"Actually," he said quietly, "I do. Unfortunately."

But almost as quickly as it had appeared, the shadow passed, and he was once again Derek Diche, raconteur of the mysterious. Too smooth. Too suave. Men who were smooth and suave always made her skin crawl; life had taught her they were rarely what they seemed. She had come to prefer awkward, stumbling, bumbling geeks. That way, what she saw was what she got—even if it didn't trip her trigger.

Diche, unfortunately, did seem to trip her trigger. And that, she told herself sternly, was only because she'd been celibate so long. Regardless, she wasn't about to fall for some smooth-talking, egotistical, self-important personality boy. He had a lot of Q, as she'd heard the entertainment industry call charisma, but she doubted he had much else. Except, possibly, the nature of a shark, always seeking chum in the water.

Hmmm. She drew up short as she realized she was being awfully uncharitable to a man she didn't really know. Maybe life had made her a bit too cynical?

And maybe she was thinking entirely too much about Derek Diche.

"Is your real name Diche?" she asked him.

"Actually, no. It's Derek Peter Todd."

"Why the Diche?"

He shrugged. "It's my mother's maiden name. It seemed like a good way to separate my new career from my old one."

"Corresponding must have been a tough job."

"It was hell." He said it flatly, then seemed to brush it aside. "I'd rather wrestle with well-fed anacondas and trek through snowstorms on Everest."

"I guess I can see that. Even if they are fake."

He gave her a long look. "The anaconda wasn't fake. It was just . . . full. Sleepy. It had had a pig for dinner."

"Poor pig." That was the part of nature she didn't like to think about.

"It's reality," he said. "Bigger things eat smaller things. We all have to survive."

"What a philosophy!"

"It's not a philosophy; it's realism. Recognizing that doesn't make me unethical."

His response came so close to what she had been thinking about him that she blushed. Considering how red the sun was making her skin, though, she doubted he could tell.

At just that moment, Chief Blaise Corrigan appeared, traipsing across the sand toward them.

He reached them and turned to look at the egg and the crowd. "Good grief."

"Yes," Sam agreed.

"Here's your sunscreen." He passed her the plastic bottle. "Did you tell these people to move on?"

"On what grounds?"

"Who needs grounds? Call it a possible crime scene." Which he promptly did. "Come on, folks, it's time to move on. You don't want to disturb the evidence."

Reluctantly, the Stepford men and women began to trail away. "See?" Blaise asked Samantha. "It's easy."

"For *you*, maybe. Hey, how's the brawl going?"

"It's losing steam." He sat on the sand beside Sam and Derek. "We may never know what was going on, other than a lot of screaming and fist-shaking. I need a multilingual officer. Screaming seems to be a contagious problem lately. I didn't understand half of what the mayor screamed at me this morning. Except I think he mentioned the marines."

"He definitely mentioned them to me."

Corrigan sighed. "So I did understand that part." He shook his head. "It just keeps getting better and better, and it's not even nine o'clock yet."

Derek took the bottle of sunscreen from Sam. "Can I help you put this on?"

She frowned at him. "Drop dead."

"Ouch." But he handed the bottle back.

Corrigan watched them with amusement. "Diplomacy, Sam. Diplomacy."

"Diplomacy doesn't require me to let some idiot put his hands on me."

Derek looked over Sam's head at the chief. "She's right."

"Well, yes," said Blaise, who looked as if he were struggling to contain a laugh. "She is."

"But it never hurts to ask."

Fuming, Sam opened the bottle and slapped the lotion on. *Men.*

5

By two o'clock that afternoon, Sam realized that her life was going to hell. Not only had the sullen crowd increased, accompanied by shrieking, running kids who alternately wanted to touch the egg, throw something at it, or get too close to the choppy Gulf waters, but Derek's camera crew arrived.

Sitting on her dune, Sam watched the insanity, complete with reflecting screens to ensure that the uncertain light didn't cast unflattering shadows on Derek's handsome physiognomy. Overhead, darkening clouds roiled, threatening a great storm, but the sun kept popping out, causing the camera crew to swear as the light abruptly changed.

Sam was rooting for the storm. A good blow would send Derek and his crew heading for their rental van, and would dissolve the crowd like unwelcome clumps of dirt.

All of which would make her life more pleasant, even if she did wind up feeling like a drowned cat.

Hell's bells. Another two-year-old was wandering too near the waterline. Jumping up, she jogged across the sand for the umpteenth time and pulled a shrieking, objecting child away from the water. This one had a sagging, dirty diaper. One whiff and she held the child at arm's length.

"All right," she shouted. "Come get your child, whoever you are. And do it now or I'm going to start citing parents for neglect."

A number of Stepford moms immediately grabbed their children, sorting out a melee that had begun over the size, shape, and ownership of a lumpy sand castle.

Someone snatched the squalling child from her hands and started soothing him with, "I'll save you from the mean, nasty cop."

Great, thought Sam. Save a child from the hungry jaws of the Gulf of Mexico and this was the thanks she got. Life just got better and better.

Derek had apparently finished whatever mumbo-jumbo he'd been purring into his microphone, because now he moved on to interviewing members of the crowd. Surprisingly, a lot of them scooted away, as if reluctant to be seen on camera.

There were, however, enough blowhards to go around.

"What do I think it is?" one man said into the microphone. "I don't know for sure, but one thing I do know."

"What's that?" Derek asked.

"It couldn't have come from around here. We don't have anything that big in Paradise Beach. Nossir, it must've come from the sky, maybe like a meteor. Or some alien brought it."

"So you think it's from outer space?"

"Didn't I just say that?"

Derek turned to another man who stood nearby. "What's your take, sir?"

"I ain't gettin' nuthin' out of it."

"I meant, what do *you* think it is?"

The guy shrugged and scratched a bloated beer belly. "Looks like one of them Godzilla eggs, 'ceptin' it ain't big enough. Hey, maybe it's gonna grow."

"It's a hoax," someone else said, shoving to the foreground. "Isn't that obvious?"

The first guy shrugged. "The cops don't think so." He pointed at the yellow ribbon that surrounded the egg. "Why else they got a cop here all day?"

"Because it's a crime scene," said the man.

"Exactly my point," said the third man. "They know it's a hoax and they're collecting evidence."

The man with the beer belly harrumphed his disagreement. The proponent of alien visitation looked scornful.

"Actually," said a woman, approaching the microphone, "it's most likely the egg of some deep-dwelling sea creature that we haven't encountered before. It was probably washed up on the beach by a storm at sea." She pointed to the clouds overhead. "It's our duty to put it back."

"I don't see how you can know that," the first man said. "It could be *anything*."

"Occam's razor," said the woman. "The simplest explanation is the likeliest."

The man with the big belly spoke. "I don't see what some guy's razor has to do with an egg." He chortled. "What'd he do? Shave it?"

The dialogue deteriorated after that. Derek, Sam noticed, stopped recording and filming and just kind of stepped back as the woman who wanted to save the egg got into it with the beer drinker, who now had a can of Milwaukee's finest brew in his hands.

Man, oh, man, the crowd was getting stirred up again. The Stepford people had been easier to deal with, kids notwithstanding.

Sam was really starting to get on edge when the marines arrived. Actually, he was a pimply-faced, wet-behind-the-ears second lieutenant named Brick from the air force base across the bay. He hesitantly introduced himself to Sam.

"Lieutenant Brick," he said. "I . . . uh . . . well, they sent me out to see what's going on."

Sam shook his sweaty palm, realizing that the air force must think the mayor was losing his marbles. Community relations dictated they send someone. The someone they'd chosen indicated the level of their concern.

"Nothing's really going on," she said, feeling almost motherly toward him. He blushed every time she looked at him. "There's an egg. Well, we think it's an egg, but we're not sure. We're waiting for some experts. So far that's all that happened."

He nodded, trying to look brisk and in command, but the attempt was ruined by the way his gaze slid fearfully toward the egg. "It's awfully . . . big," he said finally.

"We're all agreed on that."

He nodded again, but apparently couldn't think of anything else to say. "Well."

"Yes. Well." Sam sighed, noting that the crowd had fixed its attention on the lieutenant. He seemed to realize it, too.

"Ummm. . . ." He trailed off.

"When are we getting the air strike?" demanded a guy in the crowd.

"Air strike?" The lieutenant recoiled. "Uh . . . unless there's been an invasion . . ."

"What the hell do you think that is?" demanded another man. "It sure as hell didn't come from around here."

A woman raised her voice. "We have to protect our children." She held a three-year-old in her arms.

Then take the kid home, Sam thought. The heat and the long hours here on the beach with nothing to do except watch a crowd were beginning to take a toll on her temper. Nor was the young lieutenant's presence any help. If anything, his presence seemed to be agitating the crowd.

She touched his arm. He looked at her, his eyes reflecting his uncertainty.

"This might be a good time to go back to the base and tell them what you saw," she suggested.

He was only too eager to leap at the opportunity to escape. In fact, it seemed to stiffen his spine, and he squared his shoulders. On his way through the crowd, he could be heard to say confidently that he would report matters to the appropriate authority.

Much to Samantha's relief, the promise seemed to have an effect. In small groups and singly, most of the crowd began to drift away. Or maybe it was the rising afternoon heat. She looked at her watch and wondered if the chief was ever going to relieve her.

"Long day, isn't it?"

Derek spoke beside her, and for the first time Sam realized he had joined her. "Endless," she admitted. "I thought you were enjoying yourself."

He shook his head. "Not really. Doing my job, just like you."

"You sure got a crew here awful fast."

He shrugged and stuck his hands into the pockets of his khaki chinos. "They came down yesterday, just in case."

She looked over at the group of men with their casual clothes ranging from T-shirts and shorts to cutoff jeans and safari shirts. "They go everywhere with you?"

"Well, not everywhere," he said with one of his patented smiles. "I do tend to go to the loo alone."

For some reason she blushed, even though the mention of a bathroom hadn't affected her since she was ten. "I meant, are they *your* crew?"

"Pretty much. We do all the location pieces for the show together. Want an introduction?"

"No, thanks. I was just curious."

"I wonder what's taking the experts so long to get here."

Sam shrugged. "They're probably trying to squirm their way out of involvement. It's not exactly something anyone would want on his academic résumé."

He chuckled. "Good point. It surely is... curious."

She looked at the egg again, just in time to catch a teenage couple ducking under the yellow tape. "Hey!" she called, trekking across the hot sand yet again. "No one's allowed in there."

The boy seemed to look at her and nod, only to return his focus to the egg. As she drew closer, she caught snippets of the couple's conversation, but it was all Greek to her. What was that last word? Epiglottis? Barysplottus? Huh?

"You have to stay outside the tape," she said, now close enough to hear them clearly, but still unable to make heads or tails of what they were saying. "It's a restricted area."

The girl shot her an impatient look. "And how are we supposed to examine the specimen from outside the tape?"

"You're not," Sam said. "That's the point."

The boy spoke. "No, the point is, we *have* to examine it."

He turned to his partner with a roll of his eyes and they resumed their conversation, as if Sam had evaporated. And presently she figured out why their conversation sounded Greek. It *was* Greek. What was that last word? Meningitis?

"Excuse me," Sam said, "but who are you?"

"We already talked to the air force guy in the parking lot," the girl answered. "He said to go on down."

Sam shook her head, still trying to catch up. "That's nice. But who *are* you?"

"Zeph Hillock and Nat Waters," the boy said. "She's Zeph."

"USF Department of Zoology," the girl added.

These were the experts? Well, that would explain the Greek. "You're students?"

"Grad students," Zeph said, nodding.

They looked like they belonged in high school. "Well, I'm Officer Samantha Bartlett and this is my crime, umm, incident scene."

"It's some incident," Nat said. "So are you going to let us get to work now?"

Were all zoologists this pushy? Sam wondered. "Yes, of course. So . . . what is it?"

More Greek words. Sisyphus? Aeschylus?

"In English?" Sam asked.

Zeph shrugged. "Damned if I know."

"It's a big egg," Nat said. "Other than that. . . ." He spread his hands.

Great, Sam thought. *Just great.*

Derek startled her by murmuring in her ear. "Looks like all we get is the second string today."

She looked over her shoulder at him. "What about you? Are you second string, too?"

He grinned. "Absolutely. *Sixty Minutes* is first string."

"Hey, don't feel bad. *They* don't cover monster stories."

He laughed. "A guy's gotta do what a guy's gotta do."

She almost liked him then. Sternly, she reined in the impulse. Derek Diche spelled trouble. "Looks like we're not going to get any answers."

"Don't worry," he said. "I'll figure it out. In one hour less twelve minutes for commercials."

Was that a twinkle in his eye? Or was his ego bigger than this egg? The latter seemed more likely.

Just then, trouble came hotfooting across the sand. The mayor had upgraded his wardrobe to shorts and a violently colorful Hawaiian shirt. The day may have been dark, but the mayor was blinding.

"Where the hell are the marines?" he asked.

Sam answered him. "They came, they saw, they left."

"*Veni, vidi,* vent-a-vay-eee," Derek said.

"That's not Latin," Sam said.

"Neither am I," he answered. He turned to the mayor. "They're sending B-52s at dusk. They said we might want to evacuate."

"Good," the mayor said. Then, after a pause, "*What?*"

"He's kidding," Sam said. "Some second lieutenant looked at the egg and went back to report to headquarters."

"No B-52s?" the mayor asked. Sam couldn't decide if he sounded disappointed or hopeful.

"They'll get back to us," Derek answered.

"Maybe we should call Diaz from marine biology," Nat offered.

"Right," Zeph said. "The one who spent an hour recording whale sounds before she found out it was a guy in the engine room who had gas?"

"It was good science," he said.

"It was *gas*," she replied. "You just like her chest."

"She's a good scientist."

"Her bras are custom-engineered. Suspension bridges don't need that much reinforcement."

"Uh . . . kids?" Sam cut in.

"And who are they?" the mayor asked.

"They're our experts," Sam said. She introduced them. "They speak Greek."

The mayor's face was nearly as purple as the oversized violets on his shirt. "Greek? Latin? What about English? What about my town? What about my tourists? *What about that egg?*"

"It's big," Zeph said.

"We'll need lab equipment," Nat added.

The mayor nodded. "Can you get that before the B-52s show up?"

"We'll try," Zeph said.

"If not, we can examine the remains," Nat offered.

"You'd have to use a microscope anyway," Derek said.

"Exactly," Zeph agreed.

The mayor was about to suffer a coronary. Sam was about to suffer heatstroke. And Diche, damn him, was simply having *fun*.

And of course, right then, the elements decided to add their blessings to the day. The sky opened up with a crack of thunder, dropping a stinging deluge. Within a minute, Sam and Derek were the only rats left on the sinking ship.

She was stuck here, but he wasn't. "Why don't you go?" she asked.

The rain had plastered his clothes to him, sculpting a tempting physique. "Who, me?" He looked up into the pouring rain. "Maybe it's time to build an ark."

"An aircraft carrier." She grinned.

"Right. For the B-52s."

All of a sudden, they both dissolved into laughter, collapsing onto the wet sand, holding their aching sides.

And Sam discovered that shared laughter was even more intimate than sex—and just as dangerous.

At three o'clock, Sam got her sixteen-hour pass from hell. Corrigan replaced her with Frank Blodgett, a good ol' boy with a Cracker accent thick enough to walk a gator on.

Frank had been raised in north-central Florida, in a town named Skeeter Hollow—he pronounced it "Skitter Hollah"—that consisted of one store, one gasoline pump, four churches, and ten billion mosquitoes. On Sundays, he'd told her, the faithful in church were outnumbered a million to one by the "skitters." There was more slapping than amen-ing, and once the pastor had inhaled a bug in the middle of his sermon and "started speaking in tongues."

He'd grown up to be a cowboy on a nearby

cattle ranch, but after his horse bit him he decided handing out traffic tickets would be a safer way to make a living.

He also believed in aliens.

He took one look at the egg and announced, "They're here."

"Right," Sam said. "And I'm outta here. See you tomorrow morning."

"Look out for the air force and the lab equipment," Derek said. "Other than that and the mayor, you shouldn't have any trouble."

"They're here," Frank said again, still staring at the egg. "I seen one of these before."

Sam froze and looked at him.

"You have?" Derek asked.

"You betchee. Down in Skitter Hollah, by the bass lake. Dayum."

"What did it look like?" Derek asked.

" 'Bout like this here. Bigger, maybe. Glowed in the dark, it did."

Sam had stepped into another reality—there was no other possible explanation. Either that or she was the only sane person left in Paradise Beach.

"How many beers did you have before you saw that egg back home?" she asked.

"Hmmmmm," Frank answered. "I guess maybe three bass worth. Or four. Yep, it was four. We had a big fish fry that night. With hush puppies and fried okra. Had the Pobecks over, and they could put away hush puppies. Must've been four bass. Big ones."

How did that translate to blood-alcohol level? Sam guessed it was pretty high.

"What happened to the egg?" Derek asked, treating Frank as if he were an unimpeachable source.

"They came back and took it," Frank said. "That's what the preacher said."

"The preacher saw it, too?" Derek asked, his eyebrows lifting.

"Nope. Me and Pete Pobeck told him about it. He said they came back and took it. We figured he'd know, being a man of God and all that."

"And you were how old?" Sam asked.

"I dunno. Twelve. Thirteen. But I 'member it. Clear as day." He slapped an invisible mosquito on his arm. "Clear as day."

Frank turned to Derek. "Them B-52s is comin', you said?"

Derek put on a solemn face. "That's what I said."

"Gonna bomb the stuffin' out of it, eh?" He looked at the egg. "Good."

Sam didn't know quite what to say. "Uh, Frank? You're on the beach with the egg."

"Don't matter none. Gotta kill them green bug-eyed monsters. Line of duty and all."

She really had stepped into a parallel universe. "Frank, there aren't going to be any B-52s. Derek was joking."

"Oh." He looked disappointed. Then, as if he'd just figured out some inside information, he whispered, "So they gonna shoot 'em down with missiles? We're keeping people off the beach in case, like, another Roswell crash happens?"

Sam shook her head. "No missiles. Just you and your .45."

He straightened to attention. "Don't you worry none. I'll deal with them bug-eyed critters. You can count on me."

"Good," Sam said, turning toward the parking lot. Then a thought struck her. She paused and looked back. "But Frank? Don't shoot the egg. They might get mad." He nodded slowly, as if with deep understanding. She hightailed it for her car, wondering how far she was going to have to drive to find sanity again.

6

The rain in Paradise Beach was much warmer than in England, a fact that Derek fully appreciated until he stepped into Aunt Mary's house. The air-conditioning hit his sodden clothes like a blast of ice and he suddenly thought of woolly mammoths.

Specifically the woolly mammoth that had been flash-frozen so fast that thousands of years later, when he was dug out of the ice, his mouth was still full of the fresh flowers he'd been about to masticate.

That fate seemed to be hovering awfully close to him. He ran up the stairs, pausing just long enough to grab some fresh clothes before jumping into a warm shower.

The rain might be colder in England, but at

least stepping indoors wasn't apt to give one hypothermia.

As he began to warm up under the spray, he devoted some of his attention to the rather unwelcome sense of disappointment he was feeling. Samantha Bartlett had driven off into the metaphorical sunset before he'd even had a chance to invite her out for a drink.

It was ridiculous to feel disappointed. If he'd invited her out, all she would have done was tell him to get lost.

It kind of piqued his interest, he had to admit. Not that he thought he was God's gift to women or anything. It was just that these days it was so easy ... well, he rather doubted the sincerity of women who were too quick to say yes. He figured they weren't interested in Derek Peter Todd, man, but in Derek Diche, celebrity.

Which didn't really matter, he reminded himself. He didn't want to trust a woman. He didn't want to get close enough to a woman ever again to feel the kind of pain he'd felt when Janine died.

The crazy thing was, though, that when Samantha gave him a hard time, he felt himself trusting her. Maybe because it was safe to trust a woman who wasn't interested in him. She'd never let him get close enough to be open to hurt again.

Now, that, he told himself, was a crazy man talking. He didn't want to get close to Sam, either. He just wanted to have sex with her. Sex was fun, sex was emotionally safe. Sex was something he could share without being at risk.

Consequently, sex was something he didn't do very often anymore. Without intimacy it was just... well, kind of sordid. He'd found that out fast enough.

So where did that leave him? Lusting after a woman who wouldn't let him close.

Just plain dumb.

But he still wanted to ask Sam out for a drink. Why not? Nothing would ever come of it, and he kind of liked the way she bristled at him. He could sit across a table from her, get an eyeful of her enticing figure, say good night, and walk away. No harm, no foul.

But at least he'd have the semblance of normalcy in his life. He could pretend he was like other men.

The truth was, however, he was squirming inside his own skin, troubled by his own confusion. Concentrating on monsters and hoaxes was easier by far.

He dressed in the local uniform of shorts and a polo shirt, then headed down the stairs.

"Aunt Mary?"

"What?" She appeared in the living room doorway, leaning on her cane.

"Do you know where Samantha Bartlett lives?"

"That pretty young policewoman?" Her cane shot out suddenly in front of him, stopping him on the bottom stair like a barricade. "She's a small-town girl, Nephew. Not up to the likes of you."

"The likes of me?" His aunt apparently shared Sam's low opinion of him. He sat down on the step behind him and looked at her. She was a beautiful woman, with a head of thick, perfectly white hair. And a backbone of steel, he suspected.

"I know you live in the fast lane," Mary said tartly. "I've always liked a bit of a rake myself, but that girl's not up to your snuff."

For some reason, he felt amused. "I don't have a particular snuff, Aunt Mary. What's more, all I want to do is take her out for a drink."

"That's what they all say, boy."

"I'm not all of them. I'm me. Besides, she has a gun."

Mary's cane wavered. "How true."

"Exactly. Put your cane down, Auntie. If you like, you can ride along and chaperone us."

Mary shook her head. "Don't josh with me, boy."

"I'm not joshing."

"Too bad. I have a meeting here this evening."

Derek's interest perked up. "Oh? About what?"

"I'm having some friends over, is all, and we'd appreciate it very much if you'd stay out of the way."

Now Derek was torn. The idea of his aunt holding a meeting she didn't want him to attend had his nose for news twitching like mad. On the other hand . . . she *was* his aunt and he was guest in her home, and he couldn't be so rude as to put himself where he wasn't wanted—even if she was rude enough to tell him to get lost.

"Hmm," he said.

She dropped her cane. "Get out of here. No hanky-panky with Sam, though."

"I promise," he said, as much for himself as her.

"Good. Go."

He went, but just as he was opening the front door, she said, "If you *do* get up to hanky-panky, just make sure she's smiling bigger than you are, boy."

He managed to hold his laughter until he got into his car. Which was when he remembered that Mary hadn't told him where Sam lived.

Sighing, he decided to go look her up in the phone book at a pay phone, rather than deal with Mary again. Next thing he knew, his aunt would be asking him which brand of condoms he preferred.

The rain had lightened to a drizzle by the time he reached Sam's house. Both her number and address had been in the phone book, and he'd spent a few minutes debating whether to call her first. But that would only make it easier for her to brush him off.

On her front porch, he knocked and waited. She lived in a small concrete-block bungalow, one of many dozens in Paradise Beach. Hers was painted shocking pink, and he wondered if that had been her choice or her landlord's. It was still a few hours before sunset, but the clouds remained thick and dark, and the pink on her walls made the house stand out like a beacon.

Samantha greeted him wearing only an oversized T-shirt and a look of sleep.

"Oh, hell," she said. Then, after a pause, "I mean, hello."

Derek took a half-step back. "I'm sorry. Did I wake you?"

"No, I had to get up to answer the door anyway."

"I should have called."

"Then I'd have had to get up to answer the phone."

"True."

He stood for a moment, looking at her. Finally she broke the silence. "You did have a reason for coming here, right? What is it? The egg has hatched and Godzillette is walking down Gulf Boulevard?"

"Actually, no. I thought you might like to join me for a drink."

"I'd rather it were Godzillette."

"I have a lizard suit in my bag somewhere." He eyed her and let a slow smile form. "You know, for when we have to manufacture a crisis."

She laughed, almost in spite of herself. "Okay, give me twenty minutes to wake up and dress. Come in and sit down. But no lizard suit."

He nodded. "Come in. Sit. No lizards. Got it."

She gave him a wry look. "I take it you've had obedience training."

"Yes. I took it with my dog. *He* passed."

Her laughter trailed after her as she disappeared down a hallway.

Derek took the opportunity to look around. The living room was small but cozy, decorated in vivid colors that somehow seemed right for Sam. The tiny kitchen was visible, through a bar, and decorated in a bright yellow. Apparently if one wanted to eat in this house, one ate at the bar, sitting on one of the two tall stools with gaily upholstered seats.

The couch, a colorful tropical print, proved to be comfortable enough to remind him that it was getting on toward his usual bedtime. His eyelids kept sagging to half-mast.

Sam returned after only a few minutes, dressed in one of those short-skirt things—what *did* they call that?—and a snug knit top, both in turquoise. Or teal. Or whatever they called that color.

Gads, his brain was skipping around like a scratched phonograph record. Dimly, he remembered it was appropriate to rise to his feet.

"Are you okay?" she asked.

"Oh, I'm fine. My biological clock is laboring under the delusion that it's bedtime."

"Ahh." She peered at him. "Maybe we should just stay here, then. I think I have a couple of beers."

Beer? His stomach rebelled. Not that watered-down lager than Americans believed was a good brew. A Guinness, maybe, but not a lager. Then he suddenly remembered this was her house. Which meant there was a bedroom nearby.

And a bedroom nearby meant . . .

He shook himself. "Let's just go out, okay?" Safer. Saner. Especially when his brain seemed to have skipped town for dreamland.

"Sure." She smiled, looking not at all tired, although a little sunburned on the tip of her nose. So much energy. He had to remind himself that for her it was six in the evening.

"How's Mary doing?" she asked as they drove toward the boulevard.

"You know, that's a difficult question for me to answer."

"How so?"

"I've known her only a few days. So I'm guessing that she's her usual self. Feisty. Outspoken. Hell-bent on some kind of mischief, I'm sure."

"That sounds like Mary. She twisted in her seat and looked at him. "What mischief is she up to?"

"I've no earthly idea." Which was true. But, remembering the call she'd made to the mayor the instant she heard about the footprints on the beach, he had an idea what his aunt was capable of. For all he knew, she was getting ready to stir things up again.

Sam chuckled. "You know, your aunt was one of the first things everyone told me about when I moved here. Look out for Mary Todd, everyone said to me. She's a dear, but she mixes things up."

"I think she enjoys the entertainment. Which," he added, having a sudden access to brilliance despite the fogged state of his brain, "puts her in a class with God."

"God?"

"Certainly. God mixes things up, too. There you are, going along swimmingly, trying to do everything right, when suddenly life blows up in your face."

Silence greeted his words, and he realized an edge of bitterness had come through in them. He felt an ardent desire to snatch the statement back, but it was too late. And now she was going to ask questions he didn't want to answer.

But she amazed him then, did Sam Bartlett. After a few moments she said only, "I'm sorry, Derek."

Sorry? What was she sorry for? That she'd

heard him expose something deep and painful within himself? Sorry to learn he had that nugget of ugliness inside him? Or sorry that he'd been hurt?

Part of him wanted to ask, and part of him knew he'd be a fool to do so. He didn't want to talk about Janine tonight. He didn't want to rake all of that up. So he didn't reply.

"Maybe," he said instead, "you ought to tell me where to go. You know the area."

"What are you looking for?" she asked. "Quiet? Noisy and busy?"

"Quiet. Please."

She directed him down a side street, about a block from the beach. They entered a small restaurant with a gated courtyard, then went inside and took a table. He looked around, noting that there were only a half-dozen people present. All of them women. A few of them smiled and waved to Sam. On a big screen TV there was a soccer match, with the sound turned down.

"Seems like a nice place," he said to Sam. "Quiet."

"Yes."

A waitress came to take their orders. It suddenly occurred to Derek that he was out with a cop, and that he was driving. Ordering anything alcoholic might not be wise. "Would you like to order a meal?" he asked Sam. It was, after all, her dinnertime, and he didn't like to patronize an establishment and order only a soft drink.

"Love to," she said cheerfully. She looked up at the waitress. "How's the minestrone tonight, Dana?"

Dana kissed her fingertips. "Superb."

"A bowl of that, please, and manicotti. And a diet cola."

"Just the minestrone for me," Derek said. It was far too late for him to eat anything heavy. "And a glass of sparkling water."

He settled back in his chair as Dana walked away, and scanned the restaurant and bar. A thought struck him.

"This isn't a, you know . . . *that* kind of bar?"

Sam looked amused. "Actually, yes. It's about the only place on the beach that isn't overrun by tourists."

"Ah." Then he had another thought. "Are you . . . ?"

"What difference does it make?"

Good question, he thought. "Well," he blurted, "if you *are*, it makes my life easier."

That made her laugh. But it also turned her bright red.

"Well?" he demanded.

"Sorry," she said. "I can't make your life easier."

"Good." Because he didn't want it to be easier. Not *that* way. Then it struck him that he'd probably spent too many years being a reporter, because he'd just asked a reprehensible question in a social situation. "My manners are appalling," he said.

"How so?"

"I shouldn't have asked those questions."

"Why not? It's what I'd expect."

From you. The absent words were nonetheless evident to him for being unspoken. "You know, I'm really too tired. I've abandoned every social grace I ever possessed."

The corners of her mouth lifted in a curious but sweet, tucked-in smile. "So you have social graces?"

"One would wonder, wouldn't one, after the way I've behaved. So let's start this evening over, shall we? It's a lovely little restaurant, nice and quiet, just what I was hoping for. A little shy on ambience"—which was an understatement—"but otherwise right on the mark."

"I'm glad you like it. It's really nice to sit in the courtyard when it isn't raining."

"I did think it looked rather charming." Certainly more charming than this scattering of wood tables and chairs, whose only claim to decor was the candles in their red jars with the plastic netting.

Dana returned with their drinks, promising the minestrone would be out in a minute. Then she walked away, falling into conversation with a couple at another table.

Leaving Derek to rack his brains for something to say. It was horrifying to realize that he hadn't had to make conversation with a woman in years. With Janine, they'd both been reporters, and from the instant of their meeting they'd had plenty to discuss. Comrades in arms, and all that.

Then there were the Derek Diche years, when anytime he was so foolish as to ask a woman out, she spent all evening trying to entertain him by talking about him. He'd developed a reasonably good patter about his program and a few of its more exciting moments, which had carried him through otherwise deadly dull dates.

But this was different and he found himself feeling—and acting—as awkward as any schoolboy on a first date. Sam didn't care about Derek Diche. In fact, she didn't care *for* Derek Diche. And while he wanted to know all about her, he didn't know how to begin. But he had to say something.

He cleared his throat. "Have you always been a police officer?" He felt like a fool since she'd already told him she hadn't.

She looked up from her glass of cola, and he saw something like relief in her gaze. It was an endearing moment as he realized she was feeling as uncomfortable as he.

"No," she said, pretending they hadn't already discussed this. "I was a faceless cog in a huge faceless corporation for a while. It wasn't very satisfying and I started to get restless. For whatever reason, I just don't seem cut out to worry about widget quotas."

"I can understand that. So now you have things to worry about besides widgets. Do you like it?"

"Well," she said wryly, "until today I did."

He smiled. "Today was . . . unusual. I wonder what will happen next."

"Aren't you going to wrestle the egg?"

"You're never going to let me live that down, are you?"

"Not if I can help it."

He pretended to sigh. "It's like this: I never wrestle anything I can't get my arms around."

That comment had a completely unintended effect. Sam's cheeks pinkened, leaving him in no doubt about where her thoughts had strayed. Which immediately caused *his* thoughts to stray in the same direction, only this time he didn't have a camera to place in a strategic location. He scooted farther under the table. He fought for a cool, level head, even as his body started cheering for something that was neither cool nor levelheaded.

Damn, how could one thorny woman have this effect on him? He didn't like it. Not even Janine had affected him this way so strongly. Theirs had been a meeting of minds and souls, with passion following later. He wasn't used to being led around by his, er, unmentionables.

Desperately, he sought for something passably intelligent to say.

But Sam beat him to the punch. "How exactly did you get into the monster business?"

"I cover things besides monsters."

"Ghosts," she said dismissively.

"Only once."

"And aliens. But they're monsters, aren't they?"

"Depends on one's point of view." Why did he feel as if he were on the witness stand?

"What *is* your point of view?"

He shrugged. "I try to stay objective. The point is to go where the facts lead me."

"What kind of facts could there be about aliens?"

"Precious few," he admitted. "We followed a lot of leads, but most of them turned out to be anecdotal. The same with the Yeti. The big footprints in the snow—well, do you know what happens to footprints when they melt a little? They enlarge. So we found a couple of scientists who felt that was the explanation for these giant bare footprints in the snow. The videotapes of the Sasquatch were more interesting."

"How so?"

"A couple of primate experts pointed out the differences between the way human beings move and the way apes move. The creature on the videotapes moved like an ape, according to a couple of experts. Of course, there were plenty of other experts who didn't even want to return our phone calls." He smiled. "Can't say I blame them."

"And what about the giant anaconda?"

"They've found tracks in the mud in some places around the Amazon that support the notion that some of these snakes grow to fifty feet in length, even though the biggest one ever caught is only thirty feet." He nodded reminiscently. "I liked that show. It's not very often that we get to deal with a well-supported mystery. Most of them blow up the minute you start really looking at them."

And here they were talking about him, which he didn't really want to do. He wanted to talk about *her*. "So, as a cop, what was your worst experience?"

"Today," she said frankly. "The worst. Bar none."

"No shoot-outs at the O.K. Corral?"

She shook her head. "This is a quiet town."

"Until the egg landed."

Dana was just bringing their bowls of soup, and she butted into the conversation as if she had every right. "Yeah, what about that egg?" She put the bowls in front of them. "Anybody going to do anything about it, or do we just have to wait and see what comes out of it?"

"It might be dead," Sam said.

That perked Derek's curiosity. "Why do you say that?"

"Well, if it's from some deep sea creature we

don't know about—which is likely, since we've never seen anything like it—it would be logical to assume that the only reason it's on the shore is that it's dead. Or that coming up on the shore killed it."

"Except for one thing," Derek pointed out. "There were those footprints two days ago."

"Yeah," Dana agreed. "Don't forget the footprints. Say, aren't you Derek Diche?"

Sam's face closed as if someone had locked the shutters. Derek didn't like seeing that, but he couldn't be rude to Dana, who wanted to do the groupie thing. He was rescued by Sam's pager, which chose that auspicious moment to start beeping.

Sam tugged it off the waistband of her shorts and looked down at it.

"Great," she said. "I need to call the station."

"Maybe," said Dana, her voice uneasy, "the egg is hatching."

Derek hoped he could be so lucky.

7

Frank Blodgett wasn't an imaginative man. Other than the one time he saw that ball of light on the lake back home, he hadn't seen one unusual thing in his life. He was a down-to-earth man, well grounded in reality, and apt to use humor to deal with the more uncomfortable parts of life.

Which is why he thought his eyes were fooling him when the egg moved.

Eyes could play tricks on you, especially in the dark. As a youngster he'd spent countless hours back in the swamps at night hoping to catch him a gator. If you stared at something hard enough, it would seem to move.

So that's what he told himself was happening with the egg. Even so, he wasn't so sanguine that he was able to tear his eyes away from the orb and give his vision a break.

It would have been easy to know what it was doing if it had rolled or something. But it didn't do anything as obvious as that. Instead it sort of . . . bulged.

"Ullp."

For a moment he wasn't sure if the egg hadn't made the sound. Then he realized it had been his own voice. If he weren't on duty, it'd be time for a drink. If he weren't on duty, it'd be time for a lot of drinks. Beer, he thought. The temperature of the creek back home, where he and Pete Pobeck had kept a six-pack dangling over the side of the boat to keep it cool, until they'd run across a submerged cypress stump and heard the crunch and pop and fizz that had led to a feeding frenzy by alcoholic alligators. Okay, one gator had swum by into the brew, made something that might have been a sneeze, and swum away. But they'd been out in the hot sun all day catching nothing but two small mud cats and two million mosquito bites, so it'd seemed like a feeding frenzy to them. It'd made a great story, too, at least until Mom and Dad heard it. From then on they'd had to buy their own beer.

"Ullp."

He made the sound again, and wondered if the egg had moved once more, or if he was gulping at the memory of Dad heading out to the peach tree for a switch. Definitely the switch. The egg hadn't moved. Had it?

He was about to draw his weapon when he saw a couple of tourists ambling his way. Northern tourists seemed to have no concept of the southern cop's . . . the southern *man's* . . . okay, *this* southern man's need to shoot something. They'd tell the chief and he'd lose his job and that wouldn't do at all. So he did the next best thing. He called for backup.

The first person to arrive was Sam. Which was a good thing, he figured, since it was *her* egg. After all, she'd been guarding it since its discovery. Besides, an egg seemed like a woman's thing.

Of course, he'd never say that out loud. Chief Corrigan was a real bear on that equality stuff. Saying anything about women was apt to get a guy suspended. Although, right now, getting suspended sounded like a good thing.

Sam came trotting up with that annoying Brit at her heels. And of course she didn't have her gun with her, or her badge, or even her nightstick. Hell, she wasn't even in uniform. Wasn't that just like a woman?

On the other hand, with those two moony tourists standing there holding hands and looking at the egg, guns were out of the question. He sighed.

"What happened, Frank?" Sam asked as she reached him.

"It moved."

Sam looked at it. "It's still in the same place."

Frank liked Sam. He really did. He thought she was a smart woman and a good cop. But right now she wasn't even understanding English.

"It moved," he said again.

"*How* did it move?" she asked.

"It bulged. Like this." He swelled out his belly to show her.

"Wow," said Derek Diche.

Sam moved her attention from Frank to the egg, staring at it. "I don't see anything."

But just then, the lovebirds who were standing on the other side of the egg jumped back.

"Did you see that?" said the guy, all excited. "Man!"

"Billy, let's get out of here," the girl begged.

"No way. I don't want to miss this."

Frank, who was hoping against hope that the rest of the police department would arrive any second in full riot gear, realized the chief wasn't going to be happy if a couple of tourists got in the way. "You'd better move on," he said, trying to sound official.

"Aw, come on," said the guy. "I want to see what it is."

But the girl was tugging on his hand. "Billy, let's go. My father will kill you if that thing eats me."

That threat seemed to get Billy's attention. "Oh, okay," he said in a grumpy voice, clearly of the opinion that she was a poor sport. They headed back the way they'd come, this time not holding hands.

"I didn't see anything," Sam said.

"I did," Derek announced. "It bulged. Just like Frank said."

"See?" Frank felt vindicated—although life would have been so much better, so much more *normal*, if that thing hadn't moved at all. And Frank cherished normal about as much as he cherished a six-pack.

"I don't believe this," Sam said. "I simply don't believe this." Frank didn't want to believe it, either. He was perfectly willing to discount what his eyes had seen, if someone else would just tell him he was crazy.

The damn Brit had a different idea, though.

"I'm getting my camera crew down here," Derek said. "We *must* film this."

An hour later, the sun had set, but the beach was bright as day. Klieg lights, driven by a generator that sounded like a bulldozer in a bathroom, blazed white-hot light on the egg. Derek was barking instructions to the light crew. Another technician held a boom microphone, standing as far from the egg as Derek would allow, and inching farther away whenever Derek turned his head away.

At the fringes of the artificial daytime stood Sam, alternately shielding her eyes and rubbing her temples. She felt a nearby presence and turned to meet the unhappy gaze of Blaise Corrigan.

"This is getting out of hand," he said.

Sam spread her hands. "Giant sea monster eggs have a way of doing that."

He sighed. "The mayor's not going to like this."

"He's hoping the air force will bomb it," she said. "Maybe we should keep him out of the decision loop."

"Or put him at ground zero." He gave her a conspiratorial wink. "You never heard me say that."

"Not to worry, Chief. With that generator, I can hardly hear myself think."

In the parking lot cars were already arriving, and a knot of gawkers had interrupted evening strolls to watch Derek's crew. "This is going to turn into a circus. I'd better set up some traffic control."

"I can direct traffic," Sam said. "You're the chief. You should be here."

He smiled. "You won't get away that easy, Officer. This is your scene. I'll be at our command post."

"Would that be the station or your living room?" she asked. "So I know where to find you, of course."

"Oh, I'll be moving around. A mobile command post."

"So if the mayor shows up, you're busy and I don't know where to find you."

He smiled. "You're a bright cop. I'll leave Mr. Diche in your capable hands. Just tell the mayor I'm . . . doing reconnaissance."

"Thanks a lot, Chief."

"No problem. You're doing just fine."

Sam suspected there was something else dancing in his eyes, but she also suspected she didn't want to know what it was. She watched him walk away, pausing for a moment to direct two silhouetted forms in her direction. Nat and Zeph, she realized as they stepped nearer the light. Perfect. Maybe they could figure out why the egg was bulging. Some perfectly simple, perfectly ordinary, perfectly *boring* explanation would be just . . . perfect.

Derek's crews would pack up their bright lights and noisy generator, and her life could get back to normal. She allowed the fantasy to spin on for a moment, thoughts of eating a normal meal before crawling into her normal bed for a normal night's sleep with normal dreams. Derek's exclamation shattered the image.

"Hell!"

Sam whirled around. "What?"

Then she saw it. The egg was vibrating. Shivering. Shaking. Acting as if it were having an internal earthquake.

The sight apparently rattled a lot of people, most notably Derek's crew, who were accustomed to filming the known and presenting it as the unknown. Confronted with the true unknown, they bolted. In the process, the klieg lights went out.

And the egg glowed.

A hush fell over the crowd...except, of course, for the sound of running feet. Those who remained simply stared at the unmistakable green glow.

Sam, who harbored a cowardly wish that she could be among the running feet, stared, too. It was...eerie. It was downright *scary*.

"That is so *cool*," Zeph said.

"Phosphorescence," Nat said.

Zeph shook her head. "Bioluminescence."

"Way cool," Nat agreed. "Of course, it might be radioactive."

The word was rather like someone making a very rude noise at a high-class party. It cast an instant hush over the beach, silencing even the surf. Was the ocean holding its breath?

Frank let out a cough. "We better get one of those, whaddayacallems, giggle counters."

"Geiger counter," Nat said. "We have one in the van."

"We should have it here," Zeph said. Her tone of voice implied that she did not intend to be the one to fetch it.

"Oh. Right." Nat trotted off toward the parking lot.

"How much sound do we really need?" asked the technician holding the boom mike.

Sam translated the question as: *Shouldn't I be farther away? A lot farther away?*

Derek answered. "That's good for right now. But I want you to record the sounds from the Geiger counter. And would somebody get the infrared camera?" He turned to Sam, a look of boyish glee on his face. "Can you *believe* this?"

Sam sighed. "At this point, I'd believe Godzilla swatting flying saucers away from the Don CeSar while King Kong built a sand castle for a Yeti to live in."

"Yetis live in the Himalayas," Derek said. "It'd be too warm for them here. But we might find Bigfoot before this is all said and done."

At this juncture, naturally, an all-too-familiar voice said from the rear of the crowd, "Radioactive? Did somebody say *radioactive*?"

The mayor emerged from behind the crowd to the forefront, where the green glow from the egg turned his Hawaiian shirt into a nightmare of weird colors. Don Ho, meet Freddy Kreuger. "Get the air force to bomb the damn thing right now!"

"But," said Sam equably enough, "if we bomb it, radioactive pieces will fly all over the place."

"That's what we have bomb shelters for! My God, I wonder if the civil defense people have been keeping the food fresh? What if all we've got in the shelters is botulism?" He paused, thinking about that. "It *has* been a long time since the Cuban missile crisis."

"So we eat lollipops," someone in the crowd said. "At least they don't glow in the dark."

"Yet," said someone else.

"We don't know the egg's radioactive," Derek said calmly, even as he waved frantically at his crew to come back to work. They seemed to be remarkably unwilling.

"So we can't bomb it," the mayor said, talking to himself as much as anyone. "Okay. Okay. I've got it." He poked a finger at Sam. "Get me the FBI right now! I want Agent Mulder here by midnight."

Sam hated to tell him that David Duchovny was hardly likely to come solve this problem. Just how out of touch with reality was the mayor? Unfortunately, she couldn't think of a sensible thing to say in response—short of calling the men with the butterfly net.

"We've . . . notified the authorities," she offered firmly, hoping the mayor, Paradise Beach's authority, would take that to mean more than it did.

"And speaking of authorities," the mayor rolled on, "where is Chief Corrigan?"

"He's doing recon," Sam said. "In case we need the bombers after all."

The mayor seemed mollified by that answer. "Okay. Well, then. Ummmm."

"Hey, who turned out the lights?" Zeph shouted.

And, sure enough, the egg had suddenly gone dark. Which would have been great, except that it started trembling again. Shaking. The mayor was suddenly doing a passable imitation of Hawaiian wallpaper on Frank Blodgett's chest.

"Get *off* me," Frank shouted, flailing his arms.

Nat tumbled out of the crowd holding a metal box in one hand, connected by a cable to a probe in his other hand. "Who turned out the lights?" he asked.

"Pete and repeat," Derek muttered.

"But they do speak Greek," Sam said. "So, can you tell if it's radioactive?"

"Sure," Nat said. "Zeph, you want to test it?"

"You're doing fine," Zeph said.

Nat looked at her for a moment, apparently deciding whether to say anything more and concluding there would be no point in it. Slowly, gingerly, he began to circle the egg in an ever-diminishing spiral.

"Hey, get back here," Derek called to the boom operator. "I want this recorded."

"We can dub it," the sound man said, still backing away. "We have lots of Geiger counter sound on file."

"That wouldn't be *real*," Derek said. "We're supposed to be journalists here."

"Like the anaconda?" the sound man asked.

"It was a *real* anaconda! Now get your butt over here and record, or I'll make sure you spend the rest of your life recording insect sounds in a swamp for one of the science channels."

Sam rather liked his masterful air.

Click. Click. The Geiger counter was ticking

irregularly, like a time bomb with a finicky mainspring.

"That's just background radiation," Nat said. "It does that all the time."

The mayor didn't look convinced. Neither did a man in the crowd wearing a Grateful Dead T-shirt. "It's all that government nuclear testing," the man shouted.

"Actually," Zeph said, "it's a combination of unstable ions in the sand, subatomic particles from solar flares, and the general background noise of the universe."

The mayor seemed somewhat mollified by that explanation, if he even understood it. Sam was sure she'd understood at least some of it. Zeph didn't *look* worried, and she ought to know. Then again, Zeph was hanging back at the perimeter with the others. It was Nat who looked worried.

"Do we have sound on that?" Derek asked.

"Yeah, yeah," said the boom operator, looking as happy as a scalded cat. "Is that enough already?"

Then, as Nat moved around the egg, the clicking speeded up.

"Hmmm," he said.

"Hmmm," Zeph said.

"What?" demanded the mayor, who'd given up clinging to Frank and was now easing backward.

"That's a little higher than normal," Nat said. He backed away from the egg a step.

The mayor stepped even farther away. "So it is radioactive?"

"Uhh..." Nat hesitated.

"See, what'd I tell you?" said the Deadhead. "It's just like in *Godzilla*. Nuclear testing makes a monster. I wonder how big this one is gonna grow."

The egg, in answer to his question, started glowing again. Greenly. And the Geiger counter quit clicking. Completely.

"Weird," said Nat, who was edging closer to Zeph. "Really weird."

Sam felt something brush her arm and looked around to realize she had eased her way over to Derek, until she was standing right next to him. He didn't say a word, just put his arm around her shoulders.

It took every ounce of her self-control not to turn and burrow into Derek's strong arms and bury her face against his hard chest. For the first time in her life, Sam felt true appreciation for a man's physical strength. At that moment she wouldn't have complained if he'd tossed her over his shoulder and carried her off to his cave. He wouldn't even need to hit her over the head with a club.

It took her a few seconds to realize the electric tingles she was feeling weren't coming from the egg, they were coming from Derek. Now she was truly in a quandary, uncertain which was more of a threat: Derek or the egg.

But Derek's arm seemed to hold her close to

his side, though he used no effort to do so. She could have broken away easily by taking just one step. But then his fingers gently rubbed her upper arm, and that one step became impossible to take. The most delightful shivers began to course through her, and she had to fight a very different urge to turn into Derek's arm.

If that egg suddenly hatched, he *was* going to have to toss her over his shoulder, to get her out of here, because she was incapable of movement.

But then the egg settled down again. No light shone from it. No movement came from it. Minutes passed, filled only with the whisper of the breeze and the gentle roar of the surf.

Zeph broke the silence. "Get a shovel," she told Nat.

"What for?"

"This thing isn't real."

He faced her, his chin thrust out. "You can't be sure of that. What are you going to do? Kill it? It might be a new species. Something we've never discovered before."

Sam, reluctant to leave Derek's embrace, nevertheless had to do so. "I can't let you hurt the egg. It's . . . evidence."

"I don't want to hurt the egg," Zeph said. "I want to find the power cord."

Derek caught on instantly. "She's right," he said. "If it's a hoax, then there's some kind of motor and light inside it. It has to be powered somehow."

"Batteries," Sam said. "It could be batteries."

"Then somebody had to put them inside it," Derek reasoned. "In which case there has to be some kind of a door or opening somewhere."

"Most likely underneath it where no one can see it," Sam agreed.

"So let's turn it over."

Unfortunately, the suggestion didn't exactly bring out a crowd of volunteers. In fact, all it seemed to do was make the crowd disappear even more. Pretty soon, Sam realized she, Derek, Frank, and the two biologists were the only ones left on the beach. Oh, and Derek's crew, which was doing a passable imitation of being invisible.

"I don't know," Nat said. "What if we break it? What if something comes out of it?"

"Like what?" Zeph asked.

"Oh, maybe a giant blob."

"Great," Zeph groaned, throwing up one hand. "*Attack of the Killer Tomatoes. The Blob.* You watch too many late-night movies."

"All I'm saying is, if it really *is* alive and we break it, we may never know what it really is."

Zeph strode forward and poked the egg with a finger. "It's pretty soft. It won't break. It's not like a chicken egg."

"I still don't think it's a good idea."

Neither did Sam. "Maybe we should start out conservatively."

"Like how?" Nat demanded.

"Like digging."

But now Mr. Suddenly-Conservative Derek Diche had second thoughts. "There's just one problem."

"What's that?" Sam asked, though she would at that moment have rather plucked out a toenail than give him any more importance than he seemed to think was his birthright.

"It's soft."

"So?"

"If you were going to build a mechanical contraption of some kind, would you make it soft like this? Wouldn't that make the whole process more difficult? And how would you keep it slimy? It should have dried out by now."

"Hmm," Sam said. Zeph and Nat echoed her. Much as she hated to admit it, Derek the Wonder Man had a point. Then she began to wonder why she was reacting so antagonistically to him again. He hadn't really done anything. Maybe because she didn't like the echoes of the tingles he'd awakened in her? Surely she was a better woman than that.

"There's only one way to find out," Zeph argued.

"I don't know," Derek said. "I'm kind of with Nat on this one. What if it's alive? Besides, what kind of idiot would run a power cord through wet sand?"

The midnight stars wheeled overhead, twinkling and fuzzy in the humidity. There was no moon to brighten the sky, and the seaside lights of all the buildings had been turned off because it was turtle nesting season.

Sam sat on her favorite dune, arms wrapped around her knees. Frank had gone home a little while ago, considering his shift finished whether he was relieved or not. Derek had decided to remain on the beach with his infrared camera, though he'd sent his crew back to their hotel. The camera sat on a tripod, taking time-lapse photos of the egg, which proved uncooperative. It did nothing at all.

Everybody else in the town seemed to be tucked safely into their beds, including Zeph and Nat, who had decided to consult other authorities before taking any action.

Which left Derek and Sam all alone in magnificent isolation with the suspect. Er, egg.

"I'm going to pick a bone with the chief in the morning," Sam announced.

"Why?" Derek dropped to the sand beside her and folded his arms across his knees.

"He should have sent relief for Frank. I shouldn't have to stay out here all night."

"You're right." He stuffed his hand into his pockets and pulled out the rental car keys. "Here, take my car and go home to bed."

"Are you kidding? If I leave this beach, something will happen."

"Are you always such a pessimist?"

Sam scowled at him. "Only since the egg arrived."

"People don't become pessimists overnight. What's wrong, Sam?"

"Other than a lack of sleep? Other than having to babysit a blob when I ought to be doing real police work?"

He nodded. "I guess those are good reasons."

She sighed, realizing she sounded like a petulant child. "Okay, I'm being unreasonable. *This* is my job. For better or worse."

He gave a soft laugh. "Hey, it's not a marriage."

"Close enough." She unfolded her arms and scooped up a handful of sand, letting it run through her fingers. "I didn't want much out of being a cop. That's why I came here. I wanted a peaceful town with a reasonably low crime rate. A place where I could mostly deal with good people. I've got no delusions about capturing serial killers or anything like that; that's not my style. I just wanted to help make people's lives better."

He nodded. "That's a good goal."

She grew embarrassed, realizing she'd let him into a private place. But how did she slam the door now? Only by shutting her mouth.

"You want to do good things, Sam," he said. "Nothing wrong with that. As for the egg. . . " He shook his head. "This could be what I've been looking for."

"What *are* you looking for?"

"A real mystery. Something new on the face of the earth."

"Why?"

He hesitated. "It's kind of hard to explain," he said slowly.

Sam waited patiently. Even as a part of her was tolling a warning bell, cautioning her that getting close to Derek promised only pain, another part of her was eager to find some saving grace in him, some proof that he was more than a handsome face and a gorgeous body.

"I guess," he said finally, "that I've given up on the human race."

Sam, who had a lot of faith in humanity—well, except for smooth-talking, handsome men, one of whom had cut a wide swath of destruction through her life in college—found the statement painful to hear. "Why?"

"I don't know. Being a war correspondent does things to you. Or it did to me, anyway. You can't help but get a little cynical."

"I imagine."

His eyes grew distant as he looked out at the sea. His voice softened, so that Sam had to strain to hear it.

"I was in a little town in the Balkans. I think the name was all consonants. I couldn't even pronounce it. Well, not like the locals did, anyway. The situation was...well...maybe what you heard on the news. Political infighting disguised as ethnic strife. Who gets to be king of the hill. And in the process, a lot of young men with more rage than reason, doing ugly things. Just because they could."

He paused for a moment as if wondering whether to go on. Sam simply sat quietly and listened. This was not the Derek Diche she had come to know. This was someone far more distant and alone. Finally he continued.

"There was a statue of the Virgin Mother in the town square, in front of a small church. Like a lot of statues in a lot of towns in front of a lot of churches. But on that morning, there was a stigmata. Blood seeping down from the eyes of the statue, like tears. It was an ironic story in the middle of an awful situation. And I guess maybe I was looking for hope. So I covered it.

"I don't know if it was the film crew, or rumors, or whatever. But . . . the town's faithful came out. Wondered. Looked. Sort of like people have looked at this egg, but . . . there was a feeling in the crowd. As if God were going to save them. I interviewed several of them. I went back to the truck to polish the piece and transmit it."

Now his fingers tightened into fists. He bowed his head for a moment. "That's when I heard the machine guns firing. I went out, and the rebels or the government or whoever it was had opened up on the people in the square. Twenty-nine people were killed. Some I'd interviewed not an hour before. They'd said the crying Virgin meant God would rescue them. It turned out the rebels or whoever had painted the blood there as a lure, to draw them out. It wasn't a miracle; it was mass murder."

"Derek," Sam said, then floundered for words. "I'm sorry."

He looked at her. "For what? You weren't there. I was the one who went around with my camera, trying to catch wonder, trying to capture hope. Instead, I called them together to die. And . . . a part of me died, too. What little was left that believed in beauty and hope and divine rescue and magic . . . died." He looked at the egg. "And now I have this."

"And now we have this," Sam echoed, not knowing what else to say. She realized the man she'd been seeing, the confident, cocky, almost arrogant know-it-all who seemed at home in any situation, was as lost inside as she was. As the surf rolled up on the sand, she wondered what to say. How to share his pain without opening herself to the very kind of pain she'd so often found in men. A few sweet words, a few sweet thoughts, and then . . . betrayal.

He seemed to sense her conflict, and shifted an inch or two farther away in the sand. That shift, barely visible, opened a gulf between them and inside her. She hugged herself and looked up at the stars, as if hoping for some guidance. She found only loneliness.

"I'm sorry," she said again.

"We're all sorry," he answered. "Maybe someday we'll stop being sorry and do something about it. But I'm not holding my breath."

Not knowing what else she could do, she slid over until she was right beside him, her shoulder pressed to his arm. Closeness was all she had to offer, the comfort of a human touch. After a moment, his arm wrapped around her shoulders.

But not the way it had before. This time it held her snugly, as if he needed her even closer. His hand was cold against hers, and she lowered her arm around her back and tucked his hand beneath her arm. To keep it warm, she told herself. Not because in this moment she ached for his touch. No. Just to keep his hand warm.

But his fingertips were brushing against the curve of her breast. She knew it. And, she was sure, so did he.

She looked at his profile. His face seemed to change moment by moment. Remembered pain mixed with present closeness. Her own heart swirled, and deep within her another pulse added its desire to the emotional stew.

"Emotional stew," she heard herself say.

"That's what we're here for," he answered. "That's what we're in for."

Answering a tiny light within her, fueled by the pulse in her loins, she tucked his hand closer beneath her arm, so that he could not help but cup the swell of her breast. "I could . . . maybe . . . enjoy stew," she said.

He chuckled. "A moonlit picnic. Stew, with a big egg."

"The egg can take care of itself," she said,

reaching up to kiss his cheek. "Life has a way of doing that, if we give it time."

"How much time do you need?"

She paused, wondering what the question meant. Taking the easy way out, she answered, "Well, it won't be dawn for a few hours."

His fingers had found the edge of her areola through her shirt and bra, and brushed ever so gently.

"We're going to get covered in sand."

She shrugged. "We'll manage."

What was she doing? The question hammered at the doors of her consciousness, but couldn't get through. His merest touch filled her with a longing that carried her down a dark, dangerous road, away from wisdom and caution. And she didn't care.

Because the night seemed to swirl all around her, shutting out everything except the feelings that had sprung to life in her body. The aching for closeness. For intimate touches. For fulfillment. For magic.

His face turned toward hers and, just for the merest instant, their lips brushed. She wouldn't even have been sure it had happened but for the swelling throb within her that answered the contact as if sent by secret courier. Again. Soft and gentle, almost like the sea breeze, but far, far more electric.

Her arm had found its way to his thigh, as if by a will of its own. Her fingertips trailed gently in the soft, curly hairs. He chuckled. Actually *chuckled*. She did it again, and he squirmed.

"Tickles," he said.

"Uh huh, right." Her fingers swirled again. When he squirmed this time, it was his hips that rose briefly. "Tickles?"

His hand shifted slightly to her side, and a fingertip traced a slow, barely perceptible path up higher, higher, until it passed over her now-erect nipple with the barest of touches. Now it was she who squirmed.

"Like that tickles," he said.

"I like tickles."

He was grinning at her now, his smile gleaming, his eyes gleaming, too, seeming to catch the starlight and transform it to a wicked glint. His hand slipped away from her breast, down to her ribs, a light feathery touch that proved to be one of the most arousing tickles she had ever felt in her life. A gasp escaped her and she tossed her head backward, baring her throat in ancient invitation.

Myths and ancestral memories of the pirates who had once plundered this coast bounced around in her brain, making the night seem otherworldly, making Derek seem dark and dangerous and, oh, so commanding as he lay her back on the sand.

The buttons of her blouse released one by one, each seeming to free her from yet another inhibition as it slipped loose of the buttonhole.

The soft night breeze caressed the bare skin of her midriff, a delicious, forbidden feeling.

His fingertips followed the breeze, brushing lightly over her skin, skin which had grown exquisitely sensitive to the lightest touch. Underlying muscle quivered in response.

She wanted him; oh, how she wanted him.

And then someone burped.

8

Derek sat bolt upright. "Who's there?"

Sam pulled her blouse together and sat up, her fumbling fingers trying to work the buttons. Humiliation began to burn her cheeks, even as fear made her heart pound.

She looked around, but nothing moved. The night was silent again, except for the rhythmic pulse of the surf.

"That was definitely a burp," Derek said. Shoving to his feet, he began to walk around, looking for anywhere a person could be hiding.

Burrp!

This time there was no mistaking the source: the egg. Sam's embarrassment began to fade. No one had been spying on them. On the other hand, she'd revealed a whole lot to Derek. But she could castigate herself later—right now she just needed to say something that would get them past the awkwardness she was feeling.

"Oh, great," she said. "An embryonic sea monster with indigestion."

"Maybe it's morning sickness," Derek offered.

Sam looked at her watch, then out at the night sky. "Then it's ahead of schedule. Won't be morning for another five hours."

"So we have an embryonic sea monster with indigestion and a lousy diurnal clock. That fits."

She laughed, deep belly laughs releasing the tension of the moment that had come upon them. He joined in, sitting on the sand and making burping noises at the egg. He looked every bit like the playful adolescent he must have been once, long ago, before the world in all its ugliness and false adoration had changed him. He burped again.

And the egg answered him.

Both of them froze for a minute. Then Derek said, "You know, this could get really gross. How am I going to get this past the network? An egg that communicates by belching."

"Better than tooting." But Sam's sense of humor was beginning to fade as she realized this egg had it in for her. It was determined to mess up her entire life. "What," she asked it, "have I ever done to you?"

"Huh?" said Derek, looking puzzled.

"Never mind." He'd only think she was paranoid if she told him what she was feeling. And maybe she was. All the darn egg had done was sit there, glow a little, shake a little, and belch. It was hardly the stuff of paranoid delusions.

Or was it?

"It certainly has some interesting bodily functions," Derek mused.

"No more than the average high school boy."

"Oh, you know high school boys who glow in the dark?"

"In my experience, that's about the only place high school boys glow," she answered. Then blushed.

He laughed. "Maybe I should've worn my lizard suit after all. Maybe it'd hatch."

Mentally rerunning nature programs she'd seen on television, Sam seemed to remember that eggs got active only when the occupants were about to spring on the world. She didn't want to be here all alone on the beach in the dark with no protection except Derek's ego when Godzilla or Rodan decided to make an appearance. Imagining the dimensions of some slimy creature that could burst out of an egg that size was enough to give her nightmares. It was probably bigger than her or Derek, no matter that it would only be a baby.

A hungry baby.

Ack.

"Derek?" she asked quietly.

"Yes?"

"How safe do you think this is?"

He looked at the egg for a moment, then at her. "You know, honestly, I don't have a clue."

"I think maybe if I'm going to be out here all night guarding this ... thing ... maybe I should go back and get my pistol. You know ... just in case?"

He paused for a moment, then nodded. "You're right, of course. I've been having so much fun playing with this thing I've forgotten what it is. Hell, I don't even know what it is. A bit of an equalizer may be in order."

He took her hand and led her back to the car.

Fifty yards away, behind a dune, peeking through saw palmettos and sea oats, Hadley Philpott watched. This was what Mary Todd wanted, God knew why. He just hoped she knew what she was up to.

Of course, he'd been questioning Mary's wisdom for thirty years now, and he still kept getting caught up her hijinks. *C'est la guerre.*

He crept quietly back up the beach, slipped across the boulevard, and entered his snug little bungalow. There he sat at his computer and typed an e-mail.

The computers had been Mary's idea, too. All of the Hole in the Seawall Gang were beyond an age where technology was welcome in their lives. Well, except for Mary. Once she'd figured out the principle that e-mail would allow her to keep in touch with her gang regardless of whether someone was at home, the phone was busy, or they were sleeping, she'd taken to it like a lemming to a cliff. And nothing would do except that they all buy computers so she could hound them whenever she felt like it.

Obediently, Hadley typed in the e-mail, even though he hoped she wouldn't see it before morning. He wanted to be done with this.

Dear Mary,

I suppose you made the egg belch. Goodness knows how you did it. However, you might want to consider a more hands-off approach, since it interrupted a rather intimate scene between your nephew and Samantha Bartlett.

By the way, next time get another voyeur. I will certainly not keep an eye on them under such circumstances again. However, you will no doubt be pleased to know that they left the beach hand in hand.

I left the beach feeling rather . . . soiled. And not just by sand. In the future, do your own dirty work.

Sincerely, Hadley

He should have known Mary wasn't asleep. Before he could even exit his e-mail program, her response zipped back to him.

Dear Hadley,

If you were a voyeur, it's your own fault. I never asked you to watch them when they were being intimate. And what do you mean, I made the egg belch?

Sincerely, Mary

P.S. How intimate?

He was a two-finger typist, but he hammered the keys hard as he replied.

Dear Mary,

None of your business how intimate. And if you didn't make the egg belch, who did? Good night.

Sincerely, Hadley

Then, before she could strike again, he switched off his computer without exiting the programs, even though he knew he wasn't supposed to. If the damn thing blew up, so much the better.

What was he doing talking to Mary at this ungodly hour, anyway?

Grumping, he made his way to the shower, swearing that the next time he saw Mary Todd, he was going to tell her precisely where to stuff her machinations.

It occurred to Sam just before dawn that if the mama who'd laid this egg decided to come back to check on it, life was going to get awfully interesting. It didn't help to remember the size of the footprints that had walked up and down the beach only a couple of days ago.

Derek was stretched out on the sand nearby, snoring just barely loud enough to be heard over the surf. He'd tried valiantly to remain awake, but he'd already stayed up all night, on British time, before he finally lost the battle. She wished she could join him. Right now her eyes felt like grit and her brain was anything but sharp. If a monster walked out of the water right now, she'd probably just stare at it in slack-jawed wonder.

The arrival of the DustBuster Brigade saved her. At a distance, Colonel Albemarle and his "troops" began to emerge from the night, marching in perfect formation. Sam watched their approach, which broke off abruptly as they apparently saw trash on the sand. Scattering, they began to pick up whatever it was and dump it into their garbage bags.

Sam hesitated, wondering if she should wake Derek. He might be embarrassed if she didn't. On the other hand, having him sleep nearby on the sand had been the best of all possible worlds for her during the night. He'd been there in case of catastrophe, but he'd been asleep so she didn't have to deal with her awkwardness about what had almost happened between them.

And boy, did she feel awkward. She couldn't

understand what had overtaken her. She'd been touched by his story, certainly. It was a revelation to her that the talking head with his too-perfect smile who seemed to have the world by a string actually had known pain, grief, bitterness, and guilt. That he'd lost his faith in humanity.

But being touched by Derek's pain wasn't reason enough to fall into his arms. Nor was passion. But she had to be honest with herself: Derek was a hunk, and she apparently wasn't any more immune to that than the rest of the world's women.

But Derek was passing through. She might entertain him for a few hours or days, but then he'd return to his world, where beautiful women hung on his every word. And she'd be left alone to nurse the wounds and humiliation.

It was so ridiculous. He wasn't even her type to begin with. Heavens, he was more of a three-ring circus than a man, anyway. Oh, he came down here pretending to be a perfectly ordinary Joe, but she'd seen his programs. All of them. Wrestling with sleepy anacondas, standing bent over in artificial blizzards, "dramatizing" some hokey UFO display. He was definitely a circus, and he himself was in the center ring.

What in the world had she been thinking of last night?

The DustBuster Brigade drew closer, and she decided to take pity on Derek. It seemed the humane thing to do, regardless of what she thought of him personally.

She poked him with her toe. He grumbled something and tried to turn over. Why did even the worst snake of a male have to look so innocent while sleeping? Alan had looked innocent, too. She'd never guessed he was making passes at her girlfriends.

She poked him again, harder. He sprawled on his back and despite herself she noticed how flat his stomach was. A warm little tingle settled between her legs. Oh, man, she was a wuss!

She poked him again. He groaned and pulled one leg up, emphasizing some pretty darn good muscles.

"Hey," she said, poking him again. "It's Bigfoot!"

He sat up in a shot. Wide awake. "Where?"

"I was kidding. But now I know what it takes to wake you up."

He yawned and tried to scowl at her at the same time. "It's still dark. Why'd you wake me?"

She jerked her chin up the beach. "The Dust-Buster Brigade. I didn't think you'd want them to find you snoring and looking just too angelic to be believed."

"Oh." He glanced in the brigade's direction, then back at her with a grin she definitely didn't like. "So you think I'm angelic?"

"I didn't say that."

"You said I looked just too angelic."

"Do you have a tape recorder for a brain?"

"It helps in my job." He smiled with satisfaction.

"Well, then replay the entire statement. You forgot the part about when you're sleeping. That's the only time it applies."

He leered at her. "I wouldn't want to be angelic when I'm awake. That's no fun."

She should have known he wasn't going to drop what had happened—what had almost happened—between them last night. "Didn't your mother teach you any manners?"

"Plenty of them. She also taught me to be honest."

"Apparently you didn't learn your etiquette very well."

He shrugged and stretched, giving her an excuse to peek at the broad wall of his chest, which looked pretty good under the stretched fabric of his polo shirt.

"Look, last night was a mistake," she said bravely. A mistake that could quickly recur if she spent too much time around him. "Let's not mention it again."

"M'lady's wish is my command."

He said it with a really upper-class British accent, sounding like the Prince of Wales. Which made her think he was pulling her leg. But since she *didn't* want to discuss the subject any longer, she let it pass. Besides, if he didn't keep the promise, she'd throw it up in his aristocratic face and tell him he was staining his family escutcheon. If he had one. But she was pretty sure he'd get the idea.

Her chin set with determination, she turned her attention to Albemarle and his cronies, who were just now reaching them.

"A fine morning," Albemarle said by way of greeting, then called his group to a halt. "Nothing's changed, I see."

Sam didn't tell him otherwise. Talk of glowing, shaking, and belching eggs was the last thing they needed getting around town— although, actually, everything but the belching *was* probably running around the rumor mill. There'd been a fair-sized crowd during the glowing and shaking part.

She sighed. Things were going to get seriously out of hand in Paradise Beach. She could feel it coming. She just hoped it didn't happen on her shift.

"Say, Colonel," said Derek. "Do you think you and your lads could perform a little relief duty here? Officer Bartlett has been watching this deuced egg all night."

"Well, certainly we shall," Albemarle said heartily. "Won't we, men?"

His troops didn't look quite as hearty or willing as Albemarle did, but they all nodded anyway. Sam noticed, however, that they none of them were getting all that terribly close to the egg.

"Just for a short while," she hastened to reassure them. "I need to get another officer down here."

"In fact," she said to Derek a few minutes later as he drove her home for the second time that night, "I'm going to drag Chief Corrigan out of bed and ask him why he never relieved Frank last night."

"Maybe he didn't expect anybody to babysit the egg all night."

"That doesn't seem like him."

"I wouldn't know." He glanced over at her. "You could hardly blame him if he was hoping the egg might meet with an accident."

"*I'm* beginning to wish it would."

"You just haven't had enough sleep."

She cast a dark look his way. "I suppose you think this is the height of adventure."

"I admit it. I do. And I can hardly wait to see the film from last night. Want me to call you when it's processed?"

Part of her wished the whole thing would just dry up and blow away. But the rational part of her knew it wouldn't. And as long as that egg and Derek were in the same town, she was his liaison. Whoopee.

"Sure," she said, fighting back a yawn. She'd been fighting back yawns for so long now, her jaws felt sore. "That'd be great."

Jillie was having nightmares. About the fourth time her arm flew out and popped Blaise Corrigan in the nose, he gave up on the idea of getting a good night's sleep. Which turned out to be just as well, because he no sooner crawled out of the bed and went to the kitchen, where he stacked a pot of strong coffee to brew, than the phone rang.

Who the devil was calling at five-thirty in the morning.

"Chief," said the familiar voice of Miss Mary Todd, "we need to talk."

Blaise loved Mary. *Everyone* loved Mary, except when they were exasperated with her, which happened often enough to anyone who crossed her path more than once. "Mary, it's still the middle of the night."

"Poppycock. The early bird gets the worm. Besides, I saw your light come on before I dialed."

It was a small town, Blaise reminded himself. Mary didn't have to look far from one of her many windows to know what most folks on the island were doing. "Okay, but I just got up. I'm making coffee right now. I don't guarantee to be intelligent."

"You'll wake up fast enough. The egg is alive."

"Alive?" He repeated the word, feeling a momentary confusion. Everybody had pretty much agreed that it must be alive, since it was difficult to explain any other way. "And?"

"Last night it was doing odd things. Haven't

you heard? It was shaking and moving and glowing, and finally it belched."

"Belched?"

"Belched."

He stood staring out the kitchen window over the sink, in the general direction of Mary Todd's house, and wondered how it was that he was always the last to hear what was going on. "How did you hear about that?"

"I have my ways."

Of course she did. Mary had an uncanny knack of knowing everything that happened in Paradise Beach. She must have a web of spies better than the CIA. "A belch seems harmless enough."

"Of course. But Derek filmed it."

Oh, great. "What was he doing out there?"

"Well, apparently the darn thing started to get active. You remember; you were there for a while. *Derek* hung around out there all night."

Blaise gave himself a mental kick in the butt. Apparently setting guards on the damn thing wasn't going to be enough. But he'd wanted to get home to Jillie. Her pregnancy was making her a little . . . volatile, emotionally, and he was very conscious of trying to be there for her as much as was humanly possible.

Now Derek had gotten it all on film. Somehow he suspected that wasn't going to be a good thing for Paradise Beach. Most people weren't too concerned about the egg, but that wouldn't last forever. As the egg remained and no one did anything about it, concerns were going to grow, and folks would start considering it a real threat.

But the question remained: Why was Mary telling him this? He didn't like the feeling that she was manipulating events toward her own ends, as she did too often.

"What do you want me to do, Mary?" he asked, hoping that she would say something to tip him off to her plot.

But Mary was cannier than that. "I'm just giving you a heads up, boy."

When he hung up, he sighed. With Mary stirring the pot, there was no telling what would happen.

He had just poured himself a cup of coffee when the phone rang again. This time it was Sam Bartlett.

"It would have been *nice*," she said tartly, "if you had assigned someone to relieve Frank last night."

He felt a moment of confusion. "What do you mean?"

"I mean I sat on that beach all night with a belching, shaking, glowing egg. Frank cut out at midnight and nobody relieved him."

"But Fritz Holder was supposed to relieve him."

"Really? Well, Fritz never showed up. And I'm exhausted and filthy, and if you'll pardon me, I'm going to shower and go to bed. Somebody else will have to take my shift."

"Who's watching the egg right now?"

"The DustBuster Brigade."

Cripes. "Take the day, Sam. I'll find out what happened to Fritz."

It didn't take very long. Five minutes later the phone was ringing again. This time it was the station. "Chief? Fritz just showed up. He's kind of a mess. He says he was abducted by aliens."

9

Mary Todd hung up the phone and looked at the Reverend Arthur Archer. He lay sprawled in her easy chair, breathing heavily, each breath drawing in and then puffing out the green alien Halloween mask he was wearing. If she hadn't known it was Arthur, she'd have sworn he was a very muscular, very deluded teenager. Muscular, because of the shoulder pads he was wearing under the silvery costume suit.

"You can take the mask off, Arthur," she said.

He nodded and struggled for a moment.

"It might be easier if you take the gloves off first."

Arthur shook the Tampa Bay Lightning hockey gloves from his hands, then tugged at the mask which he'd tucked beneath his clerical collar. When he finally had his face free, he gasped in air.

"That thing is hot," he said. A sheen of perspiration was evidence of his words. "Mary, what mortal sin have you gotten me to commit this time?"

"Arthur, dear, I told you to relax that overwound conscience of yours. It's merely a prank."

"Why do I have difficulty believing a mere *prank* should cause a grown man to faint in fright? Or that a mere prank involves leaving a police officer in a shed behind the church all night, sobbing his eyes out and praying for mercy?"

"He didn't really."

"Yes, Mary, he did." Arthur dropped the mask and it collapsed into a puddle of green felt topped by two huge black almond eyes. "At least that's what he was doing when I went to let him out this morning. Rarely have I felt so despicable. Then, of course, when he came bolting out of the shed, I was positive he was going to arrest me."

"Clearly he did not."

"Clearly," said Arthur, struggling for the Velcro tabs that held the costume together. "No, he went running and howling for the hills, as it were."

"The police station, most likely." Mary nodded with satisfaction.

"What have you gotten me into, Mary?"

"Not a thing, dear Arthur. There isn't a soul on this island who would believe a respectable minister capable of kidnapping a police officer."

"Including," Arthur said heavily, "the respectable minister himself."

"So pray for forgiveness. I'm sure you'll get it. You were an innocent dupe."

Arthur sighed. "I've been duped so many times by you that I find it hard to claim innocence any longer. Stupidity, yes, but innocence? No way."

"So tell me, Arthur. Exactly what did you say to our good officer?"

"It said, 'We need you,'" Fritz Holder said, trying unsuccessfully to find his mouth with a quivering cup of coffee. The lukewarm liquid spilled onto his uniform shirt. "And that's when it grabbed me with its huge space gloves."

"All I said," Arthur told Mary, "was that he needed to come with me. Then he passed out cold."

"I fought free," Fritz said. "And I grabbed for my gun. Before I could unholster it, the alien pulled its ray gun and zapped me. As soon as that beam hit me, I couldn't move. I was paralyzed."

* * *

"I couldn't rouse him," said Arthur. "I certainly tried. That's when I had my first qualm. But... I couldn't leave him lying in the parking lot. Anyone might have run over him. So I did what you told me to. I put him in my car and took him to the garden shed behind the church. Do you have any idea how heavy Fritz Holder is?"

Fritz swigged more coffee, then reached for the glass of water Blaise had poured for him earlier. "It carried me away on this beam of light. I was floating through space. The next thing I knew, I was in this dark room. And the alien said, 'We're going to examine you later.'"

"I left him in the shed. I didn't even lock it," Arthur continued. "I don't know at what point he woke up, but I *do* know that at five this morning he started to make a real ruckus."

"They had me strapped down on this table," Fritz said. "I couldn't see anything at all. I could hardly move. But I made up my mind I had to get out of there somehow, even if it meant taking over the entire ship. I struggled against my bonds for what seemed like hours, and finally I worked myself free."

"I figured," Arthur said, "that perhaps he couldn't get the door open from inside. Although he should have been able to. At any rate, I put on this stupid costume again—I certainly didn't want him to recognize me—and I went out to open the door."

"They came back for me," Fritz continued, his hands shaking. "A whole bunch of them. They were tall and ugly, with these huge shoulders, green faces, and big black eyes like you see on all those TV shows. But I knew I had to get out of there and warn everyone. So I charged them. I don't know how many of them I kicked and hit, but all of a sudden I pushed through this door.

"I don't know how far I fell, but the next thing I knew I was in the backyard of the church."

He wiped his brow. "I'll never forget those space gloves they wore. Big things with this symbol on the back of them."

He reached for a pad and drew a lightning bolt.

Blaise scanned it. "Looks like the Tampa Bay Lightning logo."

Fritz shook his head. "No, boss, it wasn't hockey gloves. It was space gloves."

"Anyway," Arthur finished, "he tumbled out of that shed as if his pants were on fire and went running. I don't even think he saw me."

Blaise looked over at the other officer in the room. "Get me the artist, will you?" He turned to Fritz. "You're going to have to help us draw a picture of these guys."

Fritz nodded. "Anything I can do. But if you ask me, Chief, we need the air force. Now."

Mary picked up the phone and called the mayor. "Carl? I thought you should know. Aliens abducted a police officer last night. Do you think it has anything to do with that egg?"

Behind her, Arthur put his head in his hands. "Why, Mary?" he asked when she hung up. "Why?"

"Because it's necessary." She smiled at him. "Put that suit in a garbage bag, Arthur. I'll burn it later." Then she closed the library door firmly behind her.

Just in time, too, because her nephew came in the front door as she did it.

"Where were you all night?" she asked, pretending disapproval.

"Filming an egg. I'm exhausted. So if you'll excuse me, I'll think I'll just head up to bed."

Mary clucked. "You need to get your days and nights straightened around."

"Tomorrow. Right now I'm too tired."

Mary frowned as he passed her and headed for the stairs. "Oh, by the way, Nephew?"

He paused and looked back at her. "Yes?"

"Did you hear that one of our police officers was abducted by aliens last night? Someone just called me from the station."

"Really?" Derek, whose foot was on the lowest step, removed it and faced her. "It must be a prank."

"No prank, dear boy. At any rate, I thought it would fit in with your program."

Derek was back out the door almost before she finished speaking. Humming to herself, Mary picked up the hall phone and dialed Sam Bartlett's number. All was fair in love and war, she told herself.

The Identi-Kit software didn't handle aliens, so the department had to fall back on the services of Rich Bender, a local artist who occasionally helped them out. Rich was an unconventional soul, inclined to wear beads and loose white pants and shirts à la Indian gurus. His hair resembled a tonsure, with a big, curly nimbus on top of his head encircling a large bald spot.

His small gallery on the boulevard sold only his own works, mostly prints of his pastels of the beach and sky. However, when money got tight, Rich did charcoal portraits for tourists. Depending on what he thought of a given subject, he might produce a realistic image or a caricature. As he was fond of telling the tourists, "It's a crap shoot, man. You take what you get." Surprisingly, the tourists did.

Work for the police couldn't be a crap shoot, however, and Rich seemed to understand that. Usually.

"You're kidding, right?" he said when Blaise explained what he wanted him to draw.

"Sorry," said Blaise. They were in the front office now, where officers were lingering, reluctant to go out on their patrols because they might miss something. Fritz was beginning to feel a little better, because now he was regaling his buddies with tales of his bravery.

"Look, man," Rich said. "I do portraits, not comic strips."

"Think of it as a portrait of an alien."

"Cripes." Rich rolled his eyes to the heavens. "This is beneath me."

Blaise gripped his shoulder. "Think of it as your civic duty. The drawing might give us clues about the perp."

"Perp. Right. I'm doing a drawing of a perpetrator." He seemed to be trying to absorb the idea and get comfortable with it. "Even if it looks like something out of *Independence Day*."

"Right," said Blaise bracingly.

"I don't know. Maybe you ought to call Industrial Light and Magic. They know all about aliens."

"They know all about making them up. I need someone to draw realistically. What Fritz saw."

"Are you sure Fritz shouldn't be on Thorazine?"

"All right! Where's the air force?" the mayor demanded as he burst through the door. Blaise did his level best not to laugh at the mayor's latest sartorial crime, navy blue slacks and a white jacket over a crimson shirt, a blue tie bespeckled with stars. The patriotic vision was dimmed slightly by the fuzzy bunny slippers on his feet. As he stomped in, little eyes on springs waggled around his insteps. He paused at the chief's gaze and set his jaw. "My granddaughter gave them to me." He paused again. "Cal Lepkin's dog left a stool by my car door and I stepped in it. So my real shoes are airing on my balcony."

Blaise knew the mayor owned more than one pair of shoes. Which meant he'd run out of his condo without remembering he was in slippers.

Which meant that *somebody* had told the mayor what had happened. Blaise looked around the room, wondering which of his officers had the big mouth.

"It's early yet," Blaise said to him. "I'm not sure we need anything yet."

"What's the matter with you?" the mayor demanded, stomping his foot and setting one set of eyes to wiggling wildly. "We've got a dinosaur egg on the beach, one of our officers has been kidnapped by aliens, and you don't think we need the air force?"

"I'm not even sure we need the marines yet," Blaise said calmly. "Fritz might have been the victim of a prank."

"Prank?" Fritz repeated in wounded tones. "No prankster could have carried me through the air on a beam of light."

"There, you see?" demanded the mayor. "I

want the marines. I want the army. I want the air force. I want the coast guard!"

"I think they're busy right now," Blaise said.

"Then get me Agent Mulder!"

"Tell you what," Blaise said. "I'm kind of swamped with trying to get the evidence. So it would be a really great help to the community if *you* would go call the military and the FBI. You'd be a real hero."

The mayor's chest swelled. The eyes on his slippers bounced. "Swamped? How could you be swamped? You've got the DustBuster Brigade guarding the egg. A bunch of old men armed with trash-collection sticks and garbage bags!"

Before the argument could go any further, Blaise caught sight of a glint out of the corner of his eye. Turning, he realized that Derek Diche was filming the entire scene. Oh, great. How much had he captured? The mayor's bunny rabbit slippers?

"Derek?" Blaise said in what was supposed to be a pleasant voice. "Could you turn that thing off? This is an official investigation. It's not open to the public."

Derek shrugged behind the camera. "I'm gathering the news. Besides, the way things are going, I'm going to have an entire season's worth of material from right here in Paradise Beach. Sea monsters. Giant eggs. Alien abductions. Mass psychosis. Not to mention hare-footed political maneuvering."

Blaise had the worst urge to laugh. But that would only make the mayor foot-stomp again and cause those crazy eyes to bob like mad, and they were already making him dizzy.

"Hey," said Fritz suddenly. "Those slippers look just like the aliens. Except that they're not green. Except the aliens were bigger. And had wider shoulders. And their eyes weren't on stalks."

"I get it," said Sam, who had appeared from somewhere. "It's like that joke about the elephant and the grape, right?"

"What joke?" Derek asked.

"Oh, you know. What do an elephant and a grape have in common? They're both purple . . . except for the elephant."

A roar of laughter went up from the assembled officers, except for Fritz, who looked mortally wounded, and Blaise who figured if he started laughing he might never stop.

But Derek laughed, and for a bit the merciless eye of his camera was pointed at the floor.

"Turn that thing off, Derek," Sam said. "Please. Or I'll have to evict you from the station."

"Aww, Sam."

"Now, please," she insisted.

"What do I get if I do? A real date?"

That caused another round of laughter among her colleagues. Sam flushed.

"Tell you what," she said. "If you turn it off, I won't show you my handcuffs."

"You go, Sam," an officer chortled from the back of the room. "Show him your cuffs!"

"Nobody's arresting anybody while the mayor's here," Blaise said. Then he turned to Derek. "So please, turn it off. Or I'll have to ask the mayor to leave."

"I'm not going anywhere," the mayor said, stomping his foot again. The eyes bobbed in opposing circles, like two giant love bugs deciding whether to mate on the mayor's foot. "And if there's going to be any arresting, somebody ought to arrest that egg."

"No," said Fritz. "We need to arrest the aliens."

Enough was enough. Blaise spoke firmly. "Everybody get back to work. Now."

Rich looked up from his sketch pad. "And people think artists are weird. So what did this alien look like?"

Derek aimed his camera at the sketch pad. No one seemed to notice; they were all focused on Fritz.

"It was big," Fritz said, coming over to watch what Rich drew. "Eight, maybe ten feet tall."

Rich sighed. "I can't draw this life-sized, Fritz. Save the dimensions for the report. What did it look like?"

"Big. Had these shoulders like a linebacker." He looked on as Rich drew. "Right. And he had a radio collar around his neck. Thinner than that. Okay, good. And a green face."

"It's a black-and-white sketch," Rich noted.

"It's belongs on the comics page," Sam whispered to Blaise, who nodded.

"And big, almond-shaped eyes," Fritz added. "Yes, just like that. No nose. It's like . . . it's like its whole face breathed."

"You said it was wearing a shiny silver suit?" Blaise asked as he watched the sketch take form.

"Right. And big space gloves." He paused a moment as Rich drew. "No, bigger. It had huge thumbs. And blast protectors on its wrists."

Blaise watched as Rich added the lightning bolt logo Fritz had described. Rich held up the finished product. "That look about right?" he asked.

"Except that it was ten feet tall," Fritz said.

"Except for the elephant," Sam whispered.

Blaise nodded again. The sketch was a cosmic nightmare, a hodgepodge that might have been straight out of a very bad fifties science fiction movie. *Invasion of the Low-Budget Space Creatures*. The scary part was, he had a pretty fair idea of who it was. But proving that, and figuring out Mary Todd's latest nefarious plot, was another matter. Her gang of gentle geriatrics was as tight-lipped as a gathering of tobacco executives in a congressional hearing room.

"I've been wasting my time in the Amazon," Derek said.

"Yeah, macho man," Sam retorted. "You

can't be sure the space aliens are well fed before you wrestle with them."

Derek gave her a hurt look. "I'm not stupid. I wouldn't wrestle with Wayne Gretzky, either."

"What do you mean?"

He drew her aside. "Sam," he said in a whisper, "those are *hockey* gloves."

She met his gaze. "For real?"

"Don't believe me? We can go buy a pair."

"What'll that prove? That the aliens like hockey?" She was feeling snappish. Lack of sleep did that to her.

Derek turned to Blaise and whispered, "Are you a hockey fan?"

Blaise shrugged. "I watch it sometimes, why?"

"What's the local team's colors?"

"Blue, black, and silver," Blaise answered.

"Fritz, what color was that logo?" Derek asked.

"It was blue," he said. "With a black border. They said it represented the radiant blue light of their home star, in the vast blackness of space." He paused. "It's Sirius."

"I believe you're serious," Blaise said.

"No, Sirius. That's their home star." He looked at Derek, then at Blaise. "I've read about them. They come from the dog star."

"I *knew* Cal Lepkin's beast had something to do with this!" the mayor announced.

Sam looked at Derek with resignation. He

shook his head slowly. "It's almost like somebody wants to distract us from the egg."

"My God. The egg." Sam's head snapped up. "I'll bet Colonel Albemarle is still guarding the thing."

"But dogs don't lay eggs!" the mayor said.

Blaise sighed. "Sam, you'd better go back on egg watch. Mr. Mayor, my secretary will get you the number for the FBI's alien and sea monster division. We called yesterday, but they said the agent was on convalescent leave. Maybe you'll have better luck. They might have stabilized his medication by today."

"Are you making fun of me, Chief Corrigan?" The mayor's voice was thick with suspicion. "I don't like it when other people make fun of me."

"That's why I leave it up to you," Blaise said evenly.

"And where will you be?" Sam asked.

"Yes!" the mayor added. "Where will you be?"

Blaise sighed. "I need to go pray with an alien."

Arthur was sitting in his office when Blaise arrived. He already felt two feet tall, but at the sight of the chief of police, he felt as if he shrank to two inches.

"I'm not going to ask," Blaise said. "And frankly, I don't want to know. But I do want the costume so I can cure Fritz of his delusions and save the mayor from an early coronary. Not to mention getting those bobbing eyes out of my station."

"Delusions?" Arthur asked, overlooking the mention of bobbing eyes, feeling now only a sixteenth of an inch tall.

"He seems convinced that he was carried on a beam of light, that he fought with a whole crew of aliens, and fell from a spacecraft into your backyard."

"Oh, Lord," Arthur said. It was something of a prayerful moan.

"Should I search your trash bin? In case someone just happened to leave something there?"

"You might have more luck at Mary's."

"Ahh. Why doesn't that surprise me?"

"I can't imagine," Arthur said gloomily. "She's always surprising me. Or perhaps 'horrifying' would be a better word."

Blaise patted his shoulder. "Mary's a bad influence. In the meantime, you might want to leave off that radio collar for a day or two."

"Radio collar?"

"Well, someone besides Fritz might call it a clerical collar."

Arthur groaned. "I want to confess."

"Arthur, do me a very big favor?"

"Anything."

"Don't confess. Ever."

* * *

Mary Todd wasn't at all surprised to see Blaise on her doorstep. But then, very little surprised Mary. In fact, Blaise was sure *nothing* surprised Mary.

"I want to search your garbage."

She lifted both brows. "Do you have a warrant?"

"If I have to get a warrant, this is going to get very ugly. So just let me search your trash. Let's keep this between friends."

"Oh, very well. It's out back."

He paused. "Mary, why?"

The smile she gave him was positively wicked. "I'm just getting my nephew to extend his vacation a little while, that's all."

"Nephew?"

"Derek, of course."

"Oh, God, that explains a lot. Why?"

"Why do I want him to stay longer?"

Blaise nodded with exaggerated patience.

"Well, one has to give young love time to follow its course, you know. Sort of like you and Jillie."

He'd always suspected Mary had a hand in that. "Well, save your hijinks. This town is crazy enough. Besides, I don't want my officers developing mental problems."

"I wouldn't know anything about that."

"Of course not." He headed for her trash bins out back.

* * *

Sam felt royally frosted. She sent the Dust-Buster Brigade on their way with effusive thanks, then settled down for yet *another* day of guarding the egg. And naturally, she hadn't brought her sunscreen. No. Because having worked twenty-two of the last twenty-four hours, she hadn't expected to be out here again.

She looked at the egg, indulging in mental images of shooting it, or just rolling it back into the water. Then she chided herself. It really wasn't the egg's fault. The poor thing probably wasn't even supposed to be on the beach. For all she knew, it was suffering mightily.

Derek was still at the station, covering Fritz's story. At least she didn't have to deal with *him*. Memories of last night were still making her blush.

But between blushes, there was still the exquisite memory of how he had touched her, how he had felt against her. And much as she would have liked to pretend otherwise, she knew she wanted to repeat the experience. Wanted to go even further.

The thought made her gloomy. She'd been bitten by the lust bug, something she absolutely didn't want or need. Worse, she hadn't even needed any coaxing. Her pride would have felt a whole lot better if he'd done at least a little seducing.

She sighed, wondering if she was going to be able to stay awake, or if she was going to fall asleep on her dune and wake up looking like a lobster ready for the table.

Then she saw Zeph and Nat approaching from the parking lot. This morning they were carrying equipment. The Geiger counter, she thought, a couple of shovels, and some other stuff. Last night she'd been ready to dig around the egg, but this morning she wondered if that would be wise. Besides, there wasn't a whole lot of digging they could do. High tide was lapping very close to the troublesome egg.

Which, she thought in a moment of sheer irritability, would make it easy to roll the darn thing right into the water.

Then the chief would fire her, she'd probably be charged with some ridiculous crime having to do with environmental protection laws, and her life would be ruined. Not good.

Nat and Zeph joined her on the dune, spreading a tarp to lay the equipment on and then sitting beside her.

"What's this I hear about an alien abduction last night?" Zeph asked.

"I'm sure it was a prank," she said. She, too, had noticed that "radio" collar, and Frank's mention that he'd "fallen" into the backyard of the church. The problem was, she couldn't imagine why anyone would pull such a prank.

"Probably," Nat agreed, smothering a yawn. "I just don't buy the alien theories."

"Me neither," Zeph agreed. "Except there's this egg."

"Believe me," Sam said, "the alien Fritz saw wasn't big enough to lay that egg."

Zeph sighed. "I don't believe *anything's* big enough to lay that egg. But there it is."

"Have you learned anything about it at all?"

"Besides that it's big?" Zeph shrugged. "Not really. It's weird, though. It's slimy, like fish eggs, but underneath the slime it feels reptilian. Leathery. I took some scrapings for analysis yesterday, but... I don't know. We really need to get a marine biology expert out here."

"So why don't we?" Sam asked.

Nat answered, "Because none of them are crazy enough to get involved with this until there's something factual to hang a professional reputation on. Zeph and me, we're already crazy. Why else do you think they sent us?"

"That's very reassuring."

Nat flashed her a grin.

"We're not really crazy," Zeph argued. "We're iconoclastic."

"How so?"

"Let's just say we don't agree with a few theories in our field."

"But why would that make them send you to deal with the egg?"

Nat looked gloomy. "They're trying to submarine us."

"Great," Sam said, looking at the egg. "So

the best thing you could do would be to go back to the university and say it's a hoax."

"You got it." But then he brightened. "Or stick it up their noses that it's not."

Sam, who hadn't considered the element of academic politics, wasn't sure either outcome would be in the best interests of objectivity. But she didn't say so. "So what's the plan for today?" she asked.

"Hang out and be observant," Zeph said. "Maybe take some more Geiger counter readings, and some temperature readings."

Sam eyed the equipment. "But what about the shovels?"

Zeph looked uneasy and Nat flushed.

"No," said Sam. "You're not going to dig."

"But last night you said—"

"Last night was last night. I don't think the chief would be too happy if we upset the Humane Society and the tree huggers."

"Damn," said Zeph.

"I knew it," said Nat. "Should've left the shovels in the car."

"Why?" Sam asked. "So you could bring them out when I wasn't here and claim no one told you not to dig?"

Nat looked hurt. "Hey, we're scientists, not the mob."

Zeph snorted. "Some of us are less than honest, particularly those wearing cantilevers."

Nat apparently couldn't think of a comeback, so Zeph dug around in a backpack until she came out with another black box. "Let's take temps, Nat. Watch how they change as the ambient temp changes."

"Yeah, yeah," he agreed, looking less than thrilled.

Just as they started arguing about whether evaporation was enough to explain the low temperature of the egg, relief arrived for Sam. An officer appeared, telling her she was off duty for the next twenty-four hours.

Which, thought Sam as she made her weary way home, might be just about enough sleep.

10

But Sam didn't get to sleep for twenty-four hours. Derek Diche, a.k.a. Derek Todd, had his own plans for her time. Naturally.

At around five that afternoon, as she was staggering from her bed, where she'd slept restlessly most of the day, toward her kitchen, where she hoped to find something to nibble on that didn't require cooking, her doorbell rang.

She almost didn't answer it. She was still wearing her sleep shirt and a hastily pulled on pair of shorts, and her hair probably looked like a bird's nest. She wasn't expecting anyone, and given the time of day it was probably someone selling something.

Besides, no law required her to answer it.

However, the jerk on the other side of the

door apparently had noticed her car in the driveway and deduced that she was here. So he rang the bell again, rather insistently. Then he rang it again.

This annoying person was not going to go away. Irritated, she stomped to the door and answered it.

"Hi," said Derek, giving her a brilliant smile. Without so much as a by-your-leave he walked past her and into her house.

"I've got the tape of the egg," he said, waving a videocassette at her. "Say, you look rather ... off. Didn't you sleep well?"

Being only human, a number of responses ran through her mind, most of which could have gotten her arrested. So instead she said through her teeth, "Pretty well."

He suddenly looked appalled. "Say, I didn't wake you, did I?"

She couldn't bring herself to lie to him, tempting though it was to make him squirm. "No. I just woke." A moment of shame pierced her irritation and she wondered why Derek kept bringing out the worst in her. What was the matter with her?

"I guess my timing is bad anyway. But you wanted to see the film, so I had them dump a copy onto videotape. You *do* have a VCR?"

"Sure."

"Good. You just go back to what you were doing, and when you're ready we'll pop it in and have a look."

What she had been planning to do involved making coffee and cooking breakfast. Which meant now she had to cook for two. But before she did that, there was a greater imperative.

Escaping, she headed straight for her bedroom and bath. One look in the mirror was enough to tell her why he'd been so generous about letting her go back to what she'd been doing.

Her hair not only looked like a bird's nest, it looked as if it had been constructed by an inebriated bird. The circles under her eyes made her look like a raccoon's cousin, and there were still creases in her cheek from her pillow. She closed her eyes and groaned.

Thirty minutes later, freshly showered, blow-dried, and dressed in white shorts and a yellow tank top, and layered under enough concealer to hide raccoon rings, she sallied forth, feeling better about herself.

"Wow," Derek said when he saw her. "You didn't have to go to all that trouble on my account."

"Trust me, I didn't." Or so she wanted to believe. Heading for the kitchen, she left him sitting in the living room. She should have known he would follow. He was there, leaning against the counter, by the time she'd ground the coffee beans.

"Fresh-ground," he said. "What a treat."

"Oh, come off it. You probably have it all the time."

"Only when I happen to be eating in a fancy restaurant, which is probably a great deal less often than you would believe."

"Really?" She poured the grounds into the basket.

"Yes. I eat a lot more goat cheese and mystery meat than fancy cuisine."

"Mystery meat?"

"Only because I find it more prudent not to ask the contents of the local cuisine."

She had to smile. "I hadn't thought of that."

"I have a cast-iron stomach, as long as I can enjoy ignorance. And sometimes it's wise to eat without looking at one's plate."

She laughed. "Well, all I have is bacon, eggs, and English muffins."

"No ignorance required. May I help? And why do they call them English muffins?"

"Yes, and I don't know."

"I like them regardless. So, shall I fry the bacon? I'm pretty good at that."

"Great." She got the griddle out for him, and the package of bacon, then finished pouring water into the coffeepot. Soon delicious aromas were filling the kitchen.

"So what's on the tape?" she asked him. "I don't really want to sit here for eight hours just to see what we saw last night."

"Oh, I had Phil edit it. But believe me, there's stuff we didn't see last night."

"How is that possible?"

"We don't have infrared vision."

She paused in the act of removing a carton of eggs from the refrigerator. "You can see something warm? Inside the egg? What?"

"That's the question. I have no idea what it might be. I'd dismiss it as heat retained from the day, but it seems to be moving. You'll have to see for yourself."

The meal was pleasant to cook with Derek's help, and Sam let go of her irritation at the way he'd barged in on her.

"You know," he said as they were eating, "this isn't the first time something strange has washed up on the coast."

"Nor the first time somebody's attempted a hoax. I don't remember when it was, but they found some huge footprints up at St. Petersburg years ago."

"Right. But that *was* a hoax. I was checking the papers for similar stories, and they finally solved that one when a guy took credit for it. But I'm talking about the real mysteries."

"Real?"

"Real," he repeated. "There's the St. Augustine monster. Some huge carcass washed up on the shore there back in . . . I think it was the 1890s. Folks didn't know what to make of it, so they called on a local physician. He was able to find something that looked like the remains of octopus tentacles."

"That's no mystery."

"Yes, it is." He waved his English muffin in a small circle. "The blue whale is currently believed to be the biggest creature in the sea. But if the St. Augustine monster was an octopus, it would have been fifty times larger than the blue whale."

"Fifty times!" Sam's mind boggled. "I can't imagine it."

"Few people can. Which is why it remains something of a mystery. It's not the sort of thing respectable science wants to get involved in on the basis of one old sighting."

"I can't say as I blame them. It's hard to believe there's something that big out there if we've only had one sighting."

"Until you consider the size and the depth of the Atlantic. It's actually quite possible. Then, of course, there's the Bermuda blob."

Sam gave a little laugh of surprise. "The what?"

"The Bermuda blob. That was discovered in an inlet a few years ago. No one knows what it was. It was definitely animal tissue, probably only the remains of something much larger. *Much* larger. No one knows from what, though."

Sam looked at the egg on her fork and lost interest in eating. "So you're saying the egg is . . . possibly genuine."

"I think we've all pretty much concluded that it is. Haven't we?"

Sam, who had been fighting the idea every step of the way, nodded slowly.

"The thing is," Derek continued, "I've got to prove it's a hoax. Somehow."

That brought her head up. "But why?"

"Because there aren't any real mysteries, Sam. Only things we haven't figured out yet."

That struck Sam as one of the saddest things she'd ever heard a human being say. An ache for Derek squeezed her heart. "So you don't believe in magic?"

He shrugged. "No. Oh, I'd like to. Of course I'd like to. But there isn't any magic, and there isn't any real mystery, with a capital *M*. Only ignorance."

"Maybe so," she said slowly. "But . . . that doesn't mean we shouldn't experience the mystery and magic until we figure it out."

He shrugged.

"It also doesn't explain why you need to prove this is a hoax. You'd dispel the mystery just as well if you discover it's a giant squid egg or something."

"That would just create another mystery."

Sam had the feeling that he wanted to find the magic for real, but was even more scared of what it would mean if he did. That he was torn in two directions and it was making him inconsistent.

But why? He spent his life chasing mysteries now. Yes, he debunked them, but he was still chasing them. The paradox perplexed her, and made her wonder what was going on in his soul.

How could he intimate that the egg was real, then in the next breath say he had to prove it was a hoax? She longed to question him more closely about that, but whatever struggle he was waging internally, he didn't seem ready to look it square in the eye.

They moved into her living room. Derek popped the tape in the VCR, then they sat together on the couch. The egg appeared on the screen, looking unpleasantly green.

And Sam found herself stealing looks at Derek, wishing he were here for something besides business. It was a traitorous thought, one she shouldn't allow herself to entertain for even a few seconds.

But some part of her seemed willing to ignore the fact that Derek was a mega-version of everything she'd sworn to avoid in men. He could be smooth, too smooth, and he was entirely too handsome. Given his current calling in life, he must have had an ego the size of Antarctica. How could he not? The idea that any man could be so successful and so adored by women without letting it go to his head was ridiculous.

So why did she feel as if some invisible cord were pulling her toward him? As if there were an electric tingle in the air whenever he was near? Why did her mind want to keep drifting to last night and the way she had felt when he held her and touched her?

Why this terrifying impulse to lean against

his shoulder, to feel his arms around her? Why did her nerve endings seem to be locked in the memory of last night, replaying the exquisite feelings until desire sat heavily in her, making breathing almost impossible?

She tried to tell herself that she'd been single too long, that she was having some kind of old-maid reaction. She hadn't really been serious about anyone since college, since Alan's sweet nothings had proved to be exactly that: nothing. Not since she realized he had the smoothest lines since Casanova.

It was so easy, though, to imagine Derek turning to her, reaching for her, drawing her closer, covering her with his body. Oh, geez, she had it bad!

But she didn't see how she could let him that close to her without getting seriously hurt.

That's when it struck her that Derek didn't have any of that smarminess Alan had possessed so abundantly. She just kept *expecting* him to.

"Did you see that?" Derek turned excitedly and looked at her.

Sam flushed. Painfully. She'd been staring at him so intently she hadn't seen one thing on the video. "Uh . . . I guess I missed it."

"Well, pay attention, Sam," he said impatiently. "This is fascinating."

He might as well have dumped a bucket of ice over her head. Here she'd been, lost in daydreams that had been bordering on sexy, and he'd been so far away that they weren't even on the same planet. How embarrassing!

She turned her attention to the screen while Derek backed up the tape.

"Now watch," he said, as he hit play. "There it is, just sitting there like an egg, and then . . ."

Sam felt her heart slam. Just off center in the egg, the green was considerably brighter, almost white. It had been all along, so consistently so that she hadn't noticed it. But now it seemed to grow even brighter, and then . . .

It moved.

"Wow," she said, her heart skipping a couple of beats.

"That brightening means it was getting warmer in that one spot. That it's always warmer than the rest of the egg in that one place."

"And it moved."

"Maybe."

She looked at him. "Maybe? What else could it be? I *saw* it."

"There could be other reasons for that. We don't know that *something* moved, only that the warmest spot in the egg moved."

At that moment he didn't really sound like Derek. He sounded . . . clinical. Detached. Somehow it was making her uneasy.

"It's alive," she said, trying to pierce that detachment. "What else could it be?"

"It could be some kind of small motor that

was changing cycles, thus moving the heat pattern around."

"A motor?" She could hardly believe it. Not after what she'd just seen.

"Yes, of course. Keep watching."

She once again fixed her gaze on the television. And she started to wonder if Derek had a case of multiple personalities going.

What other explanation could there be? One minute he'd seemed to be leaning strongly to the egg-is-alive theory, and the next he was talking coolly about motors. Hmm.

Unless maybe he was doing a mental about-face because he couldn't deal with the possibility that the egg really was alive? Maybe all that made him uneasy.

Well, it made *her* uneasy, too. She'd be just as happy if it turned out to be a hoax. She didn't want to think what might come out of an egg that size. Or what would happen if it didn't go back in the water.

"There," said Derek.

She saw it, too. The egg trembled, then the bright spot seemed to return to its previous position.

"I see," she said.

"It's got to be a motor."

"Maybe. Maybe we should check those temperature readings that Zeph and Nat were going to take throughout the day. It might give us a clue."

"They were? Great." He started to pat his pockets. "I know I have their card here somewhere."

Just then Sam's phone rang. Leaning over to the end table, she picked up the cordless. "Bartlett," she said.

"Sam," said Chief Blaise Corrigan, "I'd like you to come down to the beach. And if you can, please bring Diche and his crew."

"What's happening?"

"Let's just say I've had enough."

11

Derek said he'd catch up shortly with his crew, and left. Sam changed into her uniform, then drove down to the beach in her cruiser wondering what could possibly have made Blaise say he'd had enough. He didn't strike her as that kind of man, and in all the stories she'd heard of him since coming here, she couldn't remember a single one that ever made him sound as if he were capable of losing his patience.

But the closer she got to the beach, the more she began to understand.

In the condo parking lot, heedless of what was sure to be many angry residents, sat several armored troop carriers, a Humvee, and a Jeep. It looked like the mayor had gotten his wish.

More than his wish, actually, because there were also TV satellite trucks present. Not only the four local stations, but also one of the news networks. Oh, man.

But it grew worse yet. On the beach were crowds of demonstrators—which probably explained the TV news. One cluster of unhappy-looking people bore signs that screamed, "Save the Egg!" and "Don't Abort the Sea Monster Baby." Another cluster was waving placards that proclaimed, "Welcome the Rigelians!," "Take Me to Your Leader," and assorted other messages including, "Beam Me Up."

There was also a third, unhappy cluster, this one without placards. Looking closer, Sam realized it was made up mostly of local business owners. The mayor, probably wisely, was nowhere in evidence.

The marines were, though. Or maybe they were army. Wearing camouflage, they were guarding the egg with their rifles menacingly pointed in the general direction of the civilians.

"My God," Sam said when she reached Blaise. "What happened?"

"The mayor apparently has a good connection with the governor. That's the Army National Guard."

"Oh." Shaking her head in wonder, she looked around and saw some of the TV people setting up cameras, while others talked earnestly into microphones and other cameras.

On the fringes, looking utterly at a loss, were a few of her colleagues.

"What do you want us to do, Chief?" she asked.

He shrugged. "God knows. What's got me worried is the Guard. Those kids are loaded for bear, and they're frightened."

Looking past the uniforms to the faces above them, Sam had to agree. "This isn't funny."

"Hell, no." Blaise sighed. "And the mayor's running from my calls."

Sam spied a young officer, about the same age as the infantrymen. "Is he in charge?"

"Apparently so. Wet behind the ears."

"Not good." But Sam had an idea. Wandering with apparent aimlessness, she gradually made her way over to the lieutenant, a youngster who looked as if he'd been a star on his high school football team.

"Hi," Sam said to him. She smiled.

He gave her an uncertain smile in return. "Hi."

"I'm Sam Bartlett." She offered her hand and he shook it.

"Mel Childers."

"Tough job you guys got here. Bet you'd rather be home watching the game." She had no idea whether there was a game on, but it seemed a safe bet that there probably was, of one kind or another.

"I had tickets for the Rays game tonight."

"That's too bad."

He shrugged. "Can't be helped." But he sounded a little resentful, too.

"Maybe you can go to the next one." As near as she could tell, the baseball season was eternal and the games barely paused long enough for the players to grab a meal or a flight to their next game. "There's another home game soon, right?"

"Tomorrow night."

"See?"

"I might be out here tomorrow night."

"Maybe not. We can hope. So—"

She was interrupted by someone exclaiming, "God!"

Turning, she saw Derek a dozen feet away, his crew behind him, the clusters of people between him and the egg. His face was strangely ashen.

And in that instant she knew exactly what he was looking at: the guardsmen pointing their rifles at civilians. And she knew what he was remembering: Bosnia.

Her heart slammed, and every muscle in her body tensed, ready to spring in his direction, to go to him and somehow try to comfort him. But just as quickly she realized that the best thing she could do for Derek, for everyone here, was what she had been doing.

But oh, how it hurt not to run to him and try to offer comfort.

Quickly, she turned to the lieutenant. "So what were your orders, exactly?"

"To guard the egg. What's wrong with that guy? Say, isn't that Derek Diche?"

Sam put her hand on the lieutenant's elbow, dragging his attention back to her. "So your orders were to guard the egg?"

"That's what I said."

"Well, you've got it backwards."

"Huh?" He looked confused. "What do you mean?"

"You're not supposed to protect the egg from the civilians, you're supposed to protect the civilians from the egg."

He looked at the egg, at his nervous troops, then back at her. His mouth opened, then closed. Then opened again. And closed again. "You're kidding," he said finally.

"Absolutely not. That's a sea monster egg."

Childers looked at the egg again. "You're kidding. There aren't any sea monsters!"

"Look at that egg. Two days before it was laid here, we had huge footprints on the beach. The scientists think whatever made them was probably three stories tall." She hoped God would forgive her for stretching the truth a bit.

It worked, though. Childers looked at the condo building, gauging the three stories in height, then back at the egg. "Man," he said.

"The mayor's worried there might be something like Godzilla inside it."

"Wow!"

"That's right," Blaise said from behind Sam. "The mayor's worried about what that egg might do to us when it hatches."

The lieutenant was nodding, agreeing with them at last. But he had one more qualm. "You're sure?"

Sam pointed at Blaise with her thumb. "He's the chief of police."

Childers straightened and walked over to a sergeant to say something. The sergeant barked a couple of orders, and moments later, all the troops were turned around, and all the guns were pointing at the egg.

"Hmm," said Blaise. "That doesn't look much safer."

"No," agreed Sam. "If those guys shoot at the egg, they're going to shoot each other."

But Sam was more worried about Derek. Turning, she saw him sitting a distance away from everyone while his crew set up their cameras. The other TV crews were starting to pack up their equipment, apparently planning to flash the story on the evening news. The three knots of people were murmuring among themselves. Trouble brewing there, Sam thought.

"Back in a minute," she told the chief.

"No rush," he said. "God knows why, but I have a feeling this is going to go on for a while."

She couldn't argue with him. In fact, she

thought, as she strode toward Derek, it was looking like another night on the beach.

Dropping down in the sand beside Derek, she sat cross-legged. "Are you okay?"

"Yes. Of course."

But he didn't look okay. He was still a little pale, and there was a tightness around his mouth that she hadn't seen before. Impulsively, she touched his arm. "They're not pointing their guns at the crowd anymore."

"I saw. Good job, Sam."

"It was a misunderstanding. The lieutenant got orders to guard the egg. He thought that meant he was supposed to protect it."

"Why is it I don't believe that's what the mayor had in mind at all?"

"Probably because you've seen him hopping up and down about monsters."

He gave her a small smile, then blew a long breath. "I'm okay, Sam, really. I just had a . . . bad moment. But thanks for caring."

She had no trouble imagining that for a few horrifying moments, Derek had been back in that village square in Bosnia. She squeezed his forearm, and was surprised when he covered her hand with his. Surprised at how good the warmth of his palm felt on her skin.

Man, did she have bad timing. Here Derek was, still shaken by what had probably been a terrible flashback, they were sitting on a crowded beach with a bunch of armed men a few dozen feet away, and suddenly she wanted to drag Derek down on the sand with her and find out just what that palm of his would feel like everywhere on her body.

Sheesh. She was losing it. He wasn't even her type.

Maybe she should cross her fingers and hope that half-grown air force lieutenant came back soon. Then she could drag Lieutenant Brick out to dinner, ravish him, and get the all-too-smooth, all-too-handsome Mr. Diche out of her mind.

"Are you sure you don't pronounce your name 'dish'?"

He looked at her. "What?"

Where in the world had that come from? Sam wondered, her cheeks heating. Her mouth was operating without connecting to her brain. Thank goodness he didn't seem to understand what she'd *really* meant by dish.

"Sorry," she said. "I'm still trying to adjust to your last name."

"Oh. Well, you don't have to use it. You can call me Mr. Todd."

He was teasing her, and the humor she glimpsed in his gaze warmed her and reassured her. He was okay now.

"Well, if you'll excuse me, Mr. Todd, I need to go talk to a lieutenant. Maybe I can get all those rifles pointing in a safe direction."

He glanced back toward the egg, and his face darkened. "A massacre is a massacre, and that idiot shouldn't be commanding armed men. If that egg twitches, they could all wind up shooting each other."

"Yep. So let me see what I can do about it."

"Let me see if I can help."

Her first reaction was that, of course, the mighty Mr. Diche or Todd or whatever wanted to poke his nose into things, but then she was ashamed. His offer hadn't been made arrogantly at all, and he needed distraction right now. Needed to do something about those guns.

"Sure," she said, feeling more generous. "Come on."

They rejoined Blaise and Childers in time to discover that things were beginning to heat up. Both the space cadets and the tree huggers had apparently been happier to have the rifles pointed at them than to have them pointed at the egg. The businesspeople just wanted the egg gone, and if that meant shooting it to tatters, they were all for it.

The egg had no opinion.

"All right, everybody," Blaise said. "Hold it down. Everybody gets a turn to speak, one at a time, okay? Otherwise I'm going to have to close the beach and send you all home."

Loud voices subsided, although one person said, "You can't send us home. This is a public beach and the Constitution says we can assemble."

"It says you can *peacefully* assemble. If you

start throwing sand at each other, it's not peaceful. So one at a time, folks."

Ginger Marrs, the head of the local tourist development association, stepped forward. "I understand the concerns of everyone here."

A few quiet boos from the space cadets greeted her.

"No, really I do," Ginger said. She was a gray-haired woman with a classically beautiful face. Though she usually wore conservative business clothes, this early evening she was wearing lavender capris and a matching, billowy top.

"I understand," she continued, "that this is possibly a new life-form. Something we've never seen before. It's only natural that many of you want to protect it."

Murmurs of "Hear, hear" arose from the opposing camps.

"However," Ginger continued, "there are other things to consider. "This town depends on tourism."

"*You* depend on tourism," somebody shouted back.

"A *lot* of people depend on tourism in this town," Ginger announced. "They depend on the jobs that the tourist industry provides."

"Slave wages," someone jeered.

"That's enough," Blaise said. "Let the lady speak her piece. You'll get your turn."

"People's jobs depend on local business,"

Ginger repeated firmly. "And this egg is getting in the way."

Nods backed her up from her crowd of business owners.

"It's drawing tourists," someone from the tree hugger camp called. "Folks will want to come see it."

Ginger shook her head. "If you think John and Jane Doe are going to bring six-year-old Timmy to this beach to swim when we've got soldiers with loaded rifles standing guard, you've got another think coming."

Sam found that statement fascinating. She wondered if the mayor had any idea what kind of trouble he was looking at.

"You're right," said one of the space cadets. "The soldiers have to go."

"The *egg*," said Ginger, "has to go. Tonight. I don't care what it takes. Move it to the university, throw it back in the water, chop it into little pieces—"

"Murderer!" a woman's voice shrieked.

The effect was instantaneous. Almost too quickly to see how it happened, the usually decorous Ginger was rolling on the sand, fighting with another woman. They were pulling each other's hair and screaming. Some jerk in the crowd started a chant of "Go, go, go . . ."

Wading forward, Sam grabbed Ginger and Blaise grabbed the other woman, yanking them apart. Ginger was still swinging her arms as

Sam pulled her to her feet and shoved her steadily backward.

"That's enough, Ginger," she said sharply. "Don't make me arrest you."

"That woman—"

"I said that's enough."

After a few moments, Ginger's arms stopped wheeling and she stood panting, her hair a mess, covered with sand, a suspicious red spot brightening on one cheek.

"Everybody go home *now*," said Blaise. "Nothing's going to happen to the egg tonight one way or the other. If you want a town meeting, hold it at city hall in the morning."

Lieutenant Childers looked at Sam. "I thought you said the crowd needed protecting."

The egg burped. Loudly. In fact, it sounded more like a growl. Two minutes later, the only people on the beach were the soldiers, the cops, and Derek's crew.

The sunset painted the sky in arcs of pink, red, fuchsia, and gray. The sun itself hovered just over the water, an angry red eye glaring across the waves, turning their tops crimson even as the shadows on the troughs turned midnight blue.

Blaise had put four cops around the perimeter, as much to keep an eye on the soldiers as anything else. Derek's crew had drawn the lieutenant into a poker game, on the sand. Derek, Sam, and the chief sat on a dune a short distance away. They'd carved seats for themselves in the sand in order to be more comfortable.

"It's getting dark," Derek said.

It was a statement of the obvious, but Sam had a feeling he'd said it for a reason. "Yes."

"Those soldiers are going to get really nervous when it gets dark."

Blaise nodded. "I know."

"And if the egg starts acting up like it did last night, somebody could get killed."

That haunted look was in his eyes again, Sam noted. She supposed it was a feat of courage that he could make himself stay here with those soldiers. She longed to say something comforting, but couldn't think of anything useful.

"We need to defuse this situation," Derek said.

"All ideas are welcome," Blaise agreed. "You have any?"

"Actually, I think I might. If I may?"

"Be my guest. Just let me know how you want me to play along. Sam?"

"Count me in."

They rose and started walking toward the card-playing group. "I'm just going to talk to the lieutenant," Derek said. "Basically, just agree with me whenever it seems appropriate."

When they reached the group of poker players, Derek cleared his throat. "Guys, shouldn't you be checking your cameras? We don't want to miss anything."

Good-naturedly enough, they got to their feet and went to look at the equipment. Apparently, sometime between last night and this evening, they'd lost their fear of the egg. Of course, Sam reminded herself, the egg wasn't doing anything tonight. Yet.

The sky was bloodred now, and the sun had half-vanished beneath the Gulf. That seemed to call for a lot of camera adjustments. Or maybe the crew just took hints very well.

Leaving the lieutenant, who still sat on the sand, to Derek's mercy. Which the lieutenant didn't seem to mind, because he was looking at Derek with something like awe. Sam pretended to busy herself brushing sand off her holster.

"Hi, lieutenant," Derek said pleasantly. "We haven't been formally introduced. I'm Derek Diche."

The lieutenant scrambled to his feet, brushing his palm quickly on the seat of his cammies so he could shake Derek's hand. "It's an honor, sir," Childers said. "A real honor."

"No, the honor is mine." Derek smiled that thousand-watt smile of his, the one that seemed to cast sunlight all around him. "I have the greatest respect for the job you folks in uniform do. Would you mind if I interviewed you for my show?"

"Uh . . ." Childers flushed, and scuffed his feet. "Well, sir, I'd really like that. But . . . uh . . .

I'm not allowed to be interviewed when I'm in uniform."

"Really?" Derek expressed interest. "Why is that?"

"Well, sir, if I say anything when I'm in uniform, people might think I was speaking for the Guard, sir. Officially."

"Ah. That does present a problem, doesn't it?" Derek tilted his head and appeared to think. "I know, I can interview you when you're off duty. Would you like that?"

"Yes, sir!" Childers looked thrilled.

"But it's okay if I get you on film a bit now, right?"

"Yes, sir. I'm just doing my job, sir."

"Good." Another one of those smiles. It was probably blinding the spy satellites overhead, Sam thought with amusement.

"Speaking of doing your job," Derek said slowly, "I wanted to talk to you about that. Off camera, of course. Why don't we all step over here a ways and discuss it where you can be sure I'm not filming you?"

Childers went meekly. The sun had sunk completely now, and only the red of the sky above marked its passing. The water had turned nearly black. Mysterious. Even a little threatening.

When they were out of earshot of everyone else, Derek halted them. "I don't know how much you know about this affair, Lieutenant, but Chief Corrigan, Officer Bartlett, and I decided that for your own safety, and the safety of your men, you need to know the *whole* story."

Childers's eyes widened. Sam wondered what cockamamie tale Derek was concocting. Much to her surprise, he didn't concoct one at all.

"The thing is," said Derek, his tone conveying that he was imparting privileged information, "that egg has a mother."

12

That thoroughly obvious statement had an amazing effect on Lieutenant Childers. He seemed to shrink a little, and he darted a furtive glance toward the egg. "Uh, well... uh... yes. I guess it does."

"Of course it has a mother. How else would it get here?" Derek said earnestly. "And look at the size of that thing."

Childers looked. He shrank a little more. "It's... big."

"That's an understatement," Derek said.

"It sure is," Sam offered. "Somebody figured the mom had to be at least three stories tall."

"Maybe bigger," Derek said.

"Look," interrupted Blaise. "We don't want to make the lieutenant too nervous."

Derek shook his head. "I'm not trying to make him nervous. But I figure he's got a right to know the whole story. He's the one up against it, after all. He and his soldiers. They shouldn't be kept in the dark."

"I suppose not," Blaise agreed.

"So," Derek continued, "the mother has to be huge. Really huge. I mean, if a chicken had laid that egg, it might be three stories tall. But chickens lay really large eggs for their size. And this wasn't a chicken."

Childers licked his lips. "Man," he said.

"Right," Derek agreed. "Maybe ten or twelve stories tall."

Childers craned his neck, looking upward.

"Maybe bigger," Sam said.

"Of course, from the footprints—"

Childers swung his head around, looking at Derek. "Footprints?"

"Didn't anybody tell you about that? They were on the beach two days before the egg was discovered."

"Huge," said Sam.

"Humongous," agreed Blaise.

Sam nodded. "Professor Plum from the university thinks the thing weighed tons."

"It had a heavy tail, too," Derek said. "Probably for balance so it could stand on its hind legs."

Sam, who hadn't thought of that possibility, felt a quiver of unease herself.

"Oh, man," said Childers.

"Anyway," Derek continued, "whatever it was, it was probably the egg's mother. What if she comes back to check up on junior?"

Childers swallowed hard.

"That's why I'm thinking," Derek said, "that it might be better if you and your men guard the water."

Childers swallowed again, visibly. He looked from the egg to the immensity of the Gulf of Mexico, and probably had no difficulty at all in imagining a gigantic sea monster. When he spoke, his voice was brittle, cracking. "Did you see what Godzilla did to the military?"

Derek shrugged. "I'm afraid I missed that film."

"We need something more than rifles and a machine gun. Man, oh, man..."

Sam looked at Derek wondering what he was going to do now. Whatever he was hoping to accomplish didn't involve bringing in nuclear weapons, she was sure. In fact, she saw a flicker of distress on his face. Then it was gone.

"No," said Derek. "Look, Lieutenant. They're not going to give you any more than you have right now. As far as the brass are concerned, there's nothing to contend with but a blob that might be an egg. You follow?"

Childers nodded. He looked very much like a man caught between the devil and the deep blue sea.

"The most you can hope to do is make yourselves safe and sound an alarm if the mother comes back."

Childers nodded again. He seemed to be deprived of speech.

"So what you need to do is guard the water. Keep your eye out there. Believe me, if the egg starts to hatch, we'll get plenty of warning of that. It's the mother who might be the real problem."

Childers seemed to find his voice. He looked at Derek. "Entrenchments."

"There you go."

"Sentries."

"That's the idea."

"Maybe we can slow it down."

"You certainly might make it think twice about coming ashore."

A man suddenly filled with purpose, Childers strode across the beach to his troops. Thirty seconds later their rifles were slung. Five minutes later they had retrieved trenching tools from their transports. Ten minutes later the beach was beginning to resemble Normandy before the invasion.

"Oh, my God," said Blaise. "The mayor is going to have a cow."

The earthworks extended a hundred yards along the shore. Because the water level was so high, the soldiers hadn't been able to dig down very far into the sand, so they built upward, carting sand from other parts of the beach. The labor was intensive, conducted under the glare of spotlights, but by midnight they had a wall three feet high to sit behind. Barbed wired curled along the top of it, held in place by metal rods. Derek's crew filmed the entire process.

Chief Blaise Corrigan studied it gloomily. "It's turtle nesting season."

"They wouldn't nest here regardless," Sam said reassuringly. "Too many people about because of the egg."

"I know, I know." He sighed. "Oh, well. The mayor asked for this one; now he's stuck with it." Then he suddenly grinned. "I can hardly wait to hear how he explains it tomorrow."

"He's probably going to wonder why they didn't build the wall behind the egg, to protect him."

"Could be." Blaise shook his head. "I'm outta here. Go home and get some sleep, Sam. And take the day off tomorrow."

"Thanks."

But after Blaise left, Derek turned to her. "Stay?" he asked.

Her heart gave a little flutter. "Aren't you going to go home?"

"No, I don't think so. Something might happen. I keep remembering how the egg became so active last night."

"True."

Sam returned to her hand-carved seat in the dune and waited for Derek to join her. She ought to go home. She ought to get some sleep. But somehow the fact that Derek was here kept her planted.

"The tide's going to wash out all their hard work," Derek remarked as he sat beside her.

"Not before morning. It certainly gave you some interesting film footage, though." As soon as the words were out, she realized how they sounded.

Derek spoke, his voice level. "At least they're not going to be shooting each other in the dark if the egg belches."

She realized that, and it made her feel small. She felt an apology was in order, but she didn't know how to phrase it. *Gee, Derek, I'm such a bitch?* Or, *I'm sorry, Derek, I'm scared to death of you?*

Because she was. Terrified. Appalled. Quaking in her boots. Wondering how she could feel such a strong attraction to a man who was the antithesis of everything she believed herself to want in life. Good heavens, he was just here on vacation. In a week or so, he'd head back to the bright city lights of the world's capitals, and to all the beautiful women who probably hung on his every word. Getting involved with him, even in the most minimal way, was a guarantee of painful regrets.

But it was hard to remember that, sitting here on the beach as the moon began to rise, even with the presence of all those soldiers. The breeze was balmy, gentle, a soft caress on her skin. Stars gleamed overhead, ageless, while the sea sang its eternal lullaby.

It was a romantic setting, despite the egg, the army, and the barbed wire. Sam found herself wishing that everything else would vanish, so that she and Derek could feel alone in the world. So they could wander down paths they had begun to follow last night. Her body ached for him. Her emotions yearned for him. The enchantment seemed to bypass all the hindrances. Even the turmoil in her mind and heart quieted.

"Wow," Derek said. "Beautiful."

Her heart skipped a beat. She looked at him, feeling as if the world suddenly held its breath.

Then she realized he was looking past her. She turned and her heart skipped another beat. This time, however, it was not from wonder. It was from fright.

The egg was glowing. Not greenly, as it had last night, but rather a pale, very white light, as if it were filled with bottled moonlight.

"What *is* that thing?" she heard herself ask.

"Magic."

The word seemed to hang on the air around them, bringing with it a sense of hushed expectancy.

"Wow," Derek said again, his voice quiet.

For a man who a short while ago had been claiming that he was going to prove this egg a hoax, he seemed to be feeling rather differently now. She caught the wonder in his voice, along with a bit of yearning.

And for a moment, she almost shared his feelings. But then her uneasiness returned. There was no way to know what was inside that egg, what they might face when it hatched.

The glow was fading away. Already it was almost gone. Soon nothing but the moon and stars illuminated the night.

"Come on," Derek said. "I'm going to see you home."

It was a courtly offer, one she didn't really need. But she accepted it anyway. It had been a long time since anyone had showed concern over her safety. It had been a very long time since anyone had looked out for her. It was a really nice feeling.

Mary Todd was an unhappy woman. Well, not exactly, because Mary didn't really know the meaning of unhappiness. In her more than eighty years, she'd been frustrated, disappointed, angry, irritated, disgusted, and even downright disapproving, but she'd never been unhappy.

At the moment she was irritated. Frustrated. Because that damned nephew of hers had come home early. For a man his age, Mary considered mere midnight a sin, especially when a woman like Sam Bartlett was involved.

Or not involved, as it appeared. Despite her

plotting to throw the two of them together as much as possible, there he was, climbing the stairs like a monk on the way to his solitary cell.

She would have wondered if there was something wrong with him, except that he'd been married before, for nine years. And widowed. It was probably that widowed thing that was causing problems.

It wasn't that Mary didn't understand grief. At her age, she'd buried quite a few dear friends, all of whom were sorely missed. She kept their photos and other mementos in a drawer upstairs, and from time to time she would look at them, taking a journey down a beautiful memory lane.

But the key was, you had to move on. You had to continue to live. Derek wasn't really doing that. His parents were worried, and they'd conveyed their concern to Mary, who'd alighted on Sam as a perfect solution.

Derek had lost his wife, and had given up his original profession to become a shill who chased mythical monsters. And while Mary rather liked that—it was a nutty enough occupation to make Derek seem like a true Todd—it was a way for him to hide from the world. He dealt with fantasy, instead of reality, and demolished it, depriving others of their dreams.

The brilliance of that last thought gave Mary a sense of satisfaction. She was still better than a Freudian analyst any day; she pretty much had Derek figured out.

Samantha Bartlett was another kettle of fish. The girl was entirely too closemouthed about her past. As many times as Mary had tried to peck out kernels, Sam had never confided anything. Mary loathed it when any person was opaque to her sharp eyes and mind.

Sam was a beautiful young woman who rarely dated, and when she did date, she seemed to pick losers. A good way to protect her heart? Mary wanted to think so. However, with no evidence in hand, there remained a possibility that Sam was simply stupid.

Mary rapped her ebony cane on the floor and wondered what kind of miracle she was going to have to work. The alien abduction thing hadn't worked very well, thanks to Blaise Corrigan. A shame, too. She'd been hoping the mystery would draw both Sam and Derek in together as they tried to solve it. Instead they seemed . . . disinterested?

Arthur just hadn't done it right. Imagine him wearing his clerical collar for all the world to see! Sometimes Arthur didn't have the brain God gave a gnat.

Her entire gang was giving her fits right now. The bulk of them had claimed "other obligations" at their last meeting, and had simply vanished before Mary could dragoon them into helping her.

Hadley Philpott had retreated into a high dudgeon and wasn't even answering her e-mails, let alone the imperial summons she had left on his answering machine. And as for Arthur, he seemed to have withdrawn into penitential silence. She imagined he was wearing out the knees of his slacks before the altar in his church.

In general, Mary had a great relationship with God: She left the world to him, and he left Paradise Beach to her. Until now.

Arthur was giving her indigestion. Derek was giving her indigestion. Apparently she was giving *herself* indigestion, because her stupid schemes weren't working.

But what could she do without her henchmen?

She thought about calling some of them right now, dragging them out of their comfortable beds while they were still too groggy to evade her, then decided against it. That might prove to be like stirring up a hornet's nest. No, she had to coax them back into her sphere of influence somehow.

Picking up the phone, Mary called Fritz Holder.

Sam lay in bed, staring at the dark ceiling. Her diurnal rhythms were totally messed up, she thought gloomily. All those graveyard shifts she'd worked, compounded by being up in the daytime the last couple of days, then sleeping much of today away—it might be a week before her body realized it was okay to sleep again.

She certainly wasn't going to sleep tonight. It was as if her eyelids were on springs: Every time she tried to close them, they popped up again.

Scenes from the evening insisted on playing out in her memory. The glowing center in the egg on the video Derek had showed her. The Guard pointing their rifles first at innocent people, then at each other over the egg. Ginger rolling on the ground during that unbelievable fight. Those people waving their signs to welcome the Rigelians. Hadn't they seen *Independence Day*?

But mostly she kept seeing Derek. The distress on his face at the sight of those guns; the haunted expression in his eyes. She wished there had been some way she could have comforted him, but some wounds, she thought sadly, were beyond comfort.

Still, she wished she could reach out right now and take him in her arms and hold him close.

She squirmed under her sheets and wished her mind and body wouldn't keep doing this to her. Trying to remind herself that Derek wouldn't want her when he could have virtually any woman on the planet.

When the doorbell rang, she was relieved to get out of bed. Pulling on a pair of shorts under her sleep shirt, she headed for the door. Then paused, fearing it might be Derek. Who else could it be? And she didn't want to see Derek when she was in this weakened state of mind.

Paralyzed, she hesitated and the doorbell rang again, to be followed immediately by a loud hammering that sounded very un-British. In fact, it sounded like a cop.

It was. She opened to door to find a rather wild-eyed Fritz Holder standing there.

"I need to see Derek Diche now," he said.

"Fritz, Derek's not here."

"Don't lie to me; I know he's here. And he has all the answers."

Sam didn't like the way Fritz's hand wandered to the butt of the gun in his holster. He didn't grab it or anything, but if his brain wasn't ready to shoot something, his body certainly was. She couldn't send him on his way in this state.

"Come on in," she said. "I'll see if I can find Derek."

"Thanks." His agitation seemed to subside a little as he stepped inside.

"I have to ask one favor, though, Fritz."

"What's that?"

"You have to take off your gun, okay? I have a rule against wearing guns in my house."

"But you're a cop."

"Right. And I take off my gun belt as soon as I come through that door."

He looked almost hurt, but he unbuckled it and put it on the chair beside the door.

"Thanks, Fritz. I guess I just don't like to bring my job home with me." She had a very healthy respect for guns and their inherent dangers.

"So where's Derek?" he asked.

"I told you, he's not here. But I'll find him for you, okay?"

"Thanks."

"Why don't you have a seat? Are you on duty?"

"Nah. Chief says I need a few days off."

Good idea. As tense as Fritz was, he'd probably be shooting at streetlights. "How about a beer?"

"Sounds good."

She left him sitting on the sofa while she went to get his beer and call Derek. She assumed he was at Mary Todd's, probably sound asleep, since he'd told her he was going to collapse after he left her at her door.

That had disappointed her. Apparently she'd been cherishing some unacknowledged little hope that he'd want to come inside. And more.

She shook her head at her own silliness and reached for the wall phone. Waking Mary Todd was the last thing she wanted to do. Well, except for letting Fritz wander the streets with a gun looking for Derek. Or aliens.

Much to her surprise, Mary answered, and she didn't sound sleepy.

"I'm sorry to disturb you, Miss Todd."

"I was awake," Mary said. "One of the blessings of old age is that I need very little sleep. Gives me more time to enjoy life."

"Yes. Well. Um, could I speak with Derek, please? I've got a little problem."

"You do, eh? What did he do? Knock you up?"

"Miss Todd!"

"Well, an old lady can hope, can't she?"

Sam didn't know whether to remain indignant or give up and laugh. "Our relationship isn't like that."

"More's the pity. He's asleep."

"I thought he might be. But I really need to talk to him. It's urgent."

"Hmph. Not likely, if he didn't knock you up."

Sam closed her eyes, wondering why life was so determined to be difficult these past few days. Then, to her relief, she heard Mary drop the phone without hanging up. Going to get Derek, she hoped.

A minute or two later, she heard Derek's voice saying hello. He didn't sound as if he'd been sleeping either.

"Sorry to bother you," Sam said, "but could you come over here? Fritz Holder is here."

"What's going on? Did he get abducted again?"

"No, no. But he's a little agitated, and for some reason he thinks you have all the answers."

"Great. Answers are one thing I'm awfully

short on." And he didn't sound like he was kidding, either.

"Well, I didn't want to leave him on the streets looking for you."

He seemed to pick up on her concern, saying, "Give me twenty minutes. I'll be there."

Sam hung up and retrieved a beer from the refrigerator for Fritz. While she personally didn't care for the stuff, even the smell of it, she kept a six-pack on hand for times when her coworkers stopped by. Maybe this would calm Fritz down.

He certainly wasn't calm when she returned to the living room. He'd abandoned the sofa and was pacing quickly, restlessly. "Is he here?" he asked as soon as he saw her.

"He's not here, Fritz; I told you. But he's on his way over. Twenty minutes, he said."

"Okay. Okay." He sounded almost as if he were trying to reassure himself. "He'll know what's going on."

"Where did you get that idea?"

Fritz looked at her. "Don't you watch his show?"

Another devotee, Sam thought a little sourly. The world was crawling with them, apparently, making her a minority of one. Although she had to give Derek credit that his fame hadn't gone to his head.

Fritz drained half the bottle of beer in one gulp and wiped his mouth on the back of his hand. "They think I'm crazy, you know."

"Who does?"

"Everybody. Even the chief. He tried to fool me."

"Fool you how?"

But Fritz didn't answer her. He took another spin around the small living room and swigged more beer. "I know what I saw."

"I'm sure you do," agreed Sam, who was privately of the opinion that Fritz's imagination had greatly exaggerated whatever he'd experienced.

"Do you believe in aliens?" he asked her.

Sam suddenly felt as if she was standing on a precarious rock surrounded by quicksand. The wrong word from her might prove disastrous. "I, uh . . . Well, Fritz, I've never seen one. So I'm . . . sort of . . . open-minded?" She felt her way cautiously, hoping she hadn't just put her foot in the quicksand.

"Lemme tell you," he said, waving the beer bottle, "you don't ever want to see one. They're ugly. Big green faces with these huge black eyes. Like bug eyes. Like you see on a grasshopper, almost."

She nodded, hoping she looked encouraging.

"And big. They were eight feet tall. They can't fool me."

"Who can't fool you?"

"*They* can't."

Which was a singularly unhelpful answer. "They" could be almost anybody at all. But she felt reluctant to press the issue, given Fritz's agitation. She was ever so grateful when Derek knocked on her door.

"There he is," she said brightly, and went to let Derek in.

He looked surprisingly chipper, and presentable enough to go on his TV show. Sam peered suspiciously behind him, wondering if he'd brought his entourage, but not another soul was in sight. Thank goodness. She didn't want her small, somewhat untidy living room on international television.

"Hi," he said, the corners of his eyes crinkling as if he were genuinely glad to see her. Practiced charm. She needed to keep that in mind.

He greeted Fritz in a friendly fashion, offering his hand. Fritz first drained his beer, set it on the wood end table, making Sam cringe, then wiped his palm on his pants. Only then did he shake Derek's hand.

"You know, don't you?" he said to Derek.

"That depends," Derek answered, equally cryptic.

This, thought Sam, could be a great conversation: Everybody talking and saying absolutely nothing. Or maybe she'd just fallen through a rabbit hole. Anything, she was beginning to believe, was possible.

"Why don't we sit down?" she suggested brightly. Apparently there was just enough of an edge in her voice, because both men promptly obeyed her. Derek sat near the door, close to Fritz's gun belt. She found that interesting. Fritz settled in the easy chair without getting too comfortable, leaving the couch to Sam.

"So what's up?" Derek asked Fritz.

"You have all the answers," the man announced.

"Hmm." Derek rubbed his chin. "That's a nice compliment, but I'm not really any smarter than the next guy."

Fritz shook his head. "They told me. You have the answers."

Derek and Sam exchanged looks. "Who told you?" he asked.

"They called me."

"Called you?" Derek repeated. "Like on the telephone?"

"Of course on the telephone. They can contact you any way they want."

"I see." Derek rubbed his chin again. Sam had the feeling he was trying to conceal his mouth; trying to keep from smiling or laughing. She couldn't blame him, but this would have been a whole lot more amusing if Fritz had been kidding. Unfortunately, he was not.

"So, they called you on the telephone?"

"That's right. They said to come see you here, that you had all the answers."

"Well." Derek dropped his hand and sat back. "What answers am I supposed to have?"

"I don't know. But the chief thinks somebody fooled me."

"Fooled you how?"

"He thinks it was a joke." Fritz turned to Sam. "Can I have another beer?"

"Sure." Maybe she ought to just give him the whole six-pack. It might knock him out. Then she chastised herself for the unkind thought. "Would you like one, Derek?"

"No, thanks. I think I need all my wits about me right now."

"That's probably wise."

When she returned with another beer for Fritz, it appeared she hadn't missed anything, because the two men were simply staring at each other as if they were suffering from mutual perplexity.

"Well," said Derek after another minute or so, "did the chief tell you why he thinks it was a hoax?"

"Oh, he showed me this silver suit and this mask. And some gloves, too. He said he found them in a trash Dumpster."

"Did they look like what you saw?"

"Not really. I told you, the alien was eight feet tall. That suit wasn't big enough. And the gloves . . . well, they were almost right, but they were hockey gloves." Fritz snorted. "I know the Lightning's logo."

"I'm sure you do. So you don't think it could have been a hoax at all?"

Fritz gnawed his lip. Then he took another swig of beer. "I don't know," he said finally. "But it might explain why Reverend Arthur called me tonight."

"It might? How so?"

"Well, he kept saying he was sorry, and I couldn't figure out what he meant. But he wouldn't tell me. He just kept saying, 'I'm sorry, I'm so sorry.' And he also said, 'Mary made me do it.'"

Sam and Derek looked at each other. Understanding dawned in their gazes at the same time.

"Aunt Mary!" Derek said at the same moment Sam burst out, "Mary Todd!"

Frank looked from one to the other. "Miss Mary Todd?" Then understanding dawned in his gaze, too. "She did it? She made Reverend Arthur do it?" He scowled. "Well, I'll be damned. Maybe I'll go arrest her right now."

"Whoa," said Derek. "She's eighty-something years old."

"Besides," said Sam, "you have to be able to prove it."

"I know, I know." Fritz chewed his lip again and sipped some more beer. "It was a hoax," he said, sounding as if he were testing the idea.

"Probably," Derek said. "A cruel hoax."

For her part, Sam was feeling a little confused. She could have sworn that when Fritz arrived at her house, he was convinced he'd been abducted by aliens and was offended by the mere notion that it might have been a hoax. The shift in his thinking seemed too abrupt.

"Fritz?" she said. "I thought you were convinced you'd seen aliens."

"I was. I was." He looked down at his hands and sighed heavily. "I didn't want to believe somebody could make a fool of me that way."

Derek rose from his chair and went to put a hand on Fritz's shoulder. "Nobody made a fool of you, Fritz."

Fritz kind of chuckled. "I guess not. When you think about it, it was kind of funny. I probably scared them more than they scared me."

"I'm sure of it," Derek said. "But somebody certainly owes you an apology."

"Nah," said Fritz. He stood up. "I think right now they're more scared than I ever was. They could get arrested for kidnapping a police officer." He chuckled again, looking immensely relieved. "I'm gonna go home to bed. I can sleep now. But they probably can't." He paused at the door. "The aliens were right. You do have all the answers."

He said good night and departed, leaving Sam and Derek to look uncertainly at one another.

"What the hell was my aunt up to?" Derek asked.

"I don't know. But I can't believe the change in Fritz. He was so agitated when he got here."

Derek nodded. "I saw. But you know, I think he was more worried that Chief Corrigan might have thrown something together to calm him when he was still at risk of being abducted again. And when we mentioned Aunt Mary . . ."

well, I think he was actually relieved. No more abductions to worry about."

"I guess." Sam shook her head. "I don't get it."

"Well, he was right about one thing. Aunt Mary shouldn't be sleeping peacefully tonight. If she is, I may have a few words for her."

"It probably won't do any good, Derek. Mary's suspected of more hijinks in this town that you'd believe. And nobody has ever been able to pin a thing on her."

"But why does she do these things?"

"To amuse herself? I don't know."

He sighed. "I don't suppose she'd answer me if I asked."

"Probably not. But one thing I've figured out, Derek: She's a cherished institution around here. Even to the people she sometimes drives crazy."

He gave her a wry look. "I guess my father was right. He's often said we Todds are a strange bunch." He hesitated, then said, "I suppose I should go."

But he didn't move, and she didn't, either. Instead their gazes locked, and stayed locked, as time did that incredibly clichéd thing: It stood still.

13

In those timeless instants, Sam felt as if a warm, liquid heat poured through her, filling her until every single cell in her body felt soft and yielding. Her heart stopped, then slipped into a heavy, measured beat as time released a sigh and began to move again.

But she couldn't have moved to save her life. She was trapped by the look in Derek's eyes, a look that seemed to swirl with mystery, to promise both heaven and hell.

He took a step toward her, but the movement didn't release her from the warm, aching torpor; it only deepened it. All thoughts of protecting herself were gone, driven out by a yearning so intense it overwhelmed her.

Her breasts felt heavy, swollen, and at the

apex of her thighs settled a throbbing heaviness that made her knees feel weak. Part of her wanted to collapse on the sofa behind her, and part of her longed to step toward Derek.

He took another step toward her. Yearning blossomed into fearful anticipation: Fearful because he might at any moment turn away. Fearful because she would die of disappointment if he didn't touch her.

But he did. Reaching out, he took her shoulders gently and pulled her against him. Soft flesh met hard, and a long, deep sigh escaped Sam as she savored the sensation.

She was surrounded by his arms, held by his strength. Instinctively she tipped her head back, signaling her welcome. A second later his hot mouth found hers.

All the things she had been steadfastly refusing to notice about him now flooded her senses. How big he was. How hard. How muscular. How good he smelled, like soap and man, and even a faint reminder of the sun and the beach. She could almost feel the sea pounding in her veins, a steady ebb and flow that seemed to be rocking her into security.

And his hands. Not the soft hands of an office worker, but the rough, work-hardened hands of a man who really had climbed most of the way up Everest, who really had traipsed through jungles and poled his way through swamps and some of the world's greatest rivers.

Those hands slipped up beneath her sleep shirt, finding the small of her back, caressing gently. The touch was warm, just a little abrasive, and it deepened the growing hunger within her.

Reaching up, she cradled his head in her hands, feeling the silkiness of his hair, the roughness of his beard-stubbled cheek, the warmth of his skin. And the heady, heady scent of musk that was rising between them.

His hand slipped around beneath her shirt, tracing her ribs almost delicately, sending a shiver of delight racing through her. Instinctively, she arched her back, offering him more.

He accepted the invitation, his fingertips slipping to her front, tracing her midriff, causing all the muscles there to quiver with delight. Their lips broke apart, each of them gasping for air, and he whispered huskily, "You're so soft. . . ."

And he was so hard. Arching her back had brought her hips into intimate contact with his, reassuring her that he wanted her as much as she wanted him. Delight filled her, and she rubbed against him as sinuously as a cat, taking pleasure in his muffled groan.

Then his hand slipped upward until it was just beneath her breast. She caught her breath, waiting in delicious agony for the touch. But he was in no hurry. A breathy chuckle escaped him, as if he understood her impatience, and his fingers began to circle her breast in a slow, lazy navigation, promising but not delivering.

This time it was she who moaned, a sound of mixed impatience and pleasure. Oh, would he never touch her aching nipple? Every brush of her T-shirt against it was torture as his hand seemed always to pass it by, taunting her.

Then, oh, then, she felt the first electric brush of his fingertips across the swollen peak. She gasped, arching even more, and only his other arm kept her from falling. Another moan escaped her as his fingers caused electrical shocks to race through her to her very center.

"So sweet," he whispered, his fingers engaging in a lazy dance of promise. Almost delicately, he caught her nipple between thumb and forefinger and squeezed.

A mewl of pleasure escaped her. The world seemed to swim, she felt as if she were floating, and then she felt the sofa cushions beneath her back. Just in time, for she surely didn't have the strength to stand another minute.

Fabric slipped against her sensitized skin, pulling her arms up as her shirt disappeared over her head. She felt utterly soft, utterly giving, her arms over her head as if she were offering herself without reservation. As she was.

Then his touch disappeared. A pang of loss caused her to open her eyes in time to see him pull off his own shirt, revealing a well-muscled chest kissed with bronze by the sun of foreign climes. Before she could fully register his male beauty, however, he lowered himself over her, fitting himself between her legs.

Then skin met skin, and it was as if the last tension fled from Sam's body. So good . . . oh, it was so good. How could she have lived without this for so long?

Priceless. Perfect. Exquisite. All pretenses were gone and they were just a man and a woman, meant for this moment since the beginning of time.

His mouth found her breast, treating her to an entirely wonderful experience. Gasping with pleasure, she arched upward against him, and the vee of her legs met the hardness of his hips, increasing the welling need in her. So good. *Too* good. As if an irresistible force filled her, she arched against him again and again, forgetting everything in the world except for her need for completion.

As if he shared it, he pressed against her each time she rose to meet him. His mouth on her breast sucked gently, drawing her deeply into him, meeting the rhythm of their hips in perfect counterpoint.

The ache between her thighs grew, becoming stronger and harder, driving her to move more insistently. He met her, matched her. His teeth found her nipple, nipping gently, sending a frisson of pleasure-pain racing through her, dragging a moan out of her from the depths of her lungs.

A flicker of fear danced through her as part of her realized just how vulnerable she'd become. But nothing could stop her now. Nothing.

Not even when his hand slipped down beneath her shorts, finding her damp furrow, seeking the most intimate of touches.

The first brush of his finger was almost too exquisite to bear, bordering on pain. The next one cast her up and over the pinnacle, sending gripping waves of release through every cell of her being.

An instant later he groaned and shuddered, joining her.

Sam couldn't believe what she had just done. As the haze of desire cleared from her brain, her rational mind started kicking in. Or maybe it was her conscience. She felt humiliated by the way she had just behaved, and angry at herself.

With hardly any prompting, forgoing even the clichéd persuasion of dinner dates, flowers, and candy, she had just given herself to a man who had no use for her except to satisfy his sexual urges.

Right now there wasn't a hole deep enough to hide herself in. And even if there had been, she couldn't do it, because he was lying on top of her, still shuddering, still breathing raggedly, too heavy to push away.

Well, maybe her rational mind wasn't the problem. Maybe it was her irrational mind. After all, they were two adults, and they'd just engaged in a mutually consenting sex act. Never mind that they'd both behaved . . . well, there was just something embarrassing about the fact that they were both still wearing their shorts.

Sheesh. She squeezed her eyes shut, but she couldn't quite evade the sexy tingle that came in response to the memory of the last few minutes. Couldn't quite deny that she *liked* the fact he'd been so hungry for her that he hadn't bothered with finesse.

And given half a chance, she'd probably do it again. Good grief, she was a grown woman now—she ought to be in better control of herself than this. But she'd given way to driving hormones like a sixteen-year-old.

It was very lowering to realize that she *hadn't* come a long way, baby.

Double sheesh.

Derek moved. Skin brushed against skin. And all of a sudden she was wondering what she was so embarrassed about. If she was embarrassed, so should he be. And she seriously doubted he was.

But then he lifted his head. "I'm sorry," he said. "I got carried away. That was rather . . . crude of me."

She wanted to bean him. She wanted to grab a pillow cushion and beat him about the ears with it. Did he *have* to agree with her?

"What? You mean that wasn't your usual suave and debonair coupling?"

His face darkened. For the first time, she got an inkling that Derek might actually be capable of real anger. It didn't help that her own words made her want to wince.

"Sorry to disappoint you," he said, levering himself off of her and showing her his back. "I haven't practiced since last week."

Last week? *Last week?* Seething, Sam twisted until she found her shirt lying in a heap on the floor beside the couch. It seemed to mock her, a reminder of her own . . . easiness, for lack of a better word. Snatching it up, she tugged it over her head and stood, staring at his back. A smooth, beautifully muscled back, damn him.

"Well, I'm not up to your usual standards," she said waspishly. "But don't let me detain you any longer."

He grabbed his own shirt and tugged it on before facing her. "Don't worry. You'll never have to see me again."

"Good!"

"Good!" he agreed, storming toward the door.

Just then, the phone rang. Sam stomped her foot and said a very nasty word. Derek paused at the door. "Want me to answer it?" he asked civilly.

"What? And have the whole world know that the noble Derek Diche has deigned to enter my house in the middle of the night? I think not. I've got better things to do with my life than appear on the front page of the *National Gossip Rag*."

"And I don't?"

Glaring at him, she snatched for the phone, snapping, "Bartlett!"

"Sam," said the unwelcome voice of the dispatcher, "the chief's at the hospital with Mrs. Chief. She's having the baby."

"I needed to know this?" Sam demanded. Though, if she hadn't been so upset at the moment, she would have been thrilled.

"Well, uh, yeah. Because I can't get a hold of him right now. But, uh, he said if there were any problems with the egg, I should call you."

"The egg can go to hell."

"Sam?" he said. "You'd better get down there. I'm serious. The mayor's already called twice, and it's only been forty-five seconds."

"Forty-five seconds since what?"

"Since the mayor called the first time. Sam, please."

It didn't at all strike her as odd that he was pleading with her. What was odd was her response. "The mayor, the egg, and this whole town can go to hell."

"Sam . . ."

"I'll be there in fifteen minutes."

She slammed the phone down and looked at Derek. "Saddle up, Lone Ranger. The egg needs our attention."

"What happened?"

"Damned if I know. But the mayor's having a fit."

Ten minutes later, once again in uniform, toting her gun and ready to rip the egg limb from limb—or shell from shell—Sam drove down to the beach in her patrol car, Derek hot on her bumper.

This, she thought, had better be good.

Lord, Derek thought, Sam had some temper. But then, so did he, apparently. All he'd been trying to do was apologize for a rather rough-and-ready lovemaking, with an eye to making it up for her, and she'd practically turned it into World War Three. But again, in all fairness, his response to her initial comment hadn't exactly been bright.

Of course, they'd both been a little on edge. He didn't flatter himself that Sam had honestly wanted to have sex with him. It had just kind of... happened. Which was bound to make them both uneasy and a bit touchy. It had taken them unawares, as it were.

Which was as lousy an excuse as he could think of to make love to a woman. Maybe he shouldn't try to apologize; it might be better for them both if they stayed angry and avoided one another.

Except he wasn't angry with her. Oh, he had been, in the first flush of the moment, when she had snapped at him, but the cool night air was clearing the cobwebs from his brain—entirely too many of those, lately!—and as his thinking cleared, so did his understanding of the situation. With understanding came remorse that he may have hurt her emotionally.

But this wasn't a good time to speak of it. He'd better give her a chance to cool down, and he needed to sort out his own thinking. He did *not* want to get involved again. He knew too intimately the price of that folly. Between Bosnia and his late wife, he sometimes felt as if his entire soul had been shattered into a million pieces and bound back together with masking tape. He was, in short, an emotional Humpty-Dumpty.

He had no business inflicting that on anyone else.

Sam speeded up as they approached the south end of the beach, and after a moment he could see why. The glow coming from down there was amazing. Worrisome. Entirely too bright.

She squealed her tires as she pulled into the condo parking lot. He cornered more slowly, aware that he was in a top-heavy vehicle. The military transports were still there, and judging by the smashed eggs he saw on the side of one transport, the locals had expressed their opinion of the Guard's choice of parking. Or perhaps it had been some youths with more testosterone than wisdom.

The beach was as bright as day. Not, thank goodness, from some alien landing craft or a nuclear explosion, but from enough floodlights to illuminate a night football game. Derek guessed the military had become unnerved.

The mayor was there, of course, in what appeared to be a silk kimono hand-painted with peacock feathers.

"Good Lord," Derek said to Sam as they approached, "where did he get that?"

"It was a gift from our sister city in Japan. It ought to be in a museum."

"It certainly oughtn't to be on him. It's wasted."

The mayor was not, to give him due credit, hopping about and creating a scene. Instead he was standing stiffly, his hands tucked into his kimono sleeves, glaring at all and sundry.

All and sundry involved the barbed-wire-topped earthworks along the beach—which had sprouted an interesting number of crenellations and turrets, Derek noted. As if bored soldiers had begun to turn the sand bank into a sand castle. He made a mental note to get some footage of it.

Then there were the soldiers themselves, who didn't appear to be terribly impressed by the mayor. Of course, it was difficult to be impressed by a short, balding man in a peacock kimono. Sam was the only police officer present, which left Derek wondering where the others had gone.

Then, of course, there were the lights. Many, many banks of floodlights, all aimed toward the water except for two, which showered several million candlepower on the egg.

The egg, which was foaming and frothing around its base in the most unusual way. Zeph and Nat were staring at it, frowning as if there were actually something to ponder other than that it was weird.

There was also a dog. It was shaped like an Airedale, but it was as gray as chimney soot. Right now it was staring at the mayor in a way that suggested it ought not to be ignored. Indeed, its hackles were raised.

"Somebody," said the mayor when he spied Sam, "get that hound from hell out of here."

"It's just Rover, sir," Sam replied, as if she had a close acquaintance with the mutt.

"I know what dog it is. But I want it out of here now."

Zeph stirred from her contemplation of the foaming froth. "It bit the egg, Sam."

"Bit it?" Sam stepped cautiously closer. Derek followed suit, noting that while all his cameras seemed to be operating, his crew was nowhere to be seen. Except for the long-suffering sound man, Bruce.

"Right there," Zeph said. "See that little tear?"

"I'm surprised he could get his mouth on it."

"It's soft enough; I guess he was able to nip it. This stuff has been coming out ever since."

"What is it?"

"Damned if we know."

"Exactly," said the mayor, as if that explained everything. "You don't know what it is. What if it's dangerous? What if it's some kind of acid? People could get hurt."

Lieutenant Childers, who'd been standing a respectful distance away, cleared his throat. "We won't allow that to happen, sir."

"No? You mean those children you call soldiers can actually do something besides tear up my beautiful beach to build sand castles?"

"Sir!" said Childers, sounding angry.

"Quit sirring me. Good God, man, you use that word as if it's the only one in the English language." The mayor rounded on Sam. "Somebody has to do something about this, and they have to do it now. That egg is contaminating the beach. It might be poisonous! Has the EPA approved its emissions?"

Sam looked at the dog. "It's not poisonous enough to hurt Rover, apparently."

"*Nothing* can kill that dog. It's demon spawn. Probably in cahoots with the egg!"

Derek suddenly found it difficult to maintain a straight face.

But Sam, beautiful Sam, remained as calm as a placid summer day in the face of the mayor's fulminations and foolishness. "Yes, sir, I'll take care of it right now. Lieutenant, do you have a medical kit?"

"Yes, ma'am, of course."

"Could I have it, please?"

Childers called out and a soldier came running up with a metal briefcase. Kneeling in the sand at the lieutenant's orders, he opened it.

Childers turned to Sam. "Help yourself, ma'am."

She did. Moments later she slapped a large Band-Aid over the hole in the egg. She didn't even seem worried about the goo on her boots.

"There," she said, brushing her hands together and looking at the mayor. "I stopped it."

"That's not enough." Pulling one of his hands out of his kimono sleeve, the mayor jabbed his finger at the egg. "That has to go. Now. This minute."

"We'd need EPA approval for that," Sam said. "It might be an endangered species."

Derek had never before seen a man turn quite that shade of magenta. It was so bright that it clashed with his kimono. The mayor began to froth at the mouth almost as badly as the egg.

"First aid for an egg!" the man ranted. "First aid for a monster that will probably devour half the city, trample all the beach hotels, and smash the statue of me in front of city hall!"

Just then, Derek realized why the mayor had been so unnaturally motionless when they arrived. As the man waved his arms in irritation, his kimono lifted and the bunny rabbit slippers with the bobbing eyes suddenly emerged.

Rover growled deep in his throat and leapt for the slippers. The mayor shrieked. Sam threw herself through the air and caught Rover around his middle, rolling to pull him on top of her so she didn't injure him.

Rover licked her face in a mighty slurp, then started wiggling like mad to escape her hold.

As he wiggled, he barked and growled at the mayor's slippers.

"Shoot that dog!" the mayor shouted. "Shoot him now!"

Derek noted that the soldiers at their posts were looking nervous, as if they weren't sure what they should do about the dog attack.

"Darn it!" Sam said. "Nobody is going to shoot anybody."

Rover licked her face again, his tail wagging, then returned to trying to lurch toward the offending slippers.

"Mr. Mayor," Derek said, "it might be best if you got those slippers out of here now. The dog thinks they're a toy."

"A toy—that hell hound wants to kill me!"

"No, sir, he just wants to play with them."

"Somebody," said Sam, struggling with the dog, "please get rid of those slippers."

Derek stepped toward the mayor. "Sir?"

The mayor uttered something unpleasant, then turned to storm up the beach toward the condos, swearing that he would be back.

14

Sam had apparently found a good place to scratch Rover, right behind his ears. The dog had forgotten the slippers and was moaning in ecstasy.

As soon as he was sure the mayor was out of sight, Derek bent over and lifted Rover into his arms, freeing Sam. Rover, who at first looked confused, suddenly went limp in Derek's arms and started licking his chin.

"Why," Derek wondered, "would anyone think this dog was a hellhound?"

"Beats me." Attaining her feet, Sam tried to brush sand from her uniform. "It seems to be a pretty common attitude around town, though. Darn this gun belt."

"Why?" he asked.

"*You* try falling on all this stuff. My waist and hip feel bruised."

"I'm sorry. But I meant, why does everyone think badly of this mutt?"

"I don't know. I gather there was some kind of dustup over him before I got here, but I don't know what it was about."

"He's such a sweetheart." The sweetheart was now nuzzling his neck, as if he wanted to burrow closer. The strain of holding the dog was beginning to tell on Derek's arms, and he reluctantly put Rover down. The dog, evidently deciding that Derek was good people, immediately lay down on his feet.

"Here, let me help," Derek said to Sam. "Move a little closer and give me your back."

Of course, brushing the sand off her had the unwanted effect of reminding him of the intimacies they'd shared. His groin immediately felt heavy again, and he found himself wishing he could go back just a short while in time, make up for his rather crude lovemaking to her, and sweep her off to her bed.

But she was standing stiffly under the brush of his fingers, as if she loathed his merest touch.

He was an idiot. A first-rate, world-class idiot. Why hadn't he kept his distance like the smart man he liked to believe he was? He knew full well that he could never again offer a woman a real relationship. Sam deserved that from him, and he had betrayed both of them by forgetting that fact. He had used her as if she were some plaything, all the while knowing he was incapable of offering any more.

Self-disgust made his hands move more quickly, almost angrily, over her backside. But what a sweet backside.

Zeph spoke. "It's oozing through the bandage."

"The dog killed it," Nat observed. "It can't possibly survive this."

"We'll see about that," Sam said. She retrieved a thick gauze pad from the medical kit and a large elastic bandage. "Help me?"

It took Zeph's, Nat's, and Derek's hands to accomplish the task, but a few minutes later they had a thick bandage over the puncture, held in place by the elastic wrap that went twice around the egg.

They stood back to admire their handiwork.

"Pathetic," said Sam.

"It's the best we can do." Zeph shrugged.

"Maybe I should call the medic," Childers said. "Maybe he could do stitches."

"You're kidding, right?" said the medic, who happened to be standing only a few feet away. "I'm not a veterinarian."

"Maybe that's who we should call," Nat suggested.

Zeph glanced scornfully at him. "How many monster eggs do you suppose he's sewn up in his day?"

The medic said, "Probably more than I have."

They stared at the egg.

"Hey," Nat said. "We ought to get samples of that ooze. Do a DNA analysis on it."

"Sure," said Zeph. "And in three weeks we'll know exactly what it *isn't*."

"You never know," Nat said philosophically. "We might find out what it's related to."

Derek spoke. "It *would* be revealing to know what it's not. To know with reasonable certainty, I mean. Right now, we're making a lot of guesses."

"Exactly," said Nat. "We don't even know enough to make a good hypothesis right now. What if a DNA sample proved that this egg is ninety-nine percent sea turtle?"

"It's the other one percent I'm concerned about," Zeph said. "Humans and chimpanzees are separated by, what? One or two genes? Something ridiculously small. That knowledge alone wouldn't necessarily be enough for us to hypothesize the chimpanzee."

"No," Nat argued. "But we'd know it wasn't a dog."

Zeph sighed. "When it hatches—"

"*If* it hatches," Nat interrupted. "If it already isn't dead from dog bite."

At that moment they were joined by two more people. A man and a woman approached, both of them dressed in charcoal-gray suits. The man wore a dark tie, the only distinguishing feature other than a great disparity in height. Derek felt his hackles rise. He recognized government dweebs when he saw them.

"Halt. Who goes there?" said Childers belatedly. So much for his sentries, Derek thought. His men were all so busy building sand castles that they weren't paying attention to much of anything.

The long and short clone reached in their pockets and produced badges. "Special Agents Muldoon and Sullivan, FBI," she said. "He's Sullivan. We understand you have a problem."

"Actually," said Sam, "we have an egg. Whether that's a problem remains to be seen."

"Hey," said Nat, "Are you two from the X-Files?"

"Sorry, sir," said Agent Sullivan. "We don't have an X-Files group. That's purely fictitious."

"Told you so," Zeph said.

"No," said Muldoon, tossing her shoulder-length bob. "We're from the Sea Monster and Alien Abduction Investigative Task Force."

"Also known as Z-Files," Sullivan added.

"Oh, cool" said Nat, looking pleased. "But why the Z-Files?"

Sullivan blinked. "Why not?"

Derek felt a bit of suspicion wafting up his nostrils. "Get real," he said. "There's no such thing."

Sullivan looked at him. "Not officially, no. Say, aren't you Derek Diche?"

"Yes," he said, stepping forward. "You won't mind if I interview you, will you?"

But both agents shook their heads. "Sorry, sir," said Muldoon. "We're not here to talk to the press. We just want to get the facts, sir."

Hmmm. This surpassed his credibility. Glancing at Sam, he though she wasn't any more ready than he to bite on this one. "Could we see your badges again?"

"Certainly." The agents promptly presented them again. Sam studied them.

"They look real."

"Of course they're real," Muldoon said. "We'd have been here sooner, except I missed my medication. But don't worry about it, I'm stable now."

"Can we look at the egg?" Sullivan demanded impatiently.

"Sure," said Nat, waving grandly toward it.

Derek drew Sam aside. "I smell something rotten."

"Me, too." She looked at the two agents. "The badges and ID cards are genuine, though. Or a very expensive forgery."

"Hmmm." Derek rubbed his chin thoughtfully. Stubble rasped against his fingers.

"Lieutenant Childers?" Sam called out. "Could I have a minute, please?"

The lieutenant obediently trotted over to them. "Yes, ma'am?"

"I'm going to go check on the credentials of

these two agents. Will you and your men keep an eye on them while I'm gone?"

"Sure." Childers looked at the agents, who were deep in absorbed conversation with Nat and Zeph. "You think they're phonies, huh?"

"I don't know, but I want to be certain."

"Good idea."

Derek wanted to go with her, but she didn't ask him to. As he watched her walk away, he had plenty of opportunity to consider his own stupidity, which had apparently ruptured his fragile friendship with Sam.

Sam was relieved to have an excuse to get away from Derek. He put her so on edge, primarily because she couldn't help feeling that she'd behaved badly from beginning to end this evening.

He was just a man, after all. She'd practically thrown herself at him, and men were notoriously weak about such things. Or at least they claimed to be. Compounding her iniquity, she'd behaved badly afterward because she was embarrassed, acting like a juvenile rather than a grown woman.

Oh, well. Live and learn. She was never going to get herself into that position again.

The station was quiet, as it usually was at this time of night. There was a DUI in holding awaiting a breath test, an officer sitting in there with him waiting the required twenty minutes.

Other than that, there was the dispatcher and the shift supervisor, Sergeant Halloran. Halloran was deep in a paperback thriller and scarcely nodded when Sam showed up.

At the desk, she called the local FBI field office and got an answering machine. Sighing, she dialed the bureau headquarters.

"You're kidding right?" said the person who answered the phone. Sam had asked for someone in the Sea Monster and Alien Abduction Investigative Task Force.

"I wish I were," Sam said. "But I've got two people down here flashing FBI credentials who claim that's where they're from."

"Cripes," said the man on the other end of the line. "That TV show is a pain in the butt."

"So they're fakes?"

"I don't know. I don't know *everything* that goes on around here."

"Are you an agent?"

"Didn't I say so? But I'm a rookie. Which is the whole damn reason I'm answering telephones at this hour. They never told me at Quantico that it could be like this. Do you have any idea how boring this is?"

"Actually, yes," Sam commiserated. "But I've got this problem in the form of two people claiming to be Agents Sullivan and Muldoon."

"Oh, spare me," the guy groaned. "This is too much. But the credentials look real?"

"As real as any I've seen. But there's no task force?"

"Not that I know about, but that's meaningless. I mean, look how many years it was before anybody knew that J. Edgar wore dresses. We keep secrets pretty good around here."

"Well, there must be some way I can find out if these two are genuine."

"Yeah, yeah. But there are probably a dozen agents named Sullivan and Muldoon. It's not like they're unusual names." He sighed. "Look, can I eat my sandwich while we talk? I'm starved."

"Go ahead."

"Thanks. Okay, let me see what the computer will tell me. If I can get it to work. This darn thing is as hypersensitive as my girlfriend. You can't even look at it without sending it into a pout. Okay . . . Hang on, there . . ."

Sounds of chewing, followed by a slurp that presumably was a drink of some kind. In the background, the clacking of keys.

"Okay," the guy said. "Here we go. I can uncross my toes now. It's working. Oh, man. We've got nineteen agents named Sullivan."

"Great."

"Yeah. So tell me more. Age, sex, approximate height, hair color . . ."

"Male, about six feet, dark brown hair a little on the long side, two hundred pounds. Maybe thirty to thirty-five."

"Hmm, hmm, no . . . okay . . . maybe . . . no way . . ."

Sam tried to hang on to her patience, but she

kept worrying about what might be going on back at the beach if these two characters were phony.

"Down to three," he said finally. "You should have gotten the guy's first name."

"I guess so." Sam kicked herself. Her upset with Derek had apparently clouded her brain. "I guess I could go back and ask."

"You might have to. But wait a minute more. Let's see. All right, one of these guys is out. He's in the Middle East right now. The other one is stationed in Hawaii. That leaves one. Maybe he's your guy."

"Can you tell me any more about him?"

"I'll check. No . . . Hey, his file is sealed!"

Now he sounded excited, Sam realized. Even the background chewing stopped.

"You said the other one was Muldoon?"

"Right. Female, about thirty-five, shoulder length hair, dark. About five-six, one-ten."

"Checking . . ." A minute passed. "Bingo! Seven Muldoons, but only one female . . . and she fits the description."

"So they're real."

"It seems that way. But wait a minute."

She waited. Sergeant Halloran turned the page in his book and slurped some coffee. The dispatcher answered a call.

"Woohoo," said the agent. "Her file is sealed, too. A real mystery."

"I take it that's not usual."

"Well, I can usually find out the basics, like

where they're assigned. It's not like I can read their personnel files, though. Privacy rules, you know. But these two, it doesn't even list a current assignment. I mean, there's *nothing*."

Sam felt her heart sinking. "So maybe this task force really exists?"

"It's possible. But I'll tell you right now, if it does, they've got it hidden better than J. E.'s dresses. It'd be a public relations nightmare."

"So you can't really help me?"

"I'm afraid not. But what I can do is let somebody higher up know they're there, and that you were asking about it. Maybe somebody will call you."

"Great." It was a letdown. She realized she had wanted these two agents to be a fake.

"I'll keep checking, too," the agent said. "Man, this is interesting. A lot better than the calls I usually get from people who want the FBI to check up on their neighbors because they're un-American." He sighed. "Maybe I can noodle my way into something on the computer. What's your number?"

Sam gave it to him, then warned, "Don't get yourself into trouble."

"I didn't ace my computer security class for nothing. Meanwhile, I'll send a rocket upstairs."

After she hung up, Sam sat for a few minutes, pondering. It appeared possible that Sullivan and Muldoon could be exactly what they said they were. Why not? The government had once had a project for remote viewing—or clairvoyance, as most people called it—for the CIA. Why not a Sea Monster Task Force?

How many sea monsters were there, anyway? And was there a government cover-up?

Almost laughing at herself, she got to her feet. "Hey, Sarge?"

Halloran looked up. He'd apparently listened to her end of the call. "Sea Monster Task Force?" he repeated with an elevated eyebrow.

"Well, there *is* the egg."

Halloran shook his head. "The wife wants me to send her and the kids out of town just in case—like I can afford it. I keep telling her it's a hoax. Now you've got FBI agents checking it out? My life is going to become hell."

"You don't have to tell her about the agents."

"Hah. Gossip travels faster than light in this town. She'll know about it by the time I get home in the morning."

"Sorry. But I didn't call these guys. Our esteemed mayor probably did."

"Remind me not to vote for him. What do you need?"

"Some help. I'm down there single-handed with the National Guard and these two agents. And the chief gave me time off."

"Sorry, no can do—at least not for a couple of hours. We've got that convention going on, remember? At any minute, a thousand inebriated frat boys are going to be hitting the streets."

Sam sighed. "I forgot."

"You're lucky you're on the beach. This place is going to be a madhouse soon."

As if it wasn't already one down on the beach. She supposed she could have gone home. The chief had given her time off, after all. But her sense of responsibility wouldn't allow her to leave the situation at the mercy of an inexperienced Guard lieutenant and two mysterious FBI agents. If something went wrong, she'd feel derelict, even if she officially wasn't.

When she returned, the agents were scooping up samples into little bags and bottles. That at least looked realistic. The soldiers had added to their fantastic sand castles, and now there was a tower nearly as tall as a man. Derek's film crew had returned and were busy filming every movement the agents made. And Rover was amusing himself by digging holes hither and yon.

The egg appeared oblivious to all the activity.

Everything was going just swimmingly.

Until the growl came out of the darkness.

It was a low, booming growl. Like a thunderstorm that had eaten a bad burrito. If Sam hadn't known better, she'd have thought it came from the egg. But the egg remained placid, with nary a glow, jiggle, or belch to announce its eggish intentions. No, this growl had come from the ocean.

Guardsmen put down their shovels and grabbed their rifles. Their lieutenant seemed poised on the brink of wetting his drawers. Derek's crew was looking toward the parking lot and a quick exit. Nat and Zeph were clinging to each other. Only Sullivan and Muldoon seemed unfazed.

"Female." Sullivan said, nodding. "Postnatal but still juvenile."

"Why still juvenile?" Muldoon asked, cocking her head.

"There was no nasal flurry at the end. The adult females always have nasal flurry."

"Of course," Muldoon said. "So . . . say . . . not more than forty to fifty years old?"

"If that," Sullivan agreed. "I'd guess mid-thirties."

"If it's not too much trouble," Sam cut in, "could you clue the rest of us in on this?"

Sullivan shook his head. "National security. You understand."

"No, I don't," Sam said, standing her ground. "I don't understand *any* of this!"

"Join the club," Derek said.

"Line forms to the left," Nat announced.

"Tickets at half-price if you call now," Zeph added.

Sam nodded as if her guess had been confirmed. "National security is a code word for 'I don't know.' Right?"

"Who told you that?" Muldoon asked.

"There's a leak in the Bureau," Sullivan said. Turning to Sam, he added, "But in this case, no. What it means is, you don't want to know." He withdrew a cellular phone from his jacket pocket and pressed a speed-dial button. "McDermis. Sullivan here. Yeah, she's here with me. We have a Code Four-Ten-Eighteen. We'll need an evidence removal and whitewash detail. Right. We'll report it as mass hysteria."

"Mass hysteria?" Muldoon asked. "We used that the last three cases. Can't we call it swamp gas this time?"

Sullivan put a hand up, nodding. "Boss, she wants to report it as swamp gas. Yes, she has *that* look on her face. Right. Swamp gas it is."

As Sullivan hung up the phone, Muldoon turned to Sam. "Thanks for your help, Officer. We'll handle it from here. Nothing but swamp gas."

"Right," Sam said, her tone belying the word. "It's so swampy here on the beach. Why didn't I realize?"

"We're trained in these things."

Derek snorted. "And where do you get this training? The Spielberg Academy?"

"We really gotta find that leak," Sullivan said.

Sam turned to Derek. "Now all we need is some guy smoking a cigarette."

"He doesn't smoke cigarettes," Sullivan said with a shake of his head. "It's cigars."

"Havanas," Muldoon agreed. "We have to pretend not to know."

Derek shrugged. "And I thought my family was strange."

* * *

Sam didn't abandon her post, much as Muldoon and Sullivan seemed to want her to. They wanted to banish the National Guard, too, but Lieutenant Childers took a surprisingly strong stand.

"Not until I get orders from my superiors," he said flatly. So his troops continued building sand castles. The beach was beginning to look like a miniature fantasy land amid a battle zone.

"You know," Sam said to Derek, as they retreated to their familiar seats on the dune, "I'm beginning to feel like I have ringside seats to the circus."

"Yeah. Well, it's Florida, the land ruled by a giant mutant mouse."

"Yeah."

"You know, my seat could use a cup holder." He started digging a small hole in his "armrest."

"What for?"

"The drinks I'm going to send one of my guys out for. You want coffee? Or something cold?"

"Cold, please. Icy. And full of caffeine." The night was uncomfortably humid, the temperature in the low eighties.

"In short," Derek said, "a cola."

"You got it. Thanks."

"No problem."

Herm, the second cameraman, was agreeable to going for drinks. In fact, he had to fend off the rest of the crew, all of whom wanted the job of gofer.

"No," said Derek to the rest of them. "Herm I can trust to return. I'm not so sure about the rest of you."

Sulking, they returned to their cameras and microphones.

"Are they always this difficult?" Sam asked.

"Actually, they're usually all gung-ho. But this time is different."

"How so?"

"There's actually an egg, and growls in the night. Quite a bit different from the usual risks we take."

"Oh." Sam couldn't resist teasing. "Risks like missed planes and trains? Five-star foreign cuisine?"

He looked down his nose at her. "No. Risks like no toilet paper in the loo."

"Ahh."

"Risks like snowstorms, rock slides, bugs the size of my hand—or worse, insects so small you can't see them that want to lay eggs in your eardrum—"

"Oh, stop!"

"I thought that would get your attention." He seemed smug.

"You're kidding about the bugs, right?" she asked hopefully.

"Afraid not. There are some inhospitable places out there, at least in the view of us pampered Westerners. There were places we visited where I wadded up cotton balls and stuck them in my ears at night to avoid any unwelcome guests."

"Ugh."

"I had a particular scare in Africa once. That was back when I was a correspondent. I was sent to cover some small brush war, and the town I visited had an Ebola outbreak. I fretted the next couple of weeks, you can be sure. Every time I felt an urge to sneeze, I wondered if that was the beginning. And I sneezed a lot. The place was dusty."

Sam realized she didn't want to think about all the dangers he had faced. For her, the stories weren't merely interesting. They were frighteningly personal.

"You've seen quite a bit," she said finally.

"Too much." He leaned back in his sandy chair. "Let's forget about it, shall we? It's a beautiful night and we have a real mystery here. I'm dying to see what comes out of that egg."

"I'm not." But in a way she was. "Well, maybe I am. The sooner the darn thing hatches, the sooner I can get back to real life."

He looked at her. "Is real life so wonderful?"

The question struck her as incredibly sad. "Don't you think so?"

"I suppose I did once, when it was all fresh and new. But it's just a chemical accident, you know. None of this has any real meaning."

Sam was shocked. "Do you honestly believe that?"

He shrugged and stared out toward the sea. "I don't know. My parents are organic chemists. From the time I was small, they taught me to appreciate the fantastic chemical accident of life."

"And did you? Do you?"

He shook his head once. "I don't know. Accident just doesn't explain it, does it? Not in any way I'm comfortable with."

Which was why he was pursuing mysteries all over the globe, Sam thought. He was seeking meaning in life. She had a feeling his years as a correspondent had been counterproductive in that respect. How could they not have been?

"Anyway," he went on, "we have that marvelous egg, and something growling in the dark, and I really don't want to see that egg whisked away to some government laboratory somewhere, and the whole thing passed off as swamp gas or mass hallucination."

"On that we agree. So what do we do about Abbott and Costello there?"

"I'm pondering that one."

Just about the time that Herm returned with the beverages, Derek sat upright. "Brainstorm," he said.

"Yeah? What?"

"Are you game to roust the mayor?"

Sam groaned.

"I'm serious. He's the solution to our problem."

"He was the *source* of our problem."

"But now we can use him to our advantage. Trust me."

Surprisingly, Sam found that suddenly a very easy thing to do.

"Okay," she said. "I'll give it a whirl."

He smiled at her then, a smile that touched her to her very toes. "You're a good sport."

She just hoped she wasn't a soon-to-be-fired good sport.

15

"I don't know about this," Sam said as they stood in front of the mayor's condo door. All around them the covered balcony walkway was silent, the windows dark. The doors overlooked a silent, motionless parking lot. "He's not going to like being awakened."

"He's going to like it even less when he hears the national news if Tweedledum and Tweedledee get that egg out of town."

"He's been wanting it gone since the moment it appeared. He'll be thrilled."

"Not when he hears the spin they put on it." Derek reached out and rang the mayor's doorbell. Insistently. The kind of ring that ought to bring the man to the door in a rage.

Which it did.

The door flew open and the mayor stood there. The kimono was gone, and what was left of his hair was standing on end. He wore a candy-cane-striped nightshirt that made him look like a bulging barber pole.

And he looked with disfavor on the two of them.

"What the hell do you want?" he demanded. "It's the middle of the night." Then his face paled. "Oh, my God, the egg has hatched!"

"No," said Derek. "Far worse."

The mayor, who had looked as if he were about to run for the hills, forgetting his wife on the way out of the building, paused. "What could be worse?"

"Plenty," said Derek. He then looked around as if he didn't want to be overheard, and stepped inside the mayor's condo, drawing Sam with him. Once again he scanned the walkway outside, then closed the door.

"What's going on?" the mayor demanded.

"The FBI is here," Derek announced.

"Well, it's about time. I called them days ago."

"But it's a problem."

"How?" The man looked as if he wanted to tear out his hair with frustration, or better yet, tear out Derek's.

"Just listen," Derek said. "The FBI is here, and they want to take the egg away in the morning."

"Good! The sooner that thing is off my beach, the better."

"No," said Derek.

"No?"

"No. It'll be a catastrophe."

"Are you crazy? That *egg* is a catastrophe. The minute it hatches its little Godzilla, we're all going to be heading for the hills. This town will be dead."

"This town will be dead if you let them take the egg."

The mayor gaped at him, then flopped down in a colorful easy chair. Actually, 'colorful' didn't do it justice, or injustice. The mayor apparently chose his furniture the way he chose his clothes: with his eyes closed. "I don't believe this. You're crazy."

"No, but they're going to say the whole town is crazy."

At this the mayor's jaw dropped.

"Exactly," said Derek, taking the seat across from him. "And Sam—Officer Bartlett—is my witness. They're planning to run off with the egg and tell the world this town is full of hysterics."

"But nobody will believe that. The egg is on the news!"

"By the time they get done, everybody is going to believe the egg was a hoax. Once it's gone, nobody can prove otherwise. And they're going to tell the whole world that Paradise Beach went crazy. They're going to make fun of this town."

"Worse," said Sam, seeing where Derek was going. "They're going to say our beach is full of swamp gas."

"Swamp gas?" The mayor was stunned.

"Do you know what that stuff smells like?" Sam asked. "Rotten eggs. Who's going to want to vacation on a beach that smells like rotten eggs?"

The mayor groaned and put his head in his hands. "They'll kill the tourist industry."

"Precisely," said Derek. "But there's more."

"More?" The mayor lifted his head, looking like a man awaiting the fall of the guillotine blade. "What more could there be?"

"The egg's mother."

"The egg's mother?"

"She was offshore tonight, growling. Something tells me that if anyone tries to take her egg, she might just be willing to come ashore and wreak some havoc."

"That's right," Sam agreed. "And then they'll whitewash the whole thing by saying there was some terrible gas line explosion that blew up the town. Or something like that. But it won't matter then, because we'll all be dead or homeless."

The mayor groaned again. "What can we do?"

"It's simple," Derek said. "We need to get so many people on the beach that the FBI won't dare take the egg."

* * *

The director of emergency preparedness, whose principal duties consisted of sitting through endless county meetings about hurricanes that never arrived, wasn't any happier about being dragged out of bed than the mayor had been. After listening to the mayor's description of the possible catastrophes, however, he woke up and took charge. He promised to activate the emergency phone system that would call every resident in town.

"There," said the mayor, rubbing his hands after he hung up. "I bet that gets a bunch of people down there by dawn."

Sam, who was grateful she still had her job—at least as far as the mayor was concerned—was also grateful to get out of there.

"I'm going home to get some sleep," she announced to Derek. "I have a feeling it's going to be a long day."

"Mind if I join you?"

Sam's face flamed. She was hoping he would never allude to *that* incident again.

"I mean, I'll sleep on your couch," he said swiftly. "The problem is my aunt."

"Your aunt?"

"Yes. I have the distinct feeling that if I go home, I won't get any sleep at all. She seems hell-bent on making my life . . . interesting, for lack of a better word."

"That wouldn't surprise me." Sam smothered a yawn. "Okay, you get the couch."

* * *

Which was easier said than done. Because as soon as she'd given him a pillow and a blanket and locked herself into her bedroom, her imagination started to run wild.

Despite what had happened earlier, her body was still aching, edgy, unsatisfied. It made her restless until she was battling the sheets and blankets and only getting more tangled in them. The bed had lumps, the pillow was too hard, the blanket too hot.

Muttering under her breath, she climbed out of bed, snuck into the bathroom, splashed cold water on her face, returned to her room, closed the door, and turned on the floor fan to its highest setting.

Nothing helped. Because, as her body responded with awareness of Derek's presence only a few feet away, her mind began to toss up images that fueled the heat.

He might open the door right now and stand there in the dark. Fully naked. Oh, would she love to see him fully naked. What little she'd seen so far was fabulous. All that smooth, warm skin, all those hard muscles. Those narrow hips that she suddenly longed to grip with her hands.

She punched her pillow into submission, fit her head into the dip she had created, and screwed her eyelids shut, commanding herself to sleep.

Instead she remembered the way his skin

had felt beneath her palms, the way his hips had seemed to fit against her as if they had been made for each other. The way his weight on her had felt so good.

The knowing way he had played with her breast. . . .

Smothering a groan, she clamped her legs together against the heat that seemed to be filling her down there, filling her yet leaving her feeling empty.

Needing so much more.

She wondered if he was feeling the same way. He hadn't even attempted to make a pass at her after they'd arrived, and men always made passes. So he'd had enough. He regretted their earlier encounter as much as she did.

But that didn't keep her mind from suggesting possible scenarios. She would fall asleep . . . a light feather touch would wake her. She'd pretend to remain asleep as his lips traced her ear, awakening quivers of delight in her. As his mouth trailed down her throat, spreading warmth and heaviness through her.

She would sigh then, feeling delightfully caught between waking and sleeping, relaxed and open as his hands began to play over her, coaxing her into desire with him. Leading her along to the pinnacles of need.

Slowly, slowly, he would ease her nightshirt over her head. She would feel the cool caress of the fan-stirred air on her exposed skin like a million little kisses. . . .

No, that wouldn't do. Hopping out of bed, Sam went to her closet, ditched the nightshirt, and donned a slinky black silk gown that she had bought on an impulse and never worn.

Much better.

Back in bed, she closed her eyes. He would slip the slinky black gown over her head, so slowly. Allowing them both to savor the moments as if they were the very end in themselves.

His lips would touch her. Her breasts, her belly. Down there. A delicious quiver ran through her and she hugged her pillow tight.

He'd slip off his own clothes . . . or maybe he was already naked. He would press himself to her, meld himself to her, give her the exquisite pleasure of discovering him from head to foot with her hands.

With her mouth. . . .

A sigh like a moan escaped her. Every cell in her body felt heavy with hunger. Her mind seemed to drift on a current of pleasure. . . .

"Sam?" There was a knock on the door.

She struggled out of a deep sleep, wondering what was going on. Her alarm was supposed to wake her.

"Sam? Time to rise and shine. I checked with my crew. The reinforcements are arriving."

She groaned.

"Sam, I made coffee. It's ready." His tone

was almost wheedling. "Or do you want me to go without you?"

"No!" She sat up, blinking the sleep out of her eyes. "Give me a minute."

"Meet you in the kitchen."

She looked down at herself, wondering what the heck she was doing in a slinky nightgown. Then she remembered. A blush stained her cheeks.

Annoyed at herself, she jumped out of bed and headed for the shower. A *cold* shower.

Her belt felt heavy with its burden of gun, nightstick, speed loaders, and all the rest of it. Her *uniform* felt heavy, as if it weighed a ton. Sam wondered what was wrong with her. Then she realized she was reluctant to face Derek.

The thought stiffened her spine and she marched out to the kitchen. He was sitting at her little dinette, sipping coffee. The clock said it was four-thirty.

Stifling an instinctive groan at the hour, Sam poured her own cup of coffee, set it with a thud on the table, and sat across from Derek.

"Morning," he said. He was reading her copy of the *Times*. She hated it when anybody read her copy of the paper before she'd had a chance to look it over.

He saw the direction of her glare. "I hope you don't mind," he said. "I couldn't sleep and I heard it land in your driveway a while ago."

Contritely, he passed her the A and B sections, as neatly folded as if they'd never been opened.

She managed a nod and snapped the A section open so she could take in the full front page.

Dead center was a picture of the egg. "Oh, no."

He nodded. "And they're already speculating it's some kind of hoax."

"But it couldn't be."

"Well, it might be. If the prankster had access to about ten thousand dollars and one of the Hollywood special effects people. I know. I had my researcher talk to a few of them."

"Who'd spend that kind of money on a hoax?"

"Nobody in his right mind."

Sam looked at the photo again and decided that she didn't want to start her day by reading some insufferable journalist's attempt to make light of the whole thing. The egg had caused her entirely too much trouble so far for her to find anything about it humorous.

"It's real," she said finally.

"I think so."

"But yesterday you were saying that you were going to prove it's a hoax."

"I know what I said." He sighed and put the paper down. "I'm struggling with this, Sam. With the exception of the giant anaconda, every investigation I've done so far has led me to a dead end comprised of folk tales and scientific improbability. Note I don't say impossibility. There's nothing inherently impossible about any of the things I've investigated. But they're highly improbable, and such evidence as exists is too thin or too easily explained away. This is different."

She nodded. "And?"

"And I think I'm afraid to discover that monsters really exist."

She liked him then. She liked him a whole lot. A man who wasn't fearful of admitting he was afraid. Would wonders never cease?

"On the other hand, I'm almost equally afraid that this entire thing will go up in smoke. Frightening or not, I'd like to find some magic still exists in the world."

"The world is full of magic," Sam said. "Look at the stars in the sky."

"Massive helium fusion contained by its own gravity," he said promptly.

"So?"

"So, there's no magic to it."

"That's sad."

He met her gaze. "I know. But that's what stars are."

"And they're still magical. How did they come to be? Where did all that helium come from? Where did the universe come from? And don't tell me it's a chemical accident, because I'm not buying it. Not when I can stand out on the beach at night and see all those stars twinkling in a black sky. Or when I can watch the sun set in a blaze of colors. It's magical no matter how you explain it to me."

"I wish I had the gift to see it that way."

Her heart squeezed. "Just try, Derek. The explanations don't have to kill the magic."

But he didn't answer. Instead he rose and carried his cup to the sink. "Time to go," he said. "Time to find out what we've unleashed."

They'd unleashed quite a bit. Sullivan and Muldoon were sitting on opposite sides of the egg, pistols in hand, watching the gathering crowd uneasily.

"I wish they'd put those guns away," Derek remarked.

"Me, too." But they were, after all, federal agents with an assignment to complete.

Some of the crowd were the same people who'd been there yesterday. Some of the placards were the same. But the mood was entirely different. *No* one wanted Paradise Beach and its population to be made the butt of national jokes. No one wanted to see their city being poked fun at by Jay Leno.

They were not, however, in an ugly mood. They seemed to be having a good time.

"Oh, Lord," Derek said. "There's my aunt. I should have known she'd turn up."

"Miss Todd never misses an opportunity to be provocative," Sam answered.

"So I'm beginning to discover. Would you believe she asked me if I'd knocked you up?"

"I would. She asked me the same thing."

Derek groaned. "Where do I hide my face?"

"Nowhere around here. You're too well known. Well."

"Well, what?"

"If you can't fight them, you might as well join them."

She looked at Derek and he at her. And they both started to grin.

In two minutes, he'd whipped his crew into readiness and was thrusting a microphone in Special Agent Muldoon's face. "Isn't it true, Muldoon, that you had absolutely nothing to do with the Kennedy assassination?" Seemingly stunned, she stammered for an answer, but he was already asking the next question. "And isn't it *also* true that you took no part whatsoever in the infiltration of college campuses under J. Edgar Hoover? And isn't it *also* true that you made no attempt to participate in the Watergate investigation?"

These things were, of course, true. Special Agent Muldoon couldn't have been more than a girl when these events had happened. But the questions had had their desired effect. Mutters began to sift through the crowd.

"Kennedy cover-up."

"Spying on our own kids."

"Political witch hunt."

Derek may as well have torn a page from the campaign statements of that Florida politician who had said his opponent's wife was a "practicing thespian," and accused the man of "regular mastication." Sam realized that sometimes the truth, boldly told, can be a lie unto itself. That was happening now.

"And isn't it true," Derek continued his rapid-fire inquisition, "that you're involved in an egg cover-up that reaches the highest level of the government, including the CIA?"

Sullivan reached for his cell phone and started talking rapidly. Muldoon stiffened her shoulders. "We're going to have to confiscate your cameras."

Before she could take even one step toward the equipment, the crowd surged forward.

"Free speech!" someone shouted.

"Freedom of the press," came an echoing cry.

Muldoon hesitated.

Mary Todd turned to Arthur, who had hotfooted it down to the beach in response to her histrionic plea that he use his authority to prevent violence. She at least could still push *his* buttons. The rest of her gang continued in a state of heresy, refusing to listen to a word she said.

"You need to start a chant," she said. "It'll create solidarity."

"How will that prevent violence?"

"Trust me, it will. Those two agents won't dare do a thing if the entire crowd is against them. And the chant will keep the crowd from getting out of hand."

Arthur hesitated. "What chant?"

" 'Hell, no, the egg won't go.' Has a ring, don't you think?"

Arthur was appalled. "Mary, I can't say that! I'm a minister."

Mary rolled her eyes. "Then modify it. How about . . . 'Golly gee, leave it be'?"

"But what if it stirs the crowd up more? I can't be responsible for that."

"Trust me, Arthur, if you don't act, this crowd is going to get stirred up beyond your wildest imaginings." She paused. "Amazing, the mayor having the wit to conceive of a plan like this. I might like that boy after all."

"Mary . . ."

"Arthur," she said impatiently, "a crowd chanting 'golly gee' is hardly going to get violent. Think about it. Now do something to save lives!"

Mary didn't honestly think those agents were stupid enough to shoot into a crowd. They were too severely outnumbered. But she wasn't about to let this opportunity pass away into boredom, as so many things in Paradise Beach did. Besides, it tickled her to see the mayor make a complete turnabout. Pity she hadn't thought of how to manage that herself.

As for Derek and Sam . . . well, her nephew had been out all night. Good things were in the wind there. Which was not to say they might not need another nudge or two later on.

Arthur had apparently considered her words and taken stock of the muttering crowd, which was scarier without organization than it would be with *his* organization. Perhaps he could atone a bit for taking part in that awful abduction.

He mounted a dune, his black coat whipping in the early breeze, the sun rising right behind him. He extended his arms in a pose so many in the crowd recognized as meaning he was about to preach. The gesture had the effect of quieting them.

"Hey," said Muldoon. "Get down from there."

"He's a preacher," a man shouted. "Let him have his say."

Arthur spread his arms even wider. "Shoot me if you must," he said grandly to Muldoon, "but I need to speak to my people."

Muldoon, a math whiz, took stock of the odds and subsided.

"My fellow citizens of Paradise Beach," Arthur began in the sonorous tones that could rumble to the back of a church and maintain perfect clarity, "we are brought here today to consider a miracle, and to consider our own hearts."

A few in the front of the crowd sat down to listen. Even at the outer edges of the growing mob, people became still.

"We are being tested. Yes, tested. Look into your hearts and remember the teachings of Scripture. God spoke to Job, and told of a leviathan in the sea." Arthur didn't mention that God was in the midst of dressing Job down to size in that passage. "There is more to this world than what human eyes can see, what human hands can touch, what human ears can hear!"

The egg was, of course, perfectly visible. And touchable. And audible. It burped again, seemingly in agreement with the reverend's sermon, although only Sam and Derek and the two FBI agents appeared to hear it. Muldoon edged a step away. Sullivan dialed his c-phone with greater urgency. Sam merely smiled.

"Yes, we are presented with a *miracle*," Arthur continued. "Evidence of something greater than our ordinary existence. Evidence of the divine."

Derek looked uncomfortable at that statement. Sam reached out and squeezed his hand.

"And what does our government want to do?" the reverend asked. "Take it away! Deny it! Tell us we're hysterical, or smelling swamp gas." A smile flickered over his face. "Well, I stand here to tell you that an excess of suntan lotion does not swamp gas make."

Always get them with a joke, he'd heard in homiletics classes. The crowd broke into laughter. Now they were his.

"Nay, my fellow citizens. We have been given a mission from God." Or perhaps from Mary Todd—she was apparently His emissary to this community, even more than himself. And she indeed worked in strange and mysterious ways. He wouldn't put it past her to have rigged this whole thing somehow.

"The Lord commanded us to be stewards of all life on earth. And for us, here in Paradise Beach, on this day, that stewardship includes . . . this egg."

He paused for a moment, waiting to see how the crowd responded. Silence. A few nods. He hadn't lost them yet.

"Let us not turn to violence. Just as our Lord stayed Peter's hand in the Garden of Gethsemane, I ask you to stay your hands here on Paradise Beach. But neither let us be swayed in our duty to our Lord. This is our town. This is our beach. *This is our egg!*"

"For better or for worse," Sam muttered under her breath.

"So what must we do?" Arthur asked. "How do we carry out our mission? We stand united. We protect our egg. We let nature take care of her own. We say . . . *Golly gee, let it be! Golly gee, let it be!*"

The crowd took up the chant. It rippled through the crowd until everyone, including children, was reciting it in time while waving their fists in the air.

But it wasn't the world's best chant. It faded away after a few minutes, and the crowd stood silent, feeling lost.

Then a voice arose from their midst. Other voices took up the song. Arms linked until the crowd was united as one, swaying in time to the music. The tune was by John Philip Sousa. The words were from Mrs. Graylee's third grade:

Be kind to your web-footed friends.
For a duck may be somebody's mother.
Be kind to your friends in the swamp . . .
Where the weather is very very damp.

Mitch Miller would have been proud.

16

The mayor, of course, was not content to let the citizens of his town steal the show. It was time to make it very clear who was behind this move to protect the fine reputation of Paradise Beach.

He donned his best suit—navy blue—a red tie for assertiveness, then regarded his wingtips woefully. A march across the sand would scuff them beyond recovery, and he'd spent a whole fifty dollars on them. The fact that the tops were imitation leather increased his dread. They'd be ruined.

So he settled on deck shoes sans socks. A man had to do what a man had to do, particularly when he was facing reelection.

Suddenly remembering the dog collar incident that had saved that miserable mutt from hell, Rover, from extermination several years ago—when it had seemed nearly everyone in town had been wearing green dog collars in protest—he snuck an egg from the refrigerator, which his wife guarded as if it were a bank vault. He tucked it in his pocket, convinced that *this* time he would be at the forefront of any protest symbolism.

He arrived on the beach to discover a singalong. Hmm. That wasn't quite what he'd envisioned when he aroused a crowd to protect the town from the forces of humiliation.

He hadn't wanted anything that looked quite so . . . hippie-ish. He'd wanted a show of strength. Of stalwart pride, of valor and glory. Not some song about a duck. It sounded like his third grade field trip, when they'd all piled on the bus to Sunken Gardens, right before one of the boys—*not* him; that was his story and he'd stuck to it—had shot a spitwad at the driver, and Mrs. Graylee had decreed that field trips were *not* supposed to be fun, they were supposed to be *educational*.

This was not protest. This was fun. It was time for firm action.

"My fellow citizens!" he bellowed. Unlike the good reverend, his voice was not sonorous. It was more like the angry squawk of an egret that had been rousted from its feeding place by a stray dog. But squawk he did. "My fellow citizens!"

"Oh, no," Sam muttered to Derek.

"What is that little pissant up to?" Mary Todd muttered to Arthur.

"I'm sure he'll tell us," Arthur answered. "At great length."

"My fellow citizens!" the mayor repeated for the third time. And this time people didn't look up to see if they were about to be decorated by an egret. Safe from that defilement, they turned their attention to the mayor. "We are here in a most momentous moment of monstrosity. A veritable vertigo of viragos. A confluence of consternation. A herculean house of horror."

"At least he's alliterate," Derek said. Sam laughed.

"On the dawn of this day of destiny, this gathering of the good and godly, this . . ."

He paused for a moment, and Mary muttered to Arthur, "This paean of pandering."

"A dazzling display of disingenuity," Arthur agreed.

". . . this yearn for the yore of our youth," the mayor continued, having finally found yet more words to mangle, "I ask you to stand with me in struggle, link our loins in loyalty, and breach the bastions of bureaucratic barbarism."

"Link our loins?" Sam asked.

"Sounds good to me," Derek said with a wink.

"Me, too," she said, and blushed.

He leered, a gentlemanly leer.

Sam was quick to change the subject. "Do

you suppose he's going to go through the entire alphabet?"

"One fears so."

But the mayor was at last starting to move. Like a glacier. "We have met a monster in our midst. But it's a good egg."

"Oh, sheesh," Sam whispered, smothering another laugh.

"What has it done?" the mayor inquired. "How has it offended? Other than a belch or two. And who among us hasn't belched?"

"Or glowed in the dark, or quivered like a bowl of Jell-O?" Derek whispered.

"Well, you sure glow in the dark." Sam bit her lip as she realized what she had said.

"And I could make you quiver," Derek answered.

"But no belching," she said, straight-faced.

"Not during. Never."

The mayor was still speaking, but Sam's thoughts were running to quite a different sort of egg, and quite a different sort of intrusion. God, she had it bad! She forced her attention back to the mayor.

"And so, my fellow citizens, I urge you to join me in symbolic protest! Let the shadow government know we shall not be appeased! Let us show our solidarity by proudly carrying . . ."

He rammed his hand into his pocket. And stopped. And reddened. A stain began to appear on his trousers.

"Good heavens, he's gone and wet himself again," Mary said. "I thought he stopped that when he turned fifteen."

The mayor removed his hand, and a long trail of whitish yellow goo trailed from his fingers.

A groan of repulsion rose from the crowd.

"... an ... egg," the mayor concluded, now sounding not like an angry egret, but instead like a frightened sparrow. He paused for a moment, withdrawing a fuchsia handkerchief with chartreuse paisley print, and wiping his hand. "But maybe we should boil them, I think."

"That's our mayor," Mary said. "Going off half-cooked."

Judging by the looks on the faces of the crowd, the egg as symbol wasn't going to make it. As the mayor stuffed his sodden handkerchief into his soaked pocket, he scrambled to regain lost ground.

"Hah hah," he said, a forced laugh, the kind people make when they realize a joke has fallen flat. "I was kidding."

He was also losing their attention. A bulb went on in his brain. Unfortunately, it was so dim he didn't see the consequences just ahead. "These people want to take this egg away, to make a laughingstock of our entire community. They want to say we're crazy. That swamp gas went to our brains. That we imagined it. That it was a bad joke and we were all fools."

Disturbed mutters rose from the crowd.

"They want to put us on the front page of

every newspaper in the country, claiming we're deluded dullards."

"No," came a thunder from the crowd.

"But it gets worse yet," the mayor said, revving up. "That egg has a mother."

The crowd stilled. Many of them cast uncertain glances over their shoulders at the water.

"You've all had mothers. You know what they're like. Does anyone here really want to argue with that egg's *mother*?"

"I wish he hadn't mentioned that," Sam said, eyeing the crowd uneasily.

"My fault. I mentioned it to *him*."

Mary Todd shook her head with disgust. "Criminey, he's going to turn this into a ghost town. You have to stop him, Arthur."

"Certainly, Mary. I'll just drop down from my spaceship and abduct him."

She glared at him.

"We can't let them take the egg," the mayor screeched. "We can't let them take it and dissect it into little pieces and leave this whole town to the mercy of whatever is out there in that water."

Derek had had enough. Grabbing his microphone and telling his sound man to start recording, he dashed over to the mayor and thrust the mike into his face. "So, Mr. Mayor, are you saying that the FBI is involved in a conspiracy to wipe out Paradise Beach economically?"

"You bet your britches I am!" The mayor

fruitlessly tried to stand taller as he realized he was the focus of cameras.

"Why would they want to do that, sir?"

"It's a conspiracy!"

"To what end?"

"To wipe us out, of course."

"Right. Buy *why*?"

"How should I know? Conspiracies don't need reasons. If they have one, they hide it anyway. Look at the way they covered up Roswell. Threatening to dump those good folks in a desert to die if they talked."

"Hear, hear," rumbled the space cadet contingent.

"So what you're saying," Derek suggested, "is that they're going to do the same to us. Shut us up and threaten us, so we can't let them take the evidence the way they took the flying saucer remains."

"Exactly," said the mayor, relieved to have it explained to him.

"My, my," Mary murmured to Arthur. "That nephew of mine shows promise."

"God help us all," Arthur replied.

Sam was just glad that the attention was turning back to the egg and away from whatever might be out in the water. A panic right now would be ugly.

Someone tapped her shoulder and she whirled around. Chief Blaise Corrigan was standing there.

"Anybody care to fill me in on what's going on?"

Sam nearly stammered. "Uh, didn't you get the phone message the emergency center put out?"

"Yes, I did. But I'm still wondering what's going on."

"The FBI wants to take the egg and whitewash the entire thing. The mayor doesn't want to see the town made into a laughingstock." She hoped he'd leave it at that, otherwise she was apt to be looking for a job.

He left it at that. "So he thinks a mob scene will make things better?"

"It'll keep the egg from being taken."

The chief shook his head. "If the feds want to take something, a mob scene isn't going to stop them. But I thought the mayor wanted the egg gone."

"He changed his mind. He's also worried about the egg's mother. Derek's trying to deflect him from that right now, to keep the crowd from panicking."

Blaise sighed. "Anytime you get a crowd this size together, it's dangerous. One little thing can set off a mob."

"I know." Suddenly this didn't seem like the world's brightest idea. How in the world had she let Derek talk her into this? That man was poison to her common sense.

"Well," said Blaise, looking around. "Well."

He didn't seem to have any better ideas than

the rest of them about how to handle the current crisis-in-the-making.

Not that Sam could blame him. As long as that bleepity-bleep egg was sitting on the beach, every hour was going to bring another potential crisis.

But Derek had successfully deflected the crowd's attention from the possibility of a horror-movie mommy in the sea at their backs. Now the mayor was ordering the FBI agents to leave, and Derek was capturing the whole scene for posterity.

"You don't have the authority to tell us to leave," Muldoon told him.

"I called you here, and by golly I can tell you to leave."

"It doesn't work that way, sir," said Sullivan, ever correct. He turned to his colleague. "Muldoon, is it time for my meds?"

She pulled a pill bottle out of her pocket and passed it to him. "You'll have to swallow it dry, Sullivan."

"No way." His lower lip poked out. "I won't do that."

"Yes, you will. Remember what happens when you don't take it."

He shuddered.

"Hey," said the mayor, "what's that pill for?"

"None of your business." Sullivan popped one into his mouth, grimaced as he swallowed, and passed the bottle back to Muldoon.

"I think it's our business," Derek said, microphone preceding him like a gun. "What are you taking it for?"

"Look," said Muldoon, inserting herself between Sullivan and the threatening microphone, "it has nothing to do with you. He has a medical problem."

"What kind?"

"It doesn't matter. He's fine as long as he takes his pills."

"I'm just fine," Sullivan cut in, pushing her to one side. "I *am just fine*. Got it? There's nothing wrong with me at all. As long as I have my little green pills ... little green men ... little green monsters ..." He turned to Muldoon. "What's all this 'little green' stuff? Why am I taking little green pills? Are you one of *them*?"

"Don't mind him," Muldoon said, stepping once again between the other agent and the microphone. "His dose was late."

"Late?" Sullivan stepped in front of Muldoon and glared down at her. "It's your fault we're always late. We were late to that meeting with the ambassador from Andromeda because you had to fix your hair. We were late to that landing site in New Hampshire because you couldn't find your purse." He turned to Derek. "I always get there in time to find burned grass or something, but I never get to see them. Because of her. But now we've got this egg, and I'm not going to let it go. Period."

Just then Sam's radio squawked. She held it to her ear. "Bartlett."

"Just got a call from FBI headquarters in Washington," said the dispatcher. "I don't know what it means."

"So just tell me."

"The guy said the butterfly nets should be there any minute."

Butterfly nets? These two agents were lunatics? With *guns*? "That's the message?"

"The whole thing."

And true to the message, an unmarked pale blue van pulled into the parking lot at just that moment. Two exceptionally clean-cut men climbed out, one of them holding a small black satchel. Like a doctor's kit, Sam thought.

Sullivan apparently thought so, too, or recognized them, because he began to back away. "No. No. I took my pills this time! Honest I did! Muldoon, show them!"

Muldoon blanched and held up the pill bottle, but the men continued to advance. Sam was caught between wanting to bust a seam laughing, and a sudden sadness. Watching the mayor humiliate himself was one thing; it was virtually a town pastime. But this was something else entirely.

A rushing sound swept along the beach. A collective gasp from the crowd?

Sullivan had nearly reached the protection of the sand castle, when the two clean-cut men stopped, staring at the water. The rushing sound swelled. Sam was just about to turn when Derek threw his arms around her.

"Sam, get down!"

A huge wave broke over the beach, dissolving the sand castle, soaking Sullivan, the Guardsmen, and everyone between the waterline and the sea oats. Sam slowly rose to her knees, brine and sand and seaweed clinging to her hair.

The wet, glistening egg chirped happily.

And that, perhaps more than the drenching sea water, sent everyone running for the parking lot.

Moments later, the Gulf returned to normal.

Night settled over Paradise Beach again. All day long the beach remained deserted. The FBI agents departed in the blue van, the National Guard had been mysteriously recalled, and the mayor had decided to take a sudden vacation in Tampa.

The egg sat in splendid solitude, while rumors abounded. Some said they had seen a tail. Others claimed they had seen a huge head out on the water. Others simply argued that it was a rogue wave.

Nobody knew for sure.

"At least it's peaceful," Sam remarked as she watched the stars wheel overhead. She was lying on a chaise in her small backyard. Derek sat beside her in a lawn chair, keeping an eye on the charcoal fire.

She wasn't sure how he'd managed to come

home with her, but she was sure of one thing. She didn't want him to leave.

"Did you see my aunt?" Derek asked, apparently still ruminating over the morning. "She was so angry at getting drenched."

"I can't say I blame her. That water was cold. And stinky." She'd had to wash her hair three times to get rid of the odor. Whatever had caused that wave had churned up a lot of the sea bottom, too, with rotting vegetation and things Sam didn't want to think about. "So what's your take on the wave?"

"Oh, it was probably just one of those things that happen when for some reason a number of waves synchronize and meet in a certain way."

"So scientific."

He leaned toward her. "Well," he said confidingly, "I'd like it a whole lot better if it was mama getting mad at us."

Sam didn't know if she would or not.

"But," Derek continued. "I didn't see anything, despite what some folks were claiming. And I had a better view than they did."

"You're taking all the fun out of this," she grumped. "Here I was resting up for another day of fun and follies, maybe a full-bore monster attack."

He flashed a grin. "Sorry. Just being realistic."

"That egg is realistic. And it had to have come from somewhere."

"True."

"So tell me, O scientifically minded one, when you look overhead are you still seeing helium fusion contained by gravity?"

He tilted back his head and looked up. The sky was unusually clear tonight. The stars weren't even twinkling. And there seemed to be more of them than usual.

"Yes," he said. "I am. I can't ignore what I know about them, Sam. That would be intellectual dishonesty. But they *are* beautiful."

"Major breakthrough," she teased gently.

"I suppose so." He sighed and looked at her. "It's a defense mechanism, you know."

"What is?"

"Trying to see everything in such objective terms. Things don't hurt when they can be reduced to the accidental dance of molecules."

It was as if a window opened in her mind, giving her a glimpse of what it must have been like for him as a child. She had a vision of remote parents who considered even their emotions to be the result of chemicals in the body, parents who explained away every bit of mystery and magic a child might feel. Parents who, perhaps, held their son at a safe distance.

Her heart ached for him, but she couldn't imagine what to say. That was the kind of wound only Derek could heal for himself. Nothing she might say would remove such scars.

"Anyway," he said presently, "it only works

to a point. When my wife was killed, I didn't feel anything objective about it."

"Your wife?" Her heart stopped.

"She was on a story in Pakistan, and some Afghani militants got ahold of her." He said it calmly, but Sam guessed there was nothing calm about his feelings. "Five years ago."

"Is that why you left the news?"

"A big part of it. I couldn't be objective anymore. I . . . hurt too much."

Her heart breaking, she reached out and took his hand. He squeezed her fingers and clung to them.

"I'm sorry," Sam said. "I'm so sorry."

"Me, too." He sighed and squeezed her fingers. "That charcoal looks ready."

"Okay." She was reluctant to let go of him, but she rose and went into the house to get the hamburger patties. He'd confided a great deal to her and probably didn't want to discuss it anymore. And why should he? The bare-bones outline was enough to suggest the rest of the picture.

Poor Derek, she thought as she retrieved the patties from the fridge. How absolutely awful. And to have no comfort other than the random movement of atoms . . . She shuddered at the thought.

The burgers cooked quickly. They ate them at the dinette in her kitchen, then retreated outside again. It was as if they both somehow felt safer out there, beneath the stars, with the gentle breeze stirring the palms.

He spoke. "There are places on this planet where it's so dark on a moonless night that you can see more stars than you could possibly imagine. So many stars that it's hard to pick out the constellations."

"Wow."

"I have a theory about that, you know."

"About what?"

"About the constellations, particularly the zodiac. They're visible even with a moderate amount of light. Without all the other stars, they really stand out. So I figure our ancestors picked them out because they were visible even when they sat around their fires, even at sunset and sunrise when the light washes out all the other stars."

Sam nodded and wiggled a little, getting more comfortable. "Orion's my favorite."

"A lot of the world's cultures would agree with you."

"Some of the others . . . well, I can pick out Scorpio, and the Big Dipper, but a lot of the other constellations don't look like much of anything to me."

He gave a soft laugh. "I hear you."

"This is so peaceful," Sam remarked. "The last few days have been so frantic."

"They certainly have." He reached out and took her hand, and Sam didn't fight the magic sparkles that seemed to run through her from his touch. "But I don't think the egg is done with us."

"Probably right." She sighed and held his hand tighter, and wondered if a night had ever been more beautiful. "But at least I'm not stuck on the beach with it tonight."

"I'm sure Zeph and Nat will raise the alarm if anything happens. Did you see the two of them dumping water on the thing, trying to get it to chirp again?"

She gave a little laugh. "I think that'll take another wave."

"Maybe all it was doing was losing some air as the water washed over it."

"I prefer to think it was making happy noises."

"Sorry."

She turned her head to look at him. Had he moved his chair closer? "Don't be sorry. You can't help being a skeptic."

"It would be nice if I could."

"It would ruin your show if you could."

He shrugged. "The show's not the beginning and end of the world."

She would have thought just the opposite was true for him. He seemed to work very hard at what he did, regardless of what she thought of the end result. He'd certainly put in as many hours on the egg as she had.

Besides, as he'd already explained, the "fake" parts of his show were dramatizations. And when she was being honest with herself, she had to acknowledge that they were clearly marked as such in the words at the bottom of the screen. That was hardly the sort of deceit she'd accused him of.

Why *had* she accused him of that? Why had she taken him in such dislike from the few programs she had watched? She didn't seem able to recall her reasons now.

Maybe all she had done was tar him with the brush she seemed to apply to all good-looking, smooth-talking men. That thought had occurred to her before, but right now it seemed even more true than it had. Maybe because she knew more about Derek now.

In an instant all her thoughts scattered, because one of his fingers began to gently stroke her palm. It was subtle, perhaps even unconscious on his part, but it had the effect of silencing her mind and focusing her entire awareness on that soft, sweet touch.

She held her breath as anticipation filled her, making her at once edgy and unable to move. Everything seemed to be suspended in a moment of combined yearning and fear. Yearning for his touches, fear that he wouldn't offer them.

And why should he, after the way she'd behaved last night? But the thought slipped away, carried on currents of sweeping emotion that could barely be identified, so roiled and powerful they were.

She wanted him. She needed him. In this

moment there was nothing, absolutely nothing she wanted more. The quiet stroking of her palm continued, breaking down barriers that would never have yielded to strength, barriers that crumbled before gentleness.

The simple touch seemed to reach deep into her, spreading to every corner of her being, filling her and driving everything else away.

The kiss of the breeze seemed one with his gentle touch. The stars looked down kindly.

What was left of her mind took a dizzying spin, showing her the utter loneliness of a single soul in a universe so vast, making her feel as if she tumbled through the icy reaches of space, tethered only by that soft, sweet touch on her hand.

Loneliness. So near. Too near. Yet so easy to escape if only you could make the leap.

His touch changed, palm meeting palm, filling her with the wonder and warmth of skin on skin. Filling her with a sense of connection. The spinning of her mind through the emptiness of space ceased, and the universe seemed to hang on the hush of a single breath.

He tugged, and she came to her feet with him. Willing, eager, terrified he was only going to say good night.

But he led her slowly inside, past the solitary light burning over the stove, down the darkened hallway, and into the privacy of her bedroom. How had he known?

Had the magic she was feeling, the magic he

had created within her, taken a leap back to him, filling him with the same longing for the closeness of another human being?

They both had empty lives, she saw now. They had cut themselves off from the most basic comforts of humankind, choosing to stand alone for fear of the pain that might be unleashed.

But tonight, in a moment of sheer magic, they were going to leap beyond that loneliness and emptiness, and steal the illusion of comfort.

They didn't say a word, as if words would shatter the spell. And the kindling magic turned into a conflagration. Between one heartbeat and the next, passion took over.

Derek pressed her back against the wall and plundered her mouth. When she tried to touch him, he caught her wrists gently and pinned them over her head. Making her helpless but not helpless, because she realized she had brought the passion out in him, had invited it to life.

She loved the feeling. Loved being helpless to do anything but respond as his mouth ravaged hers, then moved on to taste every inch of her throat. There was a storm on the horizon now, and she wanted to be caught up in its wild winds, carried away to places she could barely imagine.

His body moved suggestively against hers and she responded in kind, totally caught up in the sensations of the moment.

He held her wrists with one hand, and slipped the other up under her T-shirt, up under her bra, cupping her as if he cradled something delicate. Then his thumb began to brush her nipple, sending electric shocks racing through her to her center. She squirmed, trying to get closer, trying to free her hands so she could return the pleasure.

But he held her easily, preventing her from doing anything except experiencing what he gave her. The experience was so new to her, so erotic, that her stomach muscles quivered with delight.

A soft moan escaped her as pleasure heated her every cell. The ache between her thighs was growing, becoming harder, more demanding, until she writhed against him.

He released her briefly to tug her shirt and bra over her head, and tossed them away. Then he caught her wrists again, making her feel so deliciously exposed. So vulnerable. Another quiver of delight gripped her and exploded with heat at her core.

No one had ever teased her this way. No one had ever made her feel as if she were all that mattered.

Bending down, her took her nipple in his hot mouth, flicking it with his tongue, drawing another soft moan from her. Sweet, sweet torture, and it continued until she thought she could bear no more of it. She needed more, so much more, yet he taunted and teased her, holding her suspended in a place delicious beyond imagining.

Her hands were suddenly free and she felt him tug at her shorts and panties, drawing them down until they puddled around her ankles. She was forced to grip his shoulders for balance as he lifted her feet one by one and tugged the fabric away.

Then, still kneeling, he buried his face in the tuft at the apex of her thighs. Another moan escaped her in response to the welcome pressure. A deep flowering began inside her, making her yearn to press closer, to part her legs. But he still held her against the wall, his hands firmly gripping her thighs, preventing her from moving. Preventing her from collapsing.

His tongue flicked out, burrowing through soft, damp folds until he found the exquisitely sensitive nub. A soft cry escaped her, a cry of gratitude and longing at the sharp, welcome sensation. Her fingers dug into his shoulders, clinging desperately, seeking purchase in a world that was turning head over heels.

Too good. Too sweet. Sensation held her prisoner as surely as velvet ropes. She hadn't known . . . hadn't dreamed . . .

She was quivering, gasping for air, her knees weak as water, when he took pity on her. The world turned again as he rose and lifted her high in his arms, carrying her to the soft confines of her bed. Helpless, she lay there waiting.

Then he was beside her, drawing her into the

shelter of his heat and strength, oh, so perfectly naked, as was she. The dark deprived her of the sight, but she didn't care. What her eyes couldn't do, her hands could. Her mouth could. She could touch and taste, and for now that was enough.

The air was filled with the sound of ragged breathing. His . . . hers . . . both? It added to the excitement of the moments while her hands learned him, discovering small hard nipples on the muscles of his chest. Ah, he liked that. Encouraged, she followed with her mouth, giving him a taste of what he had given her. This time it was he who moaned softly, and the sound thrilled her, enhancing her own desire. Had giving ever been so beautiful?

She found the flatness of his belly, felt muscles ripple there that most men only dreamed of. Found the power of his thighs, and the soft, surprisingly soft, hair that dusted them. Found the thicket in his groin, stiff and curly and full of delicious man-scent. Found his shaft, strong and ready, filling her hand, leaping with the same eagerness that filled her.

He groaned again, and she teased him lightly with her tongue. As if it were too much, he lifted her, lifted her as if she weighed nothing at all, and settled her so that she straddled his hips. She cried out as he filled her, a sensation so perfect, so exquisite that it was almost unbearable.

Then he spoke, his only word. Her name. "Sam . . ."

She was past hearing. Past doing anything except responding to the need that filled her. She moved, and he moved with her, and the sensations built even more. Built beyond anything she had ever thought possible.

Built and built, driving, aching, needing, breathless. . . .

Then she shattered, culmination sweeping her away on a tsunami of fulfillment.

Moments later, she collapsed, only dimly aware that he had joined her.

17

Derek held Sam close, reluctant to let her go. Cold reality lurked beyond the confines of their embrace, and he wasn't ready to face it again. He was grateful that she seemed content to lie on his chest.

Her soft, gentle weight on him was comforting, soothing. He hadn't felt this content in . . . well, he didn't want to think about that right now. If he did, the moment would be shattered, and for once in his life, Derek didn't want to face the cold, hard facts.

She sighed and wiggled against him, but not trying to move away. He ran his hands down her sleek back, over her slender hips, and heard her sigh again. "Mmm," she said.

They were in agreement about that much.

Her skin was silky, a sensuous pleasure to stroke. Her breath was a warm caress on his shoulder. At this moment, the only fear he knew was the fear that Sam would come to her senses and decide this had been a big mistake.

Which it was, but he wasn't going to be the one to acknowledge that. Not tonight.

She stretched a little. "I must be crushing you."

"No . . . no . . ." he whispered back. "You're light as a feather. Soft as a down comforter."

A little sound escaped her, almost a purr. But she slid off him anyway. Before she could escape, taking bliss with her, he rolled over and wrapped his arms around her, tucking her close.

And magic, for the first time in his life, seemed only a breath away.

He would have liked to fall asleep just like that, wrapped around her, wrapped in her, but he could feel she wasn't ready to doze off.

Then she spoke. "I'm sorry about your wife."

It was exactly the wrong thing to say. He knew she didn't mean it to be, but it shattered the spell. Made him once again aware of the things he'd been holding at bay as he tried to live in a fool's paradise. He should have known better.

But it wasn't her fault; she was reaching for an emotional closeness to match the incredible physical intimacy they had just shared. There was no way she could have known how much he feared and resisted that emotional connection.

Reminding himself of that kept him from responding sharply. He gave up the battle to hang on to bliss and let reality crash through him with all its cold isolation. He needed to deal with this before somebody got seriously hurt. Before Sam got seriously hurt.

"I loved her," he admitted readily enough. Or so he had believed. "We had the perfect marriage. Common career goals, common interests. A lot of mutual respect. Because we were both foreign correspondents, we understood the need to be apart for long stretches, and when we were apart we were both busy and involved, so we weren't pining."

"Sounds ideal," she said. But did he detect the faintest edge in her voice? He wasn't sure. He'd taken a holiday in her arms, but now it was time to get back to life. He wasn't one to live in a delusion.

She seemed to move a little away from him.

"Well," she said, her voice quiet, "it would certainly be hard to find someone who shares your career now. Your present calling is virtually unique."

Now he was sure her words were meant to sting just a little. He couldn't exactly blame her. From her standpoint, it must seem he had used her. Which was why he had avoided relationships with women. Their expectations were too high.

But he took the full blame for this. He knew his state of mind; she had no way to unless he shared it. And he hadn't done that.

He wished he could think of something to say that would make her feel better, without persuading her that she could hope for anything more. Nothing occurred to him, dunce that he was.

She lay silently beside him, a little stiff, a little farther away.

He decided he hated himself. In some essential way he was emotionally crippled, and it didn't have only to do with what had happened to his wife, or what he had seen in Bosnia. It went back a lot further than that. It was as if essential parts of himself were cut off, locked away behind some big steel door in his mind.

But he wasn't quite ready to go back to the barren room that was his emotional life. Something in him reached out, trying to leap that barrier, and he drew Sam close again, snuggling her into the curve of his body. To his relief, she relaxed after a moment, letting herself go soft.

He was crazy, maybe he was even despicable, but he couldn't let go yet.

They made love again, this time a slow symphony of touches, the concert of lovers growing more familiar with each other. It was quieter, softer, gentler; a slow rocking on the waves of a leisurely hunger that was as comforting as it was passionate.

This time even his climax was softer, more of an emotional response than a physical one. And it left him shaken to his very core.

This time they slept. And when Sam awoke, he was gone.

Sam was not in a very good mood when she went to work in the morning, and apparently everyone noticed it. She received a lot of sidelong looks and the greetings that came her way were more subdued than usual.

She marched straight back to Blaise's office.

"I want off the egg, and off Derek Diche."

He sat back in his chair, steepled his fingers, and regarded her kindly. "Close the door, Sam. Have a seat."

She obeyed, but sat on the edge of the chair.

"What happened?" he asked.

She didn't want to think about what had happened, and she *certainly* didn't want to have to explain it to her boss. Tell the man she'd been a fool and slept with a guy whose idea of the perfect relationship was sharing a career? A guy whose description of his marriage had been surprisingly passionless?

She would have felt differently if he'd said, *I miss her company*, or *We were great friends.* But,

We understood the demands of our careers? Hell, it sounded like a marriage between two sci-fi Vulcans.

If that was a perfect relationship, she had it with every other officer in the station.

And worse yet, did she want anyone at all to know she'd slept with a guy who hadn't even had the decency to hang around for breakfast? Or at least to say good-bye?

"Nothing happened," she said finally. "I'm just fed up with it. Diche is a pain in the butt, and I haven't had a decent night's sleep since that egg showed up. Let somebody else have the pleasure of dealing with it."

"I can't do that, Sam."

"You're the chief! You can do what you damn well want."

"I wish." He shook his head, looking sympathetic, and leaned forward. "I'm sorry. But it's *your* egg. And Diche is *your* responsibility."

"Why?" She wanted to shout the question, but restrained herself.

"Because you're the only officer I can trust to keep her head when faced with both the egg and a bunch of cameras."

"I'm losing my mind!"

"But I'm sure you'll lose it sensibly." He paused and smiled at her. She thought she might have seen something, some recognition, in the smile. He continued.

"In the meantime, Professor Plum has returned. He's down on the beach with those two grad students, along with some other people he brought. I want you to make sure they can do their examination without any interference."

Great. Wonderful. Marvelous. She drove her cruiser slowly down the boulevard, making the trip to the egg take as long as she possibly could. And because she drove slowly, she noticed some things she'd overlooked in the whirlwind of the last few days.

Egg T-shirts had blossomed in store windows. They were selling for nearly twenty dollars. The egg, complete with elastic bandage, was stamped on shirts in every hue of the rainbow. Some of the motels had changed their marquee signs to read, "See the Giant Egg!" for only forty or fifty dollars a night. SAVE THE EGG bumper stickers were making an appearance, too, proudly displayed on vehicles ranging from rattletraps to Mercedes. And the number of out-of-state license plates was growing, beginning to resemble the mix usually only seen during the winter season.

Paradise Beach was making economic hay from its "disaster." Didn't that figure.

Her heart seemed to grow heavier as she approached the south end of town. Derek and the egg were inextricably linked, and being with one was going to remind her of the other. Not that she was planning to spend any more time than she absolutely had to with Derek. Ever again.

Vowing to give him the cold shoulder if he

was there, she parked and walked out onto the beach. Much to her surprise, there were only a few curiosity seekers. Most of the dozen or so other people seemed to be attached to Professor Plum.

Zeph and Nat were there, too, but looking relieved not to have the full burden resting on their shoulders any longer. As Sam approached, she heard them filling Professor Plum in on all that had happened.

And yesterday's sand castles were completely gone now, washed away by the rogue wave and the tide, leaving only a few formless lumps.

The egg, however, had moved. Well, not exactly moved. It had tipped over—not that anyone would have been able to tell except for the elastic bandage around it.

"Hi," Zeph said as Sam reached them.

"Howdy," Nat offered.

"Hello," said Professor Plum.

"What happened to the egg?" Sam asked.

"It rolled a little," Zeph said.

"Probably wave action," explained Nat.

"One thing for certain," Zeph said. "Now we know it isn't mechanical."

"I thought we knew that already." Sam looked at the egg, remembering the froth that had poured out of it when Rover bit it. Had that been only yesterday? Time was running together in her mind, making it impossible to remember exactly how long ago anything had happened. Not good.

"Well, we're sure now," Zeph said. "We were able to examine the base of it because it rolled."

"It's an egg, all right," said the professor. "Amazing. Phenomenal. Stupendous."

Sam was in no mood to agree with him. "What *kind* of egg?"

"Well, that's the question, isn't it? It's leathery, almost reptilian, but at the same time, that slime coating would seem to indicate it's something else. In fact, it would be my guess that it isn't meant to be on the surface at all."

Sam felt a flicker of concern. Despite all, she was beginning to take a proprietary interest in the well-being of that monstrosity. "You mean it could be dying?"

"That's entirely possible. But one doesn't know, does one? So I wouldn't advise moving it back into the water. For all we know, *that* could kill it."

"Hmm. The mayor would probably like that."

"Judging by what he said a little while ago, that's my impression, too. But really, I can't take responsibility for that."

"Good. Because in *my* humble opinion, there's no point harming the thing unless we know for certain it's a threat to life, limb, or property."

Professor Plum beamed at her. "I *quite* agree."

"But there's no other egg like it in the world?"

"Not that we know of. Not since the dinosaurs roamed the earth."

Shades of old Japanese horror movies, Sam thought. What if it was some flying monster, like a giant pterodactyl? Except it wouldn't have come out of the sea, would it, and there wouldn't be some growling thing out there watching over it. No, it couldn't be a flying monster. Somebody would have had to see its parent or kin somewhere.

"How do we know it's still alive?" she asked.

He waved toward it. "Press your ear against it. You can hear it move."

"I'll take your word for it." She didn't want to press her ear to that slime. "What about the scrapings Nat and Zeph took?"

Nat answered. "We're still waiting for the analysis. These things take weeks. Same with the foam we collected yesterday."

Which meant they just had to wait for the egg to hatch. Which meant she was going to spend a lot of days and nights on the beach. Maybe *weeks* babysitting the egg.

She smothered a sigh, wondering if life could get any more absurd.

Just as she had the thought, it did. Mary Todd approached on her lavender golf cart.

She came riding onto the beach, kicking up gouts of sand behind her wheels, Derek riding beside her.

Of course. Whither goes the egg, there goes Derek. Natch.

Mary pulled to a screeching halt near Sam. Well, it would have been a screeching halt if she'd been on pavement rather than a beach. As it was, her tires skidded sideways, spewing sand all over. Sam brushed it off her uniform while Nat made a big deal of wiping it off his face.

"So," said Mary, her voice loud and insistent, "what are we going to do about this egg?"

Sam looked at her. Zeph, Nat, and Professor Plum looked at her. Derek sighed. "Aunt Mary," he said, "I keep telling you, there's nothing to be done about the egg until it hatches."

"Nonsense," the old woman said, rapping her cane on the floor of the golf cart. "Doing nothing is simply a sign of poor foresight and imagination."

Derek shook his head, something about his attitude saying he'd already been around this block with her more than once this morning.

"It's nonsensical," Mary continued, "to say we can't do anything at all. We could, for example, dissect it."

Professor Plum and company shuddered. Sam felt a protective instinct surge in her.

"That would be murder!" She felt stupid as

soon as the words were out, but felt strangely comforted by the fact that Nat, Zeph, Professor Plum, and the others from the university moved up to stand around her, as if supporting her.

Professor Plum cleared his throat. "Really, ma'am," he said to Mary, "this is a momentous discovery for science. We need to observe it in situ in order to maximize our learning. We could be on the cusp of discovering an entirely new species. Perhaps a new genus."

Mary harrumphed. "I see no evidence whatever that that egg is a genius. Einstein was a genius, and he was no egg."

Plum sighed.

Derek turned to his aunt. "Aunt Mary, he said *genus*, not genius."

"It would help if he talked English," Mary said tartly. "But genus or genius, it doesn't matter. We simply cannot allow things to continue as they are."

"Why not?" her nephew asked. "Sometimes life requires us to simply wait and watch."

"Not my life." Mary folded her hands over her cane and surveyed the scene. Sam could almost see the wheels spinning in her head. What was the woman up to?

"Well," said Mary finally, "I can't allow a bunch of eggheads to take over Paradise Beach's future. That egg is a threat. I'll have to take action."

"Mary—" Derek started to say, but Mary hit

the gas on her cart, jolting him to silence as she sped away down the beach.

"Strange woman," said Plum, staring after her. "Who gored her ox?"

"I don't know," Sam said. "Did that scene make any sense to you? What was she after?"

"Beats me," Nat said. "All I can figure is she wants somebody to *do* something. Anything."

"But why?" Sam asked thoughtfully. The encounter hadn't seem as crafty as Mary Todd encounters usually seemed. Was the woman's age catching up with her?

That was when she spied Derek tramping back across the sand toward them. "I can't deal with her anymore," he said as he reached them. "All I know is that somebody better keep an eye on this egg."

Professor Plum rubbed his chin and nodded. "So it would appear. She's a relation of yours?"

"My great-aunt. And she's been stewing all morning, but I can't make any sense of it. I'm not sure even *she* knows what it is."

Sam hardly cared anymore what bee might be in Mary's bonnet. Derek was back and it was as plain as the nose on her own face that she, the egg, and Derek were going to be joined at the hip indefinitely. Sometimes life had a nasty sense of humor.

However, she didn't have to speak to Derek. Nor, frankly, did he seem particularly interested in piercing her silence. He delved into a complex conversation with Plum and company about the kinds of information the scientists were hoping to gather. And like the good little reporter he was, he wrote everything down on a pocket pad.

Of course, Plum was only too eager to agree to be interviewed on camera.

"But," said Derek to him, "a great many of your colleagues might try to avoid any association with this egg at all, for fear of looking foolish."

Plum shook his head. "Then they're *being* foolish. The egg is here. It would be scientific heresy *not* to examine it."

"But dissecting it would be a mistake?"

"Certainly! We'll learn far more by watching it evolve and hatch. If we were to dissect it now, we'd be guessing about what it is and what it might become."

Sam, trying to get as far from Derek as possible, retreated to the sand dune. Yesterday's wave had washed the seats out so they were little more than hollows.

It was a lousy day. It was a miserable day. Yet the sun was rising higher in a pure blue sky and the Gulf looked as if it were dappled with splinters of pure light. She hated the beauty of it, wishing clouds would move in and dump both darkness and rain on the day. It would fit her mood better. It might even get rid of Derek.

Although she really had no right to blame him. All he'd done was take what she'd offered. Why wouldn't he? Trying to shovel the responsibility for her misery on him was a childish thing to do.

So she gave herself a mental boot in the butt. She'd broken her own rules. She'd stepped outside the confines of common sense into an illusory world that couldn't have lasted any longer than a few hours, anyway.

Damn him, why did it seem he was avoiding her as carefully as she was avoiding him? Did he regret it, too? Somehow that possibility only made her feel worse. She didn't want him to have a conscience. She wanted him to be like other men of his ilk, feeling no remorse whatever for taking her freely given tumble in the hay.

Sheesh. How dare he?

Somewhere in the midst of this mental morass, it occurred to Sam that she was thinking as strangely as Mary Todd had been acting. She was making no sense whatever.

And that frightened her. She was, she realized, the kind of person who liked to keep life in neat little boxes. She was a classifier, a categorizer. She wanted to put people in slots and deal with them according to their position in her mental organization.

But Derek had broken out of the pigeonhole she'd tried to place him in since the moment they met. He didn't fit, she realized. Even after last night, which had wound up ending almost like one of her worst memories, he didn't fit any of her classifications. Which meant what?

That she needed a new category labeled *Derek Diche Todd*?

Maybe so.

Or maybe she just needed to quit categorizing. Maybe she needed to face the fact that nobody really fit into any of her slots perfectly. Maybe she needed to react to people on a play-by-play basis, rather than on a projection of outcome. Or a projection of their motives.

Derek, for example, might have had an entirely different motive for being gone when she woke this morning than The Jerk had had. He might not have been using her at all.

What if, for example, he was as afraid as she was?

That was most definitely a possibility worth pondering. The easiest thing would be to ask him if he was afraid, too—but she was terrified of what he might say. If he turned out to be as wary as she was, it would be impossible to harden herself against him. The last thing on earth she wanted to do was find out that Derek was as vulnerable as she.

The thought held her in glum preoccupation for a long time.

18

It was the summer solstice, the day on which Florida's always strong sun reached its maximum strength, creating crispy critters of the foolish and fair-skinned in a matter of minutes. On the beach, the effect was magnified by the sunlight bouncing back from white sand and water. The breeze kept the temperature a deceptive eighty-five, but the ultraviolet radiation was working like a microwave on overtime.

Sam sweated in her uniform and reapplied her sunscreen, a maximum SPF 50 and supposedly sweat-proof, every hour. She could still feel her skin shriveling. Swimmers and sunbathers dotted the beach, keeping a safe distance from the egg. At least she didn't have to worry about crowd control today.

Apparently the egg had enjoyed its fifteen minutes of fame and now was going to sink into the background like cosmic radiation. People had more important things on their minds... like getting crusted with salt and sand, and turning themselves into lobsters.

Derek left, allowing her to breathe easily for the first time since he'd showed up. But it didn't last. He returned with his crew, and while they set up their cameras and other equipment, he came over to Sam, carrying a large beach umbrella.

He popped it open and stuffed it into the sand behind her, casting her into welcome shade. "Here," he said, and walked away again.

The gesture both irritated her and made her want to cry. How dare he show concern for her?

Of course, he was British. Maybe he couldn't stop being a gentleman even when he was a cad.

Then again, maybe he'd just gotten in over his head, the way she had. Maybe he was as confused as she was. Maybe last night had been as unexpected to him as to her.

And maybe she had unfair expectations of him. She hadn't exactly been acting any better than he, this morning. Who was to say that if they'd been at *his* place last night, she wouldn't have been the one who was gone this morning?

In fact, she admitted unhappily, she probably would have been. In her heart of hearts, she realized that she had been no more ready than he for a postmortem—or anything else—this morning. So maybe, right now while it was safe thanks to all the other people around, she ought to go over to him and be a little friendly. Try to smooth away the tension.

But she was forestalled as he began an interview with Professor Plum, who stood right beside the egg, his hand resting on it in a proprietary fashion. Sam couldn't hear what they were saying, nor did she want to. She did wonder, however, if Derek intended to make a full-hour program out of the egg. She couldn't imagine how it would be anything less than boring. Twenty minutes of egg talk, yes, but an hour? No way. Not unless he went for cheap laughs and made fun of the whole situation.

Which, she had to admit, *was* pretty funny. Looking over the last few days, she began to feel her spirits improve. The people of this town were going to be telling this story for many years to come.

Just as Derek was beginning to wrap up his interview with Plum, city trucks rolled onto the beach. Sam rose to her feet, wondering if they were planning to roll right over the egg. She wouldn't put anything past the mayor, not after recent events.

But the huge trucks rolled to a halt some twenty feet away. Men sprang out of them and began to carry boards toward the oversized ovum. Sam trotted over to them.

"What are you doing?" she asked.

"We're supposed to build a shelter for the egg," said a burly guy in ragged shorts and a tank top that showed off a tattoo of barbed wire surrounding the word MOM. Sam was glad she wasn't this guy's therapist.

"A shelter?" Sam repeated. She didn't believe it. "Who sent you?"

"Our boss."

Big help. "Who's your boss and how do I get ahold of him?"

The guy told her, then leaned the boards against the truck, leaned himself against the truck, and took a cigarette break.

Sam broke out her c-phone and started to dial just as Derek and Professor Plum came trotting over.

"What's up?" Derek asked.

"I'm about to find out."

"Jawalski," answered a man who sounded even bigger than the guy with the tattoo.

"Mr. Jawalski, this is Officer Bartlett, Paradise Beach PD. I have two of your trucks here on the beach. They tell me they're supposed to build a shelter for the giant egg?"

"You got it."

"Who ordered that?"

"I did."

Sam restrained a sigh. "No, I mean, who *originally* ordered this?"

"What does it matter to you?"

"I'm a police officer assigned to protect the egg. I can't let anybody close until I'm sure they're on legitimate business."

"What's more legitimate than two city trucks?"

"They might have misunderstood what they're supposed to do."

There was a brief silence. "What did they tell you?"

"That they're supposed to build a shelter around the egg."

"Then they didn't misunderstand. I got a signed work order here, and it says plain as day, 'Build shelter around egg on beach.' "

"Did it say *which* egg? We have turtle nests around here. Some of which your drivers may be crushing with their trucks."

"Oh, man."

Sam couldn't tell if the guy was exasperated or merely worried. And at that moment she didn't care.

"Look, Officer," the guy said, "I don't give a flip-flying you-know-what if you want to stop my guys from doing their jobs. I get paid and they get paid, even if all they do is stand there all day. But *you're* the one who's going to have to explain the waste of city employees and city trucks."

"I know. That's why I want to know who signed the work order."

"My boss!"

"And who *is* your boss? Better yet, who's his boss?"

She got the number from him and was just about to dial it when Derek touched her arm. It was as if someone had touched her with a live wire. Shocks ricocheted through her entire body.

"Sam," said Derek, "maybe you're getting carried away here."

"Carried away?" She looked up at him, met his gaze for the first time since last night, and felt her insides turn to goo. "How do we know the shelter won't hurt the egg?"

"We don't. But there's no reason to suppose it will. In fact, it might protect it from the sun. But either way, is it worth losing your job for?"

She hesitated. "All I'm trying to do is find out what's going on. That's my job."

He nodded slowly, his gaze surprisingly gentle. "I figure the mayor's behind this. He probably wants to hide the egg, since he can't get rid of it."

"He wants to pen it in. So when it hatches, it can't get out. Derek, it could be dead in a matter of hours."

"Not if someone is here to watch and let it go when it hatches."

Her breath caught, and last night's spell was washing over her again. She tried to shove it back into the cellar of her mind, but it wouldn't stay there. It seemed to be oozing out every crack and under the door. "Are you volunteering?"

He nodded. "I have to wait for the magic."

The cellar door burst open and a whole lot of warmth and yearning flooded her. She looked quickly away so he wouldn't see it reflected in her gaze. She didn't want anyone to know how weak she was. She didn't even want to know it herself.

"Okay," she said. "Okay. They can build the shelter."

It wasn't long before it occurred to her that she might have been overly worried about it anyway. These were city employees, after all, and at the pace they were moving, they weren't apt to get the lumber unloaded before the end of the week. Looking at all the boards, however, she had another thought.

"How big is this shelter going to be?"

Derek shook his head. "I'm wondering myself. I was kind of envisioning some small lean-to."

"Yeah. But this isn't going to be small."

"Hardly."

At least they were talking again, Sam thought, feeling relieved. Even if they were talking about everything except themselves. Funny how the egg had become a *safe* topic.

Another two-by-four was stacked on the sand, followed, singly, by one-by-six planks.

And the sun was getting hotter than Hades. Work slowed even more. Professor Plum and his minions, along with Zeph and Nat, retreated to a local watering hole for lunch. Sam stood looking at the lumber trucks, and she was getting uneasier, not to mention hotter, by the minute.

"You know," she said to Derek, "that looks more like the stuff for building a stockade."

"The thought crossed my mind."

"Do you suppose someone wants to *confine* the creature?"

He spread his hands. "It could be."

"But to what end?"

"I can't imagine."

The city crew announced they were going to lunch. Work stopped. The beach was almost empty as bathers seemed to make the same decision.

"I'm going to find the mayor," Sam said.

"Do you have any idea where to look?"

She glanced at her watch. "At Chester's Bar and Grille."

"Why?"

"He owns it. He eats lunch there every day. Wings and beer."

"Let's go."

Chester's, of course, was a mile up the beach. The mayor and his partners in crime, the city council, jealously guarded the south end of the beach from all but residential development. It was no coincidence that they all owned condos at the south end. Nor was it any coincidence that they all owned businesses that had liquor licenses. Just as it was no coincidence that they were always giving Chief Corrigan hell for enforcing the DUI laws.

They found the mayor and two of his cohorts sitting at a table near the back, away from the hoi polloi on whom they made their fortunes. Tam Albright, the newest member of the council, looked a little uneasy as Sam approached, but Bill Alsop, who'd been around more than one maypole with the mayor, just kept tucking into the mound of spicy wings.

The mayor frowned as they approached. "What's wrong?" he demanded. "Did it hatch?"

"Not yet," Sam replied, trying to keep her tone respectful. The mayor was once again a billboard for bad fashion, having chosen to combine a pink shirt with a scarlet and green tie that would have looked good on Santa Claus.

"Did the aliens abduct another police officer?"

"No, sir."

"Then it can wait until after lunch."

Considering that just then another pitcher of beer was delivered to the table, and considering that the mound of uneaten wings might have served as a meal for a football team, Sam figured lunch was going to continue until dinnertime.

"Sir, I'm really sorry to bother you, but as you know, I've been assigned to protect the egg, and the beachgoers in the vicinity of the egg."

"Then what are you doing here?"

"Checking on a major construction project that might cause some harm." It was the politest way she could think of to phrase it. Derek was standing right behind her, keeping silent, but lending his support by his presence. Somehow that seemed to stiffen her spine.

The mayor waved a dismissing hand. "I ordered it."

"Yes, sir. But just exactly what did you order?"

"I don't see what business it is of yours."

Sam repressed a sigh. "Well, I could make the argument that I'm a taxpayer and this project is being built with my money."

"She's got a point," Tam said nervously. The mayor frowned him into silence.

"Or," said Sam, "I could point out that a construction project is dangerous and I need to know how much of the beach to clear to prevent bathers from getting injured."

That got the mayor's attention. Even Bill Alsop stopped chewing momentarily.

"Let's not go overboard here," the mayor

said, suddenly more friendly than she had seen him in a while. "It's not a dangerous project. Folks can still use the beach."

"Really? Well, if you're building a shelter—"

"I'm not building a shelter," the mayor said quickly. "Nothing that dangerous. Just a fence."

"A fence?"

"A fence."

"What for?"

"To keep the monster in, of course. So it can't ransack the homes of unsuspecting citizens."

"I see." Sam hesitated, deciding that to point out that the fence might cause the death of whatever was growing in the egg wouldn't sway the mayor at all. "But people are coming to town to see the egg."

"Oh, that's no problem. We'll have a gate and charge admission to anyone who wants to see it."

Sam felt indignation rising in her, and she had to grab it with two mental fists to keep it from overwhelming her sense. "You're going to charge admission? How much? Why?"

"Well, we have to pay for the fence," he said. "And it would be nice if I—uh, the *city*—could make a profit from this."

Sam was fuming royally by the time she left the bar and grille. "Twenty dollars!" she said to Derek as they drove back to the egg. "Twenty dollars a person. And did you catch that hesitation? He's not planning for a penny of that to go into city coffers."

"That would be my guess," Derek agreed calmly.

"That's malfeasance!"

"And it would probably take five years in a court of law to prove it," Derek said. "Look, Sam, I agree it stinks, but what can you do about it?"

"I could arrest him."

"He hasn't done anything wrong yet. More than half this town would probably agree that a stockade fence would be good protection from whatever is in that egg."

Sam slapped her hand against the steering wheel. "This place is crazy."

"No crazier than the rest of the world."

"No? Yesterday he wanted that thing dead. Today he's planning to get rich on it."

"He's an adaptable man."

"Are you defending him?"

"Absolutely not." Derek held up a hand as if to push away the mere idea. "I'm just trying to look at this realistically."

"I pity you, Derek. I really do. Realism is just a copout."

She glanced his way, catching a flicker of something that resembled hurt on his face. Right now she didn't care.

"Realism and pragmatism are just excuses,"

she continued vehemently. "Covers for a lack of caring and ethics."

"Low blow," he said quietly.

"Maybe. But what they're intending to do to whatever is in that egg is criminal."

"On that," he said, "we agree."

By the time they reached the parking lot, however, she was beginning to feel ashamed of herself. She shouldn't take her frustration out on Derek. Not even if she was still mad at him for leaving without a word while she slept. Not even though she was mad at him for acting as if nothing had happened between them. As if she weren't acting the same way herself.

Or was she? Would she have sniped at him, but for last night? Would he be treating her so distantly otherwise? She doubted it. Only a few short days ago he'd been offering to help her put on her sun lotion and asking her to join him for lunch.

In fact, they'd been getting along a whole lot better back when she'd been convinced he was a sleazy smooth-talker.

Now, when they *should* have been feeling close and friendly, it was as if a barbed-wire fence had gone up between them. This was insanity.

"I'm sorry," she said to him as they parked. "I shouldn't take my mood out on you."

"Why not?" he said. "I deserve it. I seem to

have an annoying habit of growing more rational as people around me become more emotional. You're not the first person to be irritated by it."

Defense mechanism? she wondered as they walked back onto the beach. Some kind of protective carapace he donned?

Oh, what did it matter, anyway? As soon as this damn egg hatched—and it couldn't hatch soon enough to please her—he was going to run back to New York, London, and Paris, and head off to climb some desolate mountain, or trek through some snake-infested jungle. And like every other gorgeous stud in the world, he was going to leave a trail of broken hearts behind him. Hers, she vowed, was not going to be one of them. She had too much sense to let him that close.

The city crew still hadn't returned from lunch. The few bathers that remained were way up the beach, a safe distance from the egg. The two trucks, still bearing most of their loads of lumber, sat where they'd been left.

As did the egg. It lay on its side, wearing its beige elastic belt, looking almost forlorn.

Sam spoke. "Being tipped over wouldn't hurt it, would it?"

"I don't know why it would." Derek looked around. "My crew seems to have done another disappearing act." Their equipment wasn't even there.

"They don't seem very reliable."

"Not this week." He sighed and put his hands on his hips. "This whole thing is a fiasco, start to finish. All I wanted to do was take a week off, get some sun, swim a little . . . and instead, *The Egg*."

"I hear you. I'm getting to the point where I don't even know which end is up anymore, even what day of the week it is. It must be lack of sleep."

She wished she hadn't said that. It inevitably reminded her why she hadn't gotten enough sleep *last* night.

But like the gentleman he could be when he chose, Derek let it lie. Sam went to sit under the umbrella, and Derek joined her. Their arms might have brushed, but they both made sure nothing of the sort happened. In fact, they each leaned away a little bit.

Their body language, Sam thought, was probably shrieking aversion.

Derek spoke. "The egg moved again."

She turned to look at it. "Did you see it?"

"No. But look, Sam. It's not exactly where it was before. Like it rolled a little toward the water."

She peered at it, and saw what he meant. "Maybe the little bugger inside is running laps, like a hamster in a wheel."

"I don't know. I suppose someone could have pushed it a little."

"You're going to think I'm crazy. . . ."

"Why?"

"I'm beginning to feel affectionate toward that thing."

He surprised her with a grin that lit up his whole face. "If you're crazy, then so am I," he said. "Because I'm getting attached to it, too."

Why couldn't he always be like this? So open and relaxed. Then it struck her that he may have been this way all along, but she'd been filtering his actions through her own perception that he had to be dishonest. Man, it was getting impossible to tell up from down. She needed some sleep. She needed some time off.

"Who's that?" Derek asked.

She looked in the direction he indicated and saw a man in a three-piece suit slogging over the sand toward them. "I hope it's not another FBI agent."

"Were those two for real? Did you ever find out what was going on with them?"

"They were real, but I have a feeling they didn't have all their oars in the water. Maybe I should call that guy in Washington again and see if I can find out the whole story."

"I'd like to know. But maybe Mr. Suit there is coming to tell us."

"We should be so lucky."

Derek chuckled, and Sam realized that he was beginning to relax with her again. Maybe she was beginning to relax with him, too.

The man, of average height and an average twenty pounds overweight, reached them. He had a receding hairline, sagging jowls, and brown eyes. "Officer Bartlett?"

"Yes, sir." Sam rose.

"I'm Andy Giancarelli, Environmental Protection Agency. We had a call—or perhaps I should say a *deluge* of calls—from one of your local conservation groups. Something about an egg?" He turned, eyeing the globe on the sand with distrust. "Is . . . uh . . . that it?"

"That's it."

"That's quite an egg."

Sam took a moment to introduce Derek. Andy Giancarelli seemed to be the only person on the globe who didn't recognize either the name or the face. "Pleasure," he said, never taking his eyes off the egg.

"What would the EPA have to do with this?" Derek asked.

Andy finally looked at him. "Actually, I don't know. There aren't any more of these around, are there?"

"None that we know of."

Sam spoke. "It's one of a kind."

"My," said Andy, wiping his brow. "I kind of expected a redheaded purple-tailed spinkaroo egg." He looked at them. "They're endangered, you know."

"Must be," Derek said. "I've never heard of it."

"That's how seriously underpopulated they are. Nobody's ever seen one. Well, not in a hundred years or so. They do make a rather large egg, though. Like maybe four inches. This is ... uh ... four *feet*." He turned to the egg again, clearly stunned. "I think somebody at the office misunderstood the messages."

"It doesn't matter," Sam said swiftly. "I'm glad you're here. You need to protect it."

He shook his head. "I can't protect it if I don't know what it is."

"Why not?"

He spread his hands. "It's not on my *list*."

Sam resisted the urge to throttle him. He looked like the type of bureaucrat who would insist that a hapless supplicant move to the next window for a different type of transaction, then himself move to the next window to handle it. Paradise Beach was definitely getting the governmental dregs.

"How," she asked slowly, as if to a child, "would the egg get *on* your list?"

He shook his head. "Hearings. Lots and lots of hearings. Committees formed to decide whether a committee should be formed to create a committee to study the situation." He looked at the egg for a moment. "Judging from the size, I'd say we'd need at least eighty pages of regulations. Perhaps over a hundred. And all of those would have to be hammered out in hearings."

Sam was reminded of a film she'd seen in a grade school social studies class, "How a Bill Becomes a Law." She now realized it must have been fiction. The reality would have been slightly longer than *Gandhi, The Longest Day,* and *Reds* viewed back to back.

"What, exactly, is your job?" Derek asked.

"Assistant vice deputy undersecretary in the Coastal Marine and Amphibious Species Department." The man fairly beamed at the opportunity to state his title.

"And where does that place you in the bureaucratic food chain?" Derek asked again.

"I'm responsible for the southwest coast of Florida, from Bayonet Point to Naples. This," he said, his hand sweeping in the coastline, "is my turf."

Derek nodded. "Perfect. Now, what is your agency's mission?"

"To protect the environment. My division, in particular, is tasked with protecting endangered species which live or breed along the coastline."

"Now we're getting somewhere." Derek was on a roll. "How many individual animals are required for a species to qualify as endangered?"

"It depends on the species," Andy said. "On how many are required to sustain a breeding population."

Sam could see where this was going. "So if there were only one known animal in existence, it would certainly be endangered, correct?"

"Of course. And soon to be extinct, I suspect."

Sam heard voices behind her, and turned to

see Zeph, Nat, and Professor Plum returning from lunch. She called them over and made quick introductions. Then Derek moved to the heart of the issue.

"Professor," he began, "how many of these eggs do you know to be in existence?"

"Just that one," Plum answered. "I told you that before. We've no idea what this is. It may be an entirely new kind of life. It's certainly unique in its zoological particulars."

"Well," Derek said, turning to Andy, "there you have it. There's only one. That's about as endangered as it can be, correct? And this is your turf, you said. This is your responsibility. This is what you went into government for, is it not? To protect and to serve? To safeguard our precious environment?"

To kill a rain forest to make enough paper to print all of the regulations? Sam asked silently.

Andy paused for a moment, as if struck by the gravity of the situation. "Why, yes, it is."

He stood for a few minutes, lost in thought, while Sam nearly held her breath, afraid the slightest thing might scare him off like a rabbit.

But Derek was not so hesitant. "Andy," he said, his voice pitched low and persuasively, "if we wait for regulations, it'll be too late for this egg."

As Sam watched, Andy's chest visibly swelled. The man straightened. Then, pulling a huge roll of orange stickers from his jacket pocket, he peeled one off and slapped it on the egg.

> ENDANGERED SPECIES.
> DO NOT TOUCH, MOVE, REMOVE, FOLD,
> SPINDLE, MUTILATE, MANGLE, SHOOT, PLAY WITH,
> STONE, ARREST, USE HARSH LANGUAGE, OR
> OTHERWISE DISTURB UNDER PENALTY OF LAW.
> BY ORDER OF U.S. ENVIRONMENTAL
> PROTECTION AGENCY.

"Great," said Professor Plum. "There goes our investigation."

The late afternoon sun was blazing. Even with the persistent breeze, it was hot, and hardly any bathers were to be seen.

The beach, however, was not deserted. The city crew had returned and finished off-loading the lumber, amazing Sam. She decided she'd never make it as a gambler. They even started building the fence, with a great deal of pounding and swearing. Andy, the EPA guy, was still hanging around. He'd stripped his coat and vest, discarded his tie, and rolled up his sleeves. He and Plum and company seemed to be having an animated conversation about the egg.

Sam and Derek were sitting under their umbrella.

"What's the Bible verse about building your house on the sand?"

"Something from Matthew," he answered.

Astonished, she looked at him. "You know the Bible?"

He shrugged. "I've read it."

"I thought you were a pure rationalist."

He shook his head. "My parents tried to make me one. You could say it didn't take, at least not perfectly."

"Wow."

"But what's this about the sand?"

"Oh, I'm just wondering how long this stockade of the mayor's is going to last, considering where it's being built."

He flashed a small smile. "Next high tide? Would you like to wager on it?"

"I recently decided not to gamble."

"Ah. Probably wise. However, you can gamble if you wager something you don't mind losing."

"And what would that be?"

There was a devilish sparkle in his eyes. "Oh, I don't know. How about dinner tonight? Loser buys."

That sounded dangerous to her. And why was he doing this? She could have sworn he wanted to pretend they'd never gotten close at all, let alone intimate.

Although . . . and here her brain stuttered . . . there were varying kinds of intimacy, and the lovemaking they'd shared was only one of them. It was the other kinds of intimacy they were lacking. They didn't know each other's hearts.

Or maybe... maybe they knew each other better than they realized. To know a person didn't necessarily mean you had to know their entire past, or every thought that flitted across their minds. You could know people just by knowing how they acted.

And Derek, she realized, had been unfailingly thoughtful. He walked the walk, even if he didn't talk the talk.

But dinner was still a dangerous proposition. The risk loomed before her, even more terrifying than the possibility of some monster emerging from that egg.

And the tide was rising higher.

"That's okay," he said, as if sensing her turmoil. "Forget I suggested it."

She looked at him, ready to thank him for his understanding, and saw something so naked in his eyes that it felt as if a dagger had stabbed her heart. He had reached out to her—and for the first time, she considered the possibility that he hadn't reached out to anyone in a long, long time.

"We can still have dinner," she said softly.

"No, it's all right," he said. "Really."

He felt rejected. She told herself she was imagining it, that her ego must be getting too big for her own good. Derek Diche feeling rejected by *her*, a mere nobody from a nowhere town? Not likely.

But he looked as if he felt rejected. Troubled, she returned her attention to the egg.

"I wonder," she said absently, "how many endangered snails, turtles, snakes, and bugs are running around this country with huge orange stickers on them."

"Andy *was* carrying a rather large roll of them." All of a sudden he grinned, a wicked sparkle in his eyes. "Hey, can't you just see one of them on a snail darter?"

"What boggles my mind is the idea of somebody trying to chase down snail darters to apply stickers."

They laughed together, and the tension eased again. They were through the minefield. Temporarily.

It was at this moment the mayor, apparently finished with his lengthy lunch, decided to come check on the progress of his "fence."

"I'm not going to even talk to him," Sam said. "If I do, I might say something I'll regret."

"You know what interests me?" Derek asked.

"What?"

"How there can be so many people in the world, like the mayor, who say any number of things they *ought* to regret, but never do. And then there are those like us who restrain ourselves all the time. What is wrong with this picture?"

"You're beginning to sound American."

"It's rubbing off on me." He sent her another look that seemed to sparkle with wicked delight. Well, she knew which direction his mind was running in. She just wished hers wasn't running in the same direction. "Rubbing" had suddenly become a word to be avoided.

The mayor, having stuffed his outrageous tie in his pink shirt pocket, where an end of it lolled like the tongue of some diseased reptile, approached the city crew and began to gesticulate. Mercifully, the surf sounds washed his words away.

The man with the tattoo gesticulated back. From a distance it looked like the meeting of a chubby David with Schwarzenegger-as-Goliath.

Apparently David prevailed. A few minutes later the city crew was back at work on the stockade and moving faster than ever.

Mary Todd, whose mental wheels had been spinning furiously all day, finally sat bolt upright. "Aha!"

She picked up the phone and dialed. "Eustace, I need to collect on that favor you owe me. Is that Flying Fortress of yours gassed up?"

The day was beginning to cool at last as the sun grew heavy in the west over the water. The sunset crowds were beginning to make their appearance, filling the beach with color, movement, and life. Sam, who was beginning to feel as if her uniform were stuck to her skin, was thinking longingly about a shower. Something, however, kept her from going.

The stockade was nearly finished, three walls complete. The fourth, facing the sea, couldn't yet be put into place because the tide had crept up close to the egg. Besides, city workers didn't put in overtime for anything less than a hurricane. Derek's crew had filmed the building of the stockade and were just about to pack up for the night. With the fence in place, they didn't appear to be in quite as much a hurry. All that remained to do, Sam thought, was to wait for the sunset and the clearing of the beach which it brought, get a hot shower, and think about how much of her heart she could salvage when Derek rode away into his own sunset.

It started as a low, ominous drone, and a speck on the horizon. Sam and Derek were sharing hot dogs with Zeph and Nat, who had set up an illegal charcoal grill, all the while sniffing in disdain at the stockade. The mayor had already put up a hand-lettered sign that read SEE THE EGG, ONLY $20. He'd hand-drawn the famous credit card symbols in the bottom right corner, although his artwork left as much to be desired as did his clothing. Sam figured it would take an archaeologist to decipher the scribblings. Not that she saw any way for the mayor to process credit cards regardless. But it didn't matter, because the rest of the sign pronounced—almost legibly—that the "Grand Opening" would be the next day.

The drone built, and the speck swelled.

Colonel Albemarle would later swear that he, or at least one of his esteemed brigade, had identified it first. Others would make similar boasts.

Regardless, within a few seconds the entire crowd was aware of the slow, lumbering, implacable approach of a huge, propeller-driven aircraft. A B-17 Flying Fortress. The "Old Fort," which had won the air war over Europe.

A bomber.

19

Most residents of Paradise Beach were familiar with old aircraft. B-17s and other World War II–era aircraft were often seen flying to and from air shows. Or just flying around. But they never approached from the water, out of the setting sun. And they never, *never* opened their bomb bay doors.

This Flying Fortress opened its bomb bay doors.

"What is he doing?" Sam asked as she watched the plane approach.

"Maybe the mayor finally got his bomber," Derek joked.

"Bomber?" the mayor shrieked. "Get it out of here! This egg is priceless."

"My," Sam murmured, "what a change of heart."

"Yeah, amazing what twenty dollars a look can do as a face-lift."

Sam had to bite back a snicker. Which wasn't too difficult when she realized that bomber was heading straight for them.

As the crowds on the beach watched, a strange silence and stillness began to spread out around the egg. Kids who had been playing with beach balls stopped and faced the plane coming out of the sun. Their parents, who had been sitting on the sand, rose to their feet.

It kind of looked like the beach scene in *City of Angels*. Except there were no angels here and it wasn't the sunset that was gripping everyone's attention.

"What *is* he doing?" someone asked.

"Well," said Colonel Albemarle with a sharp harrumph, "those of us old enough to remember 1944 can tell you."

The mayor turned on him. "Are you going to let us in on this secret?"

"No secret," said Albemarle. "He's on a bombing approach."

"Oh, my God," said Sam. She looked around, wondering how she was going to get all these people off the beach in time. And what was that lunatic going to drop on them? He couldn't possibly have any bombs. But anything he dropped could be dangerous. "I've got to get these people out of here."

"No, Sam," Derek said, gripping her arm. "That's what he wants. He wants to scare us away."

She looked up at him. "But why?"

"So he can bomb the egg."

But even as he spoke, his face changed and she knew he was remembering Bosnia. She watched the struggle play across his face. "Derek?"

"God," he said, "what if I'm wrong?"

But Sam suddenly knew he wasn't. She couldn't have explained why; she just knew. "Derek, it's not a mass murderer up in that plane. It's just some jerk who wants to scare people."

"Maybe."

She grabbed his hand and tugged until he faced her. "Derek. I believe in you."

A change came over him then. It was an amazing change, one that filled her with joy. He straightened, a man with purpose.

Derek let go of her and began to call out, "Everybody gather 'round the fence now. We can't let him hurt the egg."

Much to Sam's amazement, people began to do just that. Nat and Zeph were the first, standing along one side of the fence, their arms linked. After a moment, the mayor joined them.

"Can't let anyone destroy this opportunity," he said, looking almost embarrassed. The plane was coming closer, and he thrust out his wobbly chin.

People whom Sam thought of as the space cadets joined them. So did some of the business owners. Even Reverend Arthur, who had brought his grandchildren to the beach, linked arms with his fellow citizens. Pretty soon there were a couple of hundred people gathered tightly around the three-sided stockade, ranging in age from four to eighty.

And the plane grew closer.

"Hey," some man shouted, "he's dropping bombs!"

Sam jumped away from the group and went to look. Sure enough, something fell out of the bomb bay doors and hit the water with a big splash.

But nothing exploded.

"It's not bombs," she called out.

Derek joined her. "But what is it?"

"He's taking a test run," Colonel Albemarle remarked. He swatted his swagger stick against his thigh. "I daresay he's trying to determine just when he needs to drop one of those to hit the egg."

Sam and Derek exchanged looks. Sam suddenly didn't feel so good about all the people crowding the stockade.

"Maybe we should get everyone out of here," she said.

"Nonsense," said Albemarle. "He can't be that insane."

Sam had been a cop long enough to know that people *could* be that insane. Before she could act, the plane roared overhead, then swung out to sea again. A cheer went up from the crowd.

Derek's eyes met and held Sam's. "It's too dangerous."

She nodded, feeling his concern and worry. He was facing his demons here, she realized, and facing them head-on.

"Let's do it."

"Everybody out of here!" he called, turning to face the crowd and wave his arms. "It's too dangerous."

As he spoke, the plane was circling back toward them, presumably to drop its load of whatever on the egg.

"Come on," he said. "Let's go."

The crowd slowly started to move, then voices rose as panic seemed to strike. Arthur, however, was having none of it.

"Stop!" he bellowed in his loudest hellfire-and-brimstone voice. At once everyone froze and fell silent.

"We are stewards of the earth," he thundered. "We cannot abandon this egg, no matter how frightened we are. Who else will protect this hapless creature?"

"Oh, Lord," Derek said softly. The plane was drawing nearer again.

Then, from somewhere in the crowd, a beautiful soprano began to sing "Give Peace a Chance." For a few moments, only that one flutelike voice could be heard over the surf and the roar of the approaching engines, but then, one by one, other voices joined in.

Soon everyone was packed around the stockade once again, their arms linked, their voices lifted in song. Even the mayor, who looked like a carp out of water.

Arthur broke away from the group and mounted a dune a few feet away. Raising his finger to the sky, he pointed at the B-17 and commanded, "Begone!"

The plane, of course, didn't hear him. And Derek's face reflected the horror of his past experience in Bosnia. Looking at him, Sam had the urge to reach out and hug him to her, to comfort him, to tell him that whatever happened this time, he was not responsible. These people had made their decisions, and there was nothing he could do about it.

Then he did something that stunned her and filled her with an almost fierce pride. He stepped into the crowd and linked arms with total strangers, joining in the song with a full baritone.

A moment later, Sam stepped in beside him, linking her arm with his and with a woman on her other side.

The plane roared overhead once more, its engines deafening, its shadow consuming them. If the singing faltered, no one could tell, for the roar of the plane drowned the voices. Then it pulled away and headed out to sea once more.

The sun was a fiery globe on the horizon, about to sink into its watery grave. Its last light seemed to turn the beach red and the water black. And still the voices sang together, creating a community out of chaos.

Sam felt a warmth begin to glow within her, and realized she felt closer to her fellow Paradise Beachians than ever before. Maybe it was a silly thing to take a stand on, or maybe it was the most important stand they would ever take in their lives. Regardless, their voices grew louder and more joyful, and they began to sway together.

Derek's face was shining. He was feeling it, too, this warmth and power of a crowd united in a common cause.

The B-17 followed an arc in the reddening sky, coming at them once again. It flew in low, seeming almost to skim the water, as the sun's orb sank until it was little more than a sliver of gold-rimmed red. The engines roared overhead again, drowning the singing. No one ducked; everyone stood fast.

Then the threat rose in the sky and sailed off to the east, away from them.

And on a dune not too far away, a woman in a lavender golf cart nodded her head in satisfaction. Bringing people together through discord was her favorite activity. This time she had succeeded far beyond the usual. She turned her cart away and headed home.

* * *

Just a few minutes later, as the crowd began to think of their homes, an alien walked down the beach toward them.

It was silver-suited, with a big green head dominated by big black almond eyes that seemed to glisten. Everyone froze. A few younger children shrieked. A few older children laughed nervously.

And Arthur paled.

The alien seemed to have a mission. He walked straight up to Arthur. Oddly, he seemed to be tripping on the legs of his silver suit. Reaching the reverend, he held out a hand that appeared to be wearing a Lightning hockey glove.

"You're coming with me," said a squeaking voice.

"Oh, Lord," said Arthur, backing away.

"We need to perform tests on you."

Arthur backed up again, stepping on the mayor's toe. The mayor howled.

"Now," said the alien. "You owe me."

Arthur gulped.

As Sam was wondering whether to take police action, one gloved hand lifted, grabbed the top of the alien's head, and pulled it off.

Or rather, pulled the mask off. Fritz Holder stood there, grinning evilly at Arthur. "Fooled ya," he said.

Arthur fainted.

There was a party, of course. The Paradise Beach Bar cranked up the volume on its sound system, not caring whether the mayor and his fellow residents were disturbed, and the victorious crowd, now sure the plane wouldn't return, were soon drinking and eating and dancing in the sand.

Even the mayor patronized the establishment, finding himself a tall table at the edge of the bar's deck where he could stand and hold court. He claimed it was all his idea, naturally, and spent a great deal of time telling everyone what a wonderful thing the egg was going to be for the town. It was a significant change in tune, but no one was mean enough to say so.

Derek drew Sam down near the water, and in the light of rising moon and the glow from the bar lights, he urged her into his arms and danced with her to the sounds of a James Taylor ballad.

After an initial moment of resistance, Sam let her head rest on Derek's shoulder, and let his arms hold her close.

"That was quite an experience," he said after a while.

"It sure was. I wonder who the idiot in that plane was."

"I intend to find out. I suspect the first person to question would be my aunt."

"Why would you say that?"

"Oh, I don't know. It might have something to do with the fact that she was sitting on top of a dune a safe distance away watching the show."

"Really?" Sam lifted her head. "You don't think she wanted the egg destroyed for real, do you?"

"I doubt it. That would be too simple for a mind I'm coming to regard as Machiavellian."

She should have been irate at the idea that Mary might have put them all through those awful moments. But those moments had turned into absolute gold, and Derek's embrace somehow made it impossible to get her indignation up. "You're probably right. And I'm sure there's a law against what that pilot did."

"Probably. Are you going to arrest him?"

Sam laughed. "No, I don't think so. It was a wonderful experience."

"It was." He sighed and drew her farther into the shadows. The thin crescent moon cast only a little bit of silvery light, just enough to make him out by. "It was an incredible experience."

She tilted her head back. "It was for me, too. But I get the feeling . . ." She hesitated, unwilling to ruin the moment by treading into his nightmares.

"It was," he said after a few moments, "incredibly freeing."

"How so?" She kept her voice gentle.

"I kept thinking of those people in Bosnia. I suppose you guessed."

"It was . . . apparent from your face," she admitted.

"But then when I joined the crowd. . . . I understood something, Sam. Something fantastic."

She waited. They were no longer moving in time to the music that reached them even here. They were just standing, holding and being held. And the night around them seemed alive with... magic, Sam thought. Magic.

"I was..." Again he hesitated. "I suddenly understood that those people in Bosnia valued something more than their lives. That's why they gathered at the statue. They had to have known the risk they were taking, but they came anyway. While we were standing there tonight with our arms linked, I understood what they felt. I felt it, too."

"Oh, Derek."

"I suppose it sounds silly to compare what we did with the religious fervor those people were experiencing, but... I had a sense of it. And I realized, none of those people felt they died in vain. It's still an awful memory, Sam. But now... now there's something beautiful about it, too."

Sam felt tears prick her eyes, and she tightened her arms around him. Before she could say a word, however, a boy's voice cut across the music, crying, "The egg hatched! The egg hatched!"

Sam and Derek broke apart and began running back down the beach toward the egg.

Surprisingly few people followed them, as if they were reluctant to face what had been born. Which, considering a child had just announced the news, probably wasn't all that dangerous.

The receding tide had left the sand packed hard enough to easily run on. As they approached the enclosure, Sam drew up short and stopped Derek.

"Wait," she said, holding his arm. "I have the gun, remember? I should check first."

"Right," he said disgustedly, and stayed by her side. Short of arresting him, she couldn't prevent him.

Together, they cautiously approached the enclosure. Sam unhooked her flashlight from her belt and turned it on. Slowly, they walked around the outside of the stockade. Other than the trampling of the hundreds of feet earlier, the sand showed no sign that something had crawled this way.

Finally they stepped into the warm Gulf waters and rounded the open end of the enclosure.

There, in the beam of Sam's flashlight, lay the egg, torn and looking deflated. Whatever had been inside was gone.

Zeph and Nat caught up with them.

"Holy moly!" Nat said.

"We've got to save the shell," Zeph announced, quickly assessing the situation. "It's a valuable research subject."

"Right," said Nat, still staring. "Right."

But Sam had a different concern. Derek had been hoping to see the moment of magic, and he'd missed it.

"I'm sorry," she said.

He looked at her. "What for?"

"You missed it."

He shrugged. "It doesn't matter. Maybe it's more interesting this way, not knowing. Some things are, perhaps, better left to the imagination."

That, she thought, was quite a growth step for him. But she still felt bad that he'd missed the moment.

Just then the mayor, huffing and puffing, reached them. "Oh, no!" he moaned. "Oh, no! It's gone!"

"It certainly is," Derek said with a marked lack of sympathy. "Gone back to its home in the sea."

"No!" wailed the mayor, dropping to his knees in the water. "I was going to get rich."

Derek clucked with mock sympathy. "Time to come up with a fall-back plan."

Then he turned, took Sam's hand, and said, "It's time I took you home."

Which actually meant following her patrol car with his car. But what did it matter? Sam asked herself miserably. The egg had hatched and tomorrow Derek would probably be gone, too, departing on the first flight to New York.

The interlude was over. By next week he wouldn't even remember her.

But she would remember him. And she had a feeling that there was going to be a gaping wound in her heart for a long time to come.

20

Sam invited Derek in. She knew it was a dangerous chance she was taking, but they were both wet to the knees and smelling of eau de seafront. In short, like rotting seaweed and other dead things. Hardly conducive to an intimate interlude.

She also needed to wash off the sweat of the day, and the sand that seemed to have crept into every cranny. And somehow she wasn't ready to let Derek vanish yet. Truth to tell, he didn't seem reluctant to come inside with her, although the relief he displayed at pulling off his soaked shoes and socks may have been the explanation.

In the shower, she let the hot water pour

over her and thought about the entire messy situation. Somehow, despite all her vows to the contrary, she'd fallen in love with a handsome, smooth-talking man who was going to walk out of her life, leaving her heart in tatters.

That was not, she decided, acceptable.

But what could she do about it? She couldn't change his mind. She couldn't make him love her. She couldn't really do anything at all.

But Sam hadn't become a cop because she was prepared to play the wallflower; that didn't suit her nature.

Action suited her nature, and as she toweled off, she asked herself why she was suddenly behaving like some die-away Victorian miss. She was a woman of the third millennium. A woman who went for what she wanted, and didn't wait for the world to offer it to her.

What was the worst that could happen? Derek might *tell* her why he was leaving, instead of just vanishing tomorrow. She could handle that. At least she wouldn't have to wonder.

She dressed in a pair of oyster chinos and a purple tank top, her determination to take the bull by the horns growing. She was going to have it out with him. At the very least, he wasn't going to leave in blissful ignorance of her hurt. She owed that much to herself.

Marching out into the living room, she found Derek sitting on her couch, his damp pants legs carefully positioned so they wouldn't touch the upholstery. He looked up when she entered the room, his eyes revealing nothing.

"Look, Diche," she said.

"I'm looking." The faintest of smiles was suddenly flickering about his mouth. "You look good in purple."

No, she wasn't about to let herself be distracted.

"And by the way," he said, before she could gather steam, "don't call me Diche. The real me is Derek Todd."

Wait a minute! He was taking over this conversation. She couldn't allow that. "Okay, Todd. We're going to talk."

He elevated one brow. "I thought that's what we were doing."

For an instant she wavered, wondering what it was she saw in this man that threatened to leave her wounded for life. Then she realized *this* was what she saw in him. His annoying tendency to irritate her. His too-handsome smile. His too-gentle heart. His carefully constructed defenses, which, she decided, were definitely kicking into action right now. He was afraid of what she might say.

Oddly, that gave her heart, and increased her determination.

"No," she said, "we're going to talk about us."

"Is there an *us*?"

Last week, even yesterday, such a question might have driven her back into hiding. It might have raised her own defenses so high even she wouldn't have been able to peek over them. But tonight she was a stronger woman than that. "You damn well know there's an us."

He simply waited, for once not trying to derail her. Strangely, she wished he had. Because she was growing more terrified by the moment.

"Look," she said. Then her mind went blank. Look at what? What was she going to say? What could she say? But then words started tumbling out of her mouth, from some deep recess in her soul.

"I know you'll be leaving tomorrow," she said. "Going back to life in the fast lane. And I'm not letting you leave here until we get some things clear."

He nodded. "Be my guest."

Was he teasing her? She had the worst feeling he was, but she plunged on anyway.

"We are lovers." She made the announcement flatly, even as some part of her mind squirmed at her boldness. That wasn't something she was comfortable saying out loud.

"We certainly have been," he agreed.

"Cut it out."

"Cut what out?"

"Putting it in the past, like it's over. It's not over."

Now both of his eyebrows raised, and there was something indefinable in his gaze, something that suddenly made her feel hunted. She began to wonder if she should have brought a chair and whip to this meeting with the lion. Because he looked almost hungry right now.

"I'm listening," he said.

"When you fly out of here, I want you to know that . . . that . . . you've broken my heart."

"Really?" His eyebrows couldn't have climbed any higher.

"This wasn't a game for me, Derek. I don't have casual affairs. Maybe in your world it's different, but I don't share that kind of intimacy casually. In fact, I never do it at all. Anymore. Until you."

"Hmm." He nodded, and she thought his gaze changed again, growing . . . warmer? Was that warmth she was seeing? Her heart slammed so hard it almost knocked the breath out of her.

"Neither," he said quietly, "do I."

The words were so unexpected that she didn't register them right away. "I'm not going to let you get away so easily, Derek," she plowed on. "If you go, you're going to go knowing how badly you've wounded me."

He nodded slowly. "What is it you want, Sam?"

"I want . . . I want you to stay. I want . . ." And suddenly it all burst out of her. "I love you, Derek. I want you to marry me."

There was a silence. Seconds ticked by on leaden feet as the future hung suspended between them. Sam felt her heart preparing for the fatal blow. Her chest ached until breathing became impossible.

"You know," said Derek gently, "you really ought to kneel when you make a proposal of marriage."

Kneel? Well, why not? Wasn't that the traditional position for receiving the coup de grâce? Somehow Sam managed to stumble across the room and kneel in front of Derek. He spread his legs so that his sodden pants wouldn't touch her.

"Now," he said in that same gentle voice, "take my hands."

She did, looking at him from a place somewhere between soaring hope and terror.

"Ask me again, Sam. Properly."

"Derek," she said, her voice reed-thin with tension, "will you marry me?"

"I have to ask a question first," he said, stroking the backs of her hands with his thumbs.

She nodded dumbly.

"Will we have children? I want them, you know. Two or three, or even four, but at least two."

She nodded, her heart and soul unable to grasp what was happening.

"And will we raise them to believe in magic, Sam?"

"Of course!" The words burst from her.

"Then, Sam, sweet Sam, I joyfully accept your proposal of marriage."

For a stunned moment, his words didn't connect. Then she was in his arms, and he in hers, heedless of his damp slacks and everything else in the world except unbounded happiness.

"I love you, Sam," he murmured as he rained kisses all over her face. "I swore I'd never let it happen again, but it did. Oh, God, I love you."

"Why didn't . . . oh, Derek, why didn't you say something?"

"Because I thought you needed more time. Because I was afraid."

There was something wonderful in his willingness to admit his fear, something that made her chest swell until it was ready to explode.

"I wasn't going to leave, you know. I was going to stay right here until you would agree to have me forever. Oh, Sam. . . ."

It was a long time before exquisite contentment began to replace the knife-edge of joy. By then she was sitting in his lap, tucked closely to him.

A twinge of sorrow pierced her happy haze,

and she looked at him. "I'm sorry you didn't find the magic you were looking for, Derek."

He appeared surprised. "But sweetheart, I did. I found all the magic I could ever ask for. I found *you*."

Dear Reader,

If you've enjoyed the Avon romance you've just read, then you won't want to miss next month's selections. As always, there's a wonderful mix of contemporary and historical romance for you to choose from. And I encourage you to try a book you might not regularly read. (For example, Regency historical readers might want to be brave and give a different setting a try!) I promise that *every* Avon romance is terrific.

Let's begin with Rita Award-winning and *USA Today* bestselling writer Lorraine Heath's THE OUTLAW AND THE LADY. Angela Bainbridge has spent her life dreaming of the perfect marriage . . . but she knows that this will never be. So when she's kidnapped by the notorious Lee Raven she's angry and captivated. His powerful kisses leave her breathless, but can she ever reveal the truth about herself?

If you love medieval romances, then don't miss Margaret Moore's THE MAIDEN AND HER KNIGHT. Beautiful Lady Allis nearly swoons when she first sees the tall, tempting knight Sir Connor. She is duty-bound to wed another, someone of wealth and privilege . . . but how can she resist this tantalizing knight?

Blackboard bestselling author Beverly Jenkins is one of the most exciting writers of African-American historical romance, and her newest book, BEFORE THE DAWN, is a love story you will never forget. Leah Barnett can't believe how fate has taken her from genteel Boston to the towering Colorado Rockies . . . and into the arms of angry, ruggedly sexy Ryder Damien.

Readers of contemporary romance should not miss Michelle Jerott's HER BODYGUARD. Michelle's books are hot, hot, hot . . . and here, pert pretty Lili Kavanaugh hires sexy Matt Hawkins as her bodyguard—and soon finds herself wanting more from this tough guy than his protection.

Until next month, happy reading!

Lucia Macro

Lucia Macro
Executive Editor

ELIZABETH LOWELL

THE NEW YORK TIMES *BESTSELLING AUTHOR*

LOVER IN THE ROUGH	0-380-76760-0/$6.99 US/$8.99 Can
FORGET ME NOT	0-380-76759-7/$6.99 US/$8.99 Can
A WOMAN WITHOUT LIES	0-380-76764-3/$6.99 US/$9.99 Can
DESERT RAIN	0-380-76762-7/$6.50 US/$8.50 Can
WHERE THE HEART IS	0-380-76763-5/$6.99 US/$9.99 Can
TO THE ENDS OF THE EARTH	0-380-76758-9/$6.99 US/$8.99 Can
REMEMBER SUMMER	0-380-76761-9/$6.99 US/$8.99 Can
AMBER BEACH	0-380-77584-0/$7.50 US/$9.99 Can
JADE ISLAND	0-380-78987-6/$7.50 US/$9.99 Can
PEARL COVE	0-380-78988-4/$7.50 US/$9.99 Can
MIDNIGHT IN RUBY BAYOU	0-380-78989-2/$7.50 US/$9.99 Can

And in hardcover

BEAUTIFUL DREAMER
0-380-78993-0/$19.95 US/$29.95 Can

MOVING TARGET
0-06-019875-3/$24.00 US/$36.50 Can

Available wherever books are sold or please call 1-800-331-3761 to order.

Love and Laughter from
USA Today Bestselling Author

SUE CIVIL-BROWN

NEXT STOP, PARADISE
0-380-81180-4/$5.99 US/$7.99 Can
Love ensues when a small-town lady cop
matches wits with a smooth-talking TV journalist.

And Don't Miss

TEMPTING MR. WRIGHT
0-380-81179-0/$5.99 US/$7.99 Can

CATCHING KELLY
0-380-80061-6/$5.99 US/$7.99 Can

CHASING RAINBOW
0-380-80060-8/$5.99 US/$7.99 Can

LETTING LOOSE
0-380-72775-7/$5.99 US/$7.99 Can

CARRIED AWAY
0-380-72774-9/$5.99 US/$7.99 Can

Available wherever books are sold or please call 1-800-331-3761 to order.

SCB 0901

Discover Contemporary Romances at Their Sizzling Hot Best from Avon Books

IT HAPPENED AT MIDNIGHT 0-380-81550-8/$5.99 US/$7.99 Can	by Cait London
YOU MADE ME LOVE YOU 0-380-80789-0/$5.99 US/$7.99 Can	by Neesa Hart
THIS PERFECT KISS 0-380-81256-8/$5.99 US/$7.99 Can	by Christie Ridgway
BORN TO BE WILD 0-380-81682-2/$5.99 US/$7.99 Can	by Patti Berg
SWEETHEARTS OF THE TWILIGHT LANES 0-380-81613-X/$5.99 US/$7.99 Can	by Luanne Jones
HE COULD BE THE ONE 0-380-81049-2/$5.99 US/$7.99 Can	by Elizabeth Bevarly
SOMETHING ABOUT CECILY 0-380-81852-3/$5.99 US/$7.99 Can	by Karen Kendall
DEAR LOVE DOCTOR 0-380-81308-4/$5.99 US/$7.99 Can	by Hailey North
FOLLOWIN' A DREAM 0-380-81396-3/$5.99 US/$7.99 Can	by Eboni Snoe
MAYBE BABY 0-380-81783-7/$5.99 US/$7.99 Can	by Elaine Fox

Available wherever books are sold or please call 1-800-331-3761 to order.

CRO 0601

Delicious and Sexy Contemporary Romances from Bestselling Author

SUSAN ELIZABETH PHILLIPS

"No one tops Susan Elizabeth Phillips"
Jayne Ann Krentz

FIRST LADY
0-380-80807-2/$6.99 US/$9.99 Can

DREAM A LITTLE DREAM
0-380-79447-0/$6.99 US/$9.99 Can

IT HAD TO BE YOU
0-380-77683-9/$6.99 US/$8.99 Can

HEAVEN, TEXAS
0-380-77684-7/$6.99 US/$9.99 Can

KISS AN ANGEL
0-380-78233-2/$6.99 US/$9.99 Can

NOBODY'S BABY BUT MINE
0-380-78234-0/$6.99 US/$8.99 Can

LADY BE GOOD
0-380-79448-9/$6.99 US/$8.99 Can

JUST IMAGINE
0-380-80830-7/$6.99 US/$9.99 Can

And in Hardcover

THIS HEART OF MINE
0-380-97572-6/$24.00 US/$36.50 Can

Available wherever books are sold or please call 1-800-331-3761 to order.

Wonderful, Sassy Romance
from Nationally Bestselling Author
Susan Andersen

ALL SHOOK UP

0-380-80714-9/$6.99 US/$9.99 Can

A man who doesn't believe in love and a woman who doesn't trust it find out just how wrong they can be ...

And Don't Miss

BABY, DON'T GO

0-380-80712-2/$6.50 US/$8.99 Can

"[A] madcap and humorous romp ..."
Romantic Times

BE MY BABY

0-380-79512-4/$6.50 US/$8.99 Can

"Sexy humor and smoldering passion ...
Don't miss out!"
Romantic Times

BABY, I'M YOURS

0-380-79511-6/$6.99 US/$9.99 Can

"Sassy, snappy, and sizzling hot!"
Janet Evanovich

Available wherever books are sold or please call 1-800-331-3761 to order.